Other Books by Bradley Harper

A Knife in the Fog

Queen's Gambit

Reflections in a Dragon's Eye

Advance Praise for Maiden Voyage

"Bradley Harper's Maiden Voyage is a page turning historical crime thriller with a deadly twist. It takes place aboard the R.M.S. Titanic. With dialogue so crisp and period detail so realistic you'll feel like you're sailing on the ill-fated ship. Fantastic!"

~Bruce Robert Coffin, bestselling author of the Detective Justice Mysteries

"I love it when Brad Harper makes history come alive by giving it a creative twist. He did it in *Knife in the Fog* when Sir Arthur Doyle solves the Jack the Ripper Murders. He did it again in *Queen's Gambit,* foiling the assassination of Queen Victoria. Now, in *Maiden Voyage,* an art heist is afoot aboard the doomed *RMS Titanic.* You're in for another great read from a master writer."

~ John DeDakis, Author, Writing Coach, Former Senior Copy Editor for CNN's "The Situation Room with Wolf Blitzer."

"Being a Titanic historian for the past 45 years, this book brings the tragic events to life, Dr. Harper's characters and story make the reality of the disaster all the more compelling!"

~ W.E. Brower Jr., Author, Filmmaker and Titanic historian

"*Maiden Voyage* is a masterwork of sleight-of-hand, set amidst the historical backdrop of the ill-fated Titanic, a heist wrapped in heartbreak and history. This is genre fiction with a literary heartbeat, and I highly recommend it!"

~Baron Birtcher, award-winning author of *Knife River*

"*Maiden Voyage* by Bradley Harper is a perfect combination of Titanic fact and Titanic fiction. This book is guaranteed to grip the reader in suspense, while attempting to figure out which characters are the result of an excellent creative mind, and which characters are the result of an exceptional piece of historical research."

~ Clifford Ismay, Author: *Understanding J Bruce Ismay*

"Dr Bradley Harper's *Maiden Voyage* is a rollicking historical fiction novel that draws you into a robust and rich world of crime, tragedy, and redemption. Filled with characters that crackle with intelligence, this book puts the reader squarely in the middle of a fast-paced battle of wits and wills that I didn't want to leave."

~D. Werkmeister, Retired FBI Agent and author of the supernatural thrillers *VOLK* and *Skinwalkers*

"In a sea of Titanic retellings, *Maiden Voyage* is an absolute triumph of historical fiction that transforms the famous tragedy into a high-stakes game of cat and mouse aboard the ill-fated ship. It's a must-read for anyone who loves a clever heist, a well-researched historical setting, and a page-flipping pace."

~Carmen Amato, author of the *Galliano Club* and Detective Emilia Cruz series

"*Maiden Voyage* is everything you want in a caper and nothing you'd guess as a bold band of female thieves leaves England in pursuit of a priceless painting—aboard RMS Titanic. Award-winning historical novelist Dr. Bradley Harper transports us deep below decks, through elegant halls and perilous lifeboats, sharing the food, fashion and foppery of an upper class raided by an honorable but cutthroat band whose thievery rivals Fagin's. Titanic sinks and enemies clash but hearts will soar as *Maiden Voyage* reaches its inevitable but still surprising end."

~Mark Bergin, award-winning author of *Apprehension* and *Saint Michael's Day*, coming soon from Level Best Books

MAIDEN VOYAGE

Love and Larceny aboard the Titanic

BY

Bradley Harper

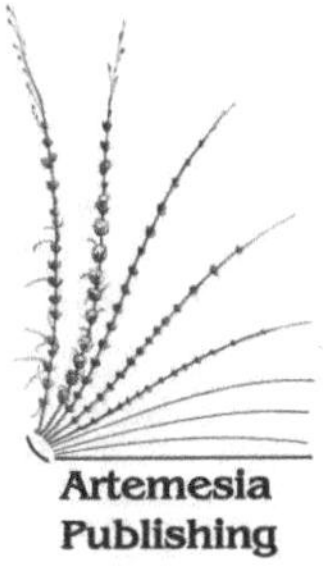

ISBN: 978-1-963832-38-9 (paperback)
ISBN: 978-1-963832-50-1 (ebook)
LCCN: 2025944537

Printed in the United States.

This book was handcrafted by skilled artisans. No AI was used in the writing or cover design for this book.

Artemesia Publishing
9 Mockingbird Hill Rd
Tijeras, New Mexico 87059
www.apbooks.net
info@artemesiapublishing.com

To my mother,

Who taught me the magic of books. And found me a wife who is equally magical.

Acknowledgements

This marks my fifth book, fourth novel, since I started writing in 2013. Each book represents its own challenges, and I say the book you write only teaches you how to write that book. *Maiden Voyage* began in Edinburgh as my thesis project for a Master's in Creative Writing at Napier University. My classmates were mainly from the UK, but we had the occasional American (I, at seventy, was one of the odder ones), as well as Canadians and a Scandinavian.

I was fortunate to have had D. V. Bishop (https://d-vbishop.com/) as my mentor for the course, a well-established writer of historical crime fiction set in Florence during the Medici period. His Cesare Aldo detective brings an authentic flavor to the place and time, and I took his input seriously.

I'm also grateful to my wife, Chere, for once again packing up what we needed to live in another country. After a life in the US Army, she thought we were done with all that, but to her credit, she made the best of it, as she always did. I could never have gone this far without her. I'd also like to mention our dear friend Beverly Bergman, whom I'd met years before when she was a physician in the Royal Army. She splits her time between Glasgow and Edinburgh, and her warm welcome and assistance to two bewildered Americans made our adjustment to life in the land of Sir Walter Scott and Robert Lewis Stevenson much less stressful.

Finally, I'm grateful to my friends, family, and faithful readers who have become like family, who have followed my journey through letters for the past seven years since my first book appeared. I write with you in mind. I hope you find something within my tale that not only entertains you but also makes you reflect on how you would have acted during that terrible night.

I know I have.

Brad

Contents

“Sing to me of the man, Muse,
The man of twists and turns
Driven time and again off course
Once he had plundered the sacred heights of Troy.”

Homer, *The Odyssey*

Chapter One

South London

March 14, 1912

THE SHABBY YOUNG WOMAN sat in the center of the dim, smoke-filled back room of the Elephant and Castle pub, a space that served many functions, most of dubious legality. Currently, it was the 'Court' of Mary Carr, leader, or "Queen" of the ruthless female gang called The Forty Elephants. Mary sat furthest from the door, smoking a small cigar while sitting in a high-backed chair dressed in a black wool suit. To her right stood a tall, lean woman in her early thirties, dressed in a man's white shirt, black wool trousers, and suspenders. She had a prominent jaw, short, light brown hair, and eyes that didn't blink much.

"What have you got to say for yerself, Maggie?" Mary asked the woman before her. "You were supposed to be on lookout but were so stinking drunk you damn near got Sally pinched. If that bobby hadn't slipped in a puddle, we'd be paying her barrister right now."

The accused twisted a plain blue kerchief in her hands before croaking her response. "I'm sorry, Mary. You're right, but me man's just been sentenced to five years, and well, I was taking it hard. Our Johnny won't see his da again 'til he's ten." She sniffed. "He might forget what his father looks like by the time he's out."

"All the more reason for you to pull your weight," Mary said, leaning forward and waiting until the woman's eyes met hers. "You'll have to earn enough for two now until your man gets out. You know The Code. No drinking on or before a job."

Maggie swallowed. "Aye, Mary, I know..." She looked down at the sawdust-covered floor, No answers there. "What's your judgment, then?"

"I like a woman who can take her medicine. One month working the docks. The stink of rotting garbage will remind you it's a privilege to work in a place like Harrods or Selfridges, while the money off drunken sailors will help feed you and your boy."

"Thank you, Mary! It won't happen again, I swears!"

"See that it doesn't." Mary nodded towards her silent companion, "or next time it'll go harder on you."

Maggie glanced at the woman beside Mary as she rose, flinched, and left without another word or backward glance.

"Who else is here to see me tonight, Sam?"

"A maid."

"We ever work with her before?"

"No."

"Then how'd she find me? Could she be working for the police?"

Samantha 'Sam' McMurphy, burglar, aide to Mary Carr, and enforcer for the Forty Elephants, snorted. "You're famous, Mary. There's not a Southie as doesn't know where you hang your bonnet. Queen Victoria, bless 'er, may be dead and gone, but we still have a queen in England. Don't worry, if she smells false, I'll get her sorted quick enough."

"All right. It's my job to worry, yours to see I've naught to worry about. Bring her in."

Sam soon returned from the pub's main room with a middle-aged woman bent as much by life as years. Her red, chapped hands declaring how she made her way in the world, the well-worn but clean clothes presented a defiant dignity the years and work had yet to take from her.

Mary rose and motioned to the chair still warm from the last visitor. "Please, Mum, take a seat. You've something to tell me?"

The woman stood a moment, looked around the

room, then straightened her shoulders and sat down.

"Yes, I do," she said, in a fine public-school accent. "I've been nanny, then maid, to a family here in London for the past twenty-five years."

"And?" Mary asked. "I reckon that's about to change."

"Yes, ma'am, it is. The Master 'invested' poorly at the racetracks and casinos, so I'm to be let go in two weeks." She spread her damaged hands. "Without severance."

Mary frowned. "And you're looking to join us, then? I'm sorry, but you're a bit long in the tooth to take to 'hoisting' now."

The maid shook her head. "I agree. Besides, I haven't the nerve, but I know something that would be of value to a woman like you and," her eyes darted to Mary's companion, "your associates."

"Ah, now we're down to it," Mary smirked, looked over to Sam standing to her right, and nodded ever so slightly before returning her gaze to the maid. "You know where they store the family jewels, is that it?"

The visitor swallowed. "I'm sorry, this is new for me. I've been loyal to this family, raised their son..."

"And you see how they've repaid that loyalty," Mary said, tapping the ash from her cigar onto the floor. "As Shakespeare said, 'to thine own self be true.' Time to take care of yourself, Mum. But you know me, what's your name? I swear it won't leave this room."

"My name is Henrietta. Henrietta Forrest. I know your reputation, Miss Carr, as a woman who keeps her word, else I wouldn't have come. I also know you by another means, for you once worked for the family that now employs me. That's why I thought of you."

Mary leaned in. "The Findlays?"

"Aye, the same, though my master is the son of the man you worked for—"

Sam's laugh was brought short by a glare from Mary. "Yes, Sam, I was once in domestic service. I was young and hungry, something you'd know nothing about."

She returned her attention to her visitor, softening her tone. "Randolph Findlay," she shook her head, "I'm surprised he's still alive and out of prison."

"Out of prison, yes, but nearly bankrupt. If I tell you

what the item is, where it is, and when it will be unguarded, how much will you pay me if you take it? A percentage I suppose?"

Mary and Sam exchanged a smile. "Well, Miss Forrest, for someone new to this, you ask the right questions. The right answer is—it depends."

She waved her hand as to dispel the maid's question before it appeared. "If it's too valuable or remarkable to sell outright, we'll need to use a fence. They usually pay half the market value. So, if I say ten percent, it's ten percent of what we get, not what you might see at an auction or in a store.

"You still want to talk with us?"

"Quite acceptable, Miss Carr. The item is a painting by the French artist Blondel, and it's scheduled to sail in two weeks to America. My employer just sold it to pay off his debts." She shrugged. "He hated that. It's of a naked woman, and he kept it in his bedroom."

Samantha smiled, showing a disturbing pair of canines. "Even I've heard o' this Blondel chap. How much then, this painting?"

Miss Forrest straightened herself in the chair. "The master sold it for one hundred thousand pounds."

Mary coughed. "You've got my interest, even before you mentioned the value. Your master and I have a bit of history and giving him some of his own would make the payout all the sweeter. Where is it now, and how will it travel to America?"

"We still live at the same place, near Covent Gardens. The ship's scheduled to sail on March 29, the same day I'm to be let go, but with the coal strike on that may change."

"It would be easier to steal it from the residence," Sam said. "You steal it on a boat, you got no place to go until it reaches harbor."

"Aye, Sam, you've the right of it." Mary turned to her visitor. "I'd like my friend here to pay a visit while you're still there. I'd go myself, but someone might recognize me."

Miss Forrest frowned. "That's possible, but if I do and the painting goes missing, I'd be suspect for having strangers in the house, don't you think?"

Sam cleared her throat. “I can come to sharpen the knives in the kitchen, and just take a gander.” She tapped her head, “after, I can draw a map. If it looks like you’ll be sacked before the painting leaves, we’ll wait ‘til you’re gone.”

The maid considered this. “Fair enough. How about tomorrow? It’ll just be cook and me after breakfast until around six in the evening, assuming Mauritz, the son, stays out all night as he often does.”

“And if he doesn’t?”

“Not to worry, Miss Carr. He’s an idiot.” She sighed. “I should know, I raised him. He’s to accompany the painting to America, which is why I said it’d be unguarded.”

“I trust your judgment,” Mary said, “but if we can’t steal it before it sails, we’ll need to consider hoisting it in transit. That’ll take a good deal more planning, however. What’s the ship in case I need to purchase passage?

“A fairly new ship of the White Star Line,” she said. “Named *Zealandic*.”

“I’ve always wanted to see America,” Sam said. “Maybe this caper will pay for a nice holiday.”

Mary shrugged. “I’ve heard the food’s terrible.”

***

Miss Forrest almost didn’t recognize Sam when she appeared dressed as a man in a leather apron, knocking at the tradesman’s entrance the next morning.

“I didn’t order this.” Cook huffed. “You should have asked me, Henrietta. Everything that happens in the kitchen is my job.”

“And everything that happens in the dining room is mine,” the maid said. “Master complained how hard it was to cut his lamb shank last week. I told him it was because his knife needed a better edge. Would you rather I’d said you’d overdone it? I was doing you a favor.”

Sam smiled to herself. *For someone new to the game,* she thought, *Miss Forrest learns quickly.*

The kitchen knives soon gleamed and when it came time to sharpen the dining room cutlery, Henrietta said she’d accompany the tradesman to keep watch over him. Once out of sight, she whispered, “Young master came in just after daybreak. His room is down the hall from his father's, so we'll need to be quiet."

"Was I being noisy?" Sam asked, as she laid her sharpening tools on the dark oak of the dining room table. "Best I do the knives first, case I need to leave quickly. Just take a moment."

Once the dozen steak knives were done and dusted, Sam softly followed her guide upstairs. The door to the master bedroom creaked slightly, and Sam produced a small oil flask to quiet the hinges before entering.

The canopied bed against the interior wall was hung with thick red velvet drapes, a bell pull on one side. Across from it was a life-sized rendering of a naked woman with vaguely Roman architecture behind. The artist, understandably, had paid more attention to the red-haired woman leaving her bath than the columns in the background.

"You didn't say it was so..."

"Large? Yes, it took a great deal of effort to hang it properly on the wall. Is that a problem?"

"Well, I certainly can't tuck it under my arm now, can I? It'll take two people to move it."

Sam estimated the painting, including its gilded wooden frame, weighed upwards of forty pounds. No way to hide something that size while walking down a street. She'd need a van and an accomplice.

Sam looked around the room and noticed what wasn't there. No vanity. No stock of cosmetics. No smell of a woman's perfume, but the slight aroma of dog. If the small water bowl beside the bed didn't confirm her suspicion, the sneeze that followed did.

"Your Master Findlay a widower?"

Miss Forrest chuckled. "Not exactly. His wife is visiting her mother in Kent."

"How long's she been gone?"

"Five years."

"Well, that simplifies things. Will he be away overnight before the ship sails?"

"Usually, he'd be off to Baden-Baden this time of year for the baths and the casino, but I've noticed letters in the mail from Germany and Monte Carlo over the past month that he's torn to shreds. I suspect his credit's no good now."

"Bugger." Sam nodded toward the water bowl. "When were you gonna tell me about the dog?"

"Oh, Samson!" the maid pinked up. "I've gotten so used to the dear thing, I forgot about him. He's a foxhound, rather long in the tooth. Samson used to be one of the master's dogs when he rode. He keeps the dog around as a reminder of his younger days. He wouldn't hurt a fly."

"He may not bite, but he can howl. I suppose he eats in the kitchen?"

"Right you are. Cook and him are best mates. She says he's the only Findlay who appreciates her."

They started at a creak of a door and feet shuffling hurriedly down the hall. Another door slammed open followed by the sound of violent retching.

"Young Master Mauritz is awake." Miss Forrest said. She checked the timepiece in her broach. "Ten o'clock. Earlier than usual."

"I need to go before he sees me," Sam whispered. "Keep him busy and I'll walk out through the kitchen."

The maid went first and found the young man with his face still drooping over the toilet.

"Help me back to bed," he groaned. "I want to die in bed."

"You haven't died yet, Master Findlay, and if New Year's didn't kill you, you're immortal."

Sam slipped quietly past. *I wonder if we could slip some Scotch into the dog's bowl?* she thought as she rolled her tools up into her leather satchel and bade the cook goodbye.

"You may want to put the kettle on," she advised. "It appears your young master has defied death once again."

Chapter Two

MARY WAS SIPPING GIN in the back room when Sam came in, her eyes still red from Samson's dander. Pulling out a handkerchief, she asked, "Can I keep the cutler fee? I'm allergic to dogs, and I'll be blowing my nose all afternoon."

"Dogs? Rudy has a dog?"

"Rudy?"

"My name for the esteemed Mister Findlay." Her jaw clenched. "I'll tell you about it sometime, when we're both very drunk."

Sam grinned. "The young Findlay had a terrific hangover this morning. Miss Forrest was helping him back to bed when I left."

"Like father, like son I suppose. But what's this about a dog?"

"The master keeps the dog, an old foxhound, in his bedroom at night where the painting is."

"And his wife allows it?"

"They live apart and have for some time, and before you ask, he's not scheduled to be away on holiday anytime soon. He's that broke. Miss Forrest says the casinos have cut him off."

"Interesting. If we steal the painting, he may think someone from the casino has taken it to pay his debts. What do you think? Can you do it?"

"Anything's possible, but it's not a one-person job, the painting is life-sized. With the frame it's more than what I can easily carry."

"Besides the maid, who else lives there?"

"The cook, who almost never goes upstairs, the son, and an old gardener who rarely gets past the kitchen. The house is going to seed, with only Miss Forrest to tend to it and two idle men."

"I have an idea," Mary said. "Can you drive a truck?" She smiled at the thought of 'Rudy' Findlay staring at an empty wall.

"I've never done it, but Elisa's man drives one and on occasion 'loses' some of his shipment for us. I reckon he can give me a quick lesson."

"Good." Mary wrote a list and handed it to her lieutenant.

"Bring me a crew tomorrow afternoon with people who can do these things. Choose carefully. We'll do a sit down then and plan this out, nice and proper."

***

A week later a van arrived at the Findlay residence shortly after ten and backed carefully up to the tradesman's entrance. If the cook had paid attention, she might have noticed a strong resemblance between the driver and the cutler who'd recently sharpened her knives.

The man had a clipboard with a form containing the White Star Line symbol on top, and the truck had 'White Star Lines Cargo Services' freshly painted on the side.

"Is Mister Findlay here to sign?" the driver asked.

"The younger is," Miss Forrest said, her face impassive. "What's this?"

"Your master reported a high value item for the trip on the..." he checked the form, "Zealandic on the 29th. That requires special handling. We're here to place it into secure storage in preparation for transfer to the ship."

"I see," the maid said. "I can't sign for it, of course. I'll wake Master Mauritz. It'll only be a moment."

"Of course, Mum. If you don't mind, we'd like to pack it up while you get him. We're on a tight schedule."

The cook shrugged, "Go ahead and take him to the painting, Henrietta. I'll wake the master."

"I think he's awake, Mildred," the maid said, then winked, "but don't walk in after you knock. I heard a woman giggling when he came up the stairs at dawn."

The cook rolled her eyes before heading up the stairs. She knocked gently and heard bedcovers rustling.

"What is it? Do you know the time?" a baritone growled from the other side.

"The time!" a woman's voice moaned. "I must be at the theater before noon."

"Then you've an hour, Missy," the cook said, "but Henrietta needs you to sign some paperwork, Master. The men from the White Star Line are here for the painting."

"What!"

A young man with a bedsheet wrapped around him like a Roman senator burst out of the door. "Tell them to stop immediately! There's been a mistake!"

Sam and her confederate had the packing frame propped up by the wardrobe and were putting their gloves on when they heard the bedsheet dragging down the hall towards them.

"Stop what you're doing, you idiots!"

Sam saw her companion reach for the cosh in her overalls pocket and shook her head slightly. They'd have to bash the cook and Miss Forrest as well. "What's this, then?" Sam said, before sneezing loudly.

"Didn't you hear? Our crossing's been delayed by the coal strike. Father told me last night. They're taking the coal off our ship so another can sail."

"I didn't know," Henrietta said. "I've been laundering and packing your things." She glared at him. "I should have been informed."

"Yes, well," he shrugged. "I'm informing you now." He turned to the cook. "My friend needs a quick breakfast before she goes to work." He noticed the two men beside the packing frame were giving him an odd look, and he adjusted his toga before striking a regal pose.

"As for you two," he sneered, "kindly bugger off. I'll be traveling in style next month, not on some tugboat."

"Shall I unpack your things?" the maid asked, stone faced.

"By all means. I'll need a better wardrobe than I'm sure you crammed into my valise. I'll be sailing on the *Titanic!*"

***

That night Miss Forrest paid another visit to the Elephant and Castle pub and found Mary in her 'office,' awaiting her.

"I'm so sorry, Miss Carr," she said. "The master never tells me anything."

Mary nodded. "Knowing him as I do, I'm sure it's not your fault. Are you still to be let go in a week?"

"Aye, I am."

"Bad news for you, or perhaps not. Once you're out of the house, we'll have a free hand. Do you have a house key with you? I've a lass who can make a copy in five minutes."

"Right here," she said, jaw clenched. "If I had any reservations before, they're gone after this morning. I only wish I could be there myself to see the master's face when he sees the painting's gone."

"Good," Mary said, rising as she reached for the key. "I'll bring you an ale while you wait." She curtsied. "We aim to please."

She paused when she reached the door. "Any idea when the *Titanic* is scheduled to sail?"

"I overheard Mauritz tell his lady friend he would be away from April 10 for a month."

"Giving us almost a fortnight after you're gone. Good."

Henrietta savored her ale as the sounds of the pub filtered through the thin wall. She remembered teaching a young Mauritz to walk and to speak his first words. Then she recalled his sneer when he said, "Well, I'm telling you now," when he told her of the change in his departure.

She took a hefty swig and waited.

After the key was duplicated and Henrietta on her way back to the Findlay estate, Mary called a council of war with Sam and a petite, dark-haired young woman.

"Well done with the key, Colette. I'll need it and you for a second story job. Sam can draw the layout. The painting's heavy, so it'll take both of you to carry it out, but we need to get a dog out of the way, first. He sleeps with his master in the bedroom with the painting we're after."

Colette frowned. "What kind of dog? A mastiff?"

"A fox hound."

"Humm. Clever. No bite but lots of bark." Colette

turned to Sam. "Draw me the map, and I'll see what I can do," then back to Mary. "How soon?"

"A fortnight."

She chuckled. "A fortnight? *Facile*, give me a fortnight to plan and I could hoist the crown jewels."

Chapter Three

New York City

March 28

HARRY WAS USHERED THROUGH the back entrance after dark, telling him more about the nature of his mission than his wealthy client was willing to admit. Ushered was the right word, he thought, for the butler/secretary/lackey who met him at the door never strayed more than ten feet from him once he entered.

You'd think I was here to steal the silverware, he thought. Though still relatively new as a Pinkerton agent, he was used to some respect. Then he considered his share of the pending fee, and his irritation faded. A thousand dollars would more than double his life savings and allow Harry to upgrade his wardrobe to something more appropriate for rubbing elbows with well-to-do clientele.

The servant escorted him to the library where a well-dressed, middle-aged man was seated at a desk heaped with files. Harry's guide tapped at the doorframe and the... librarian?... looked up from a ledger.

"Ah yes, the courier."

"Harry Worth, at your service. Do I have the pleasure of addressing Mister JP Morgan?"

The seated man exchanged smiles with the escort before standing. "You obviously aren't from New York, young man. In answer to your question, no, I'm not Mister Morgan." He looked Harry up and down, which didn't take long given Harry's five-feet-two-inch stature.

"I expected someone more... robust." The man shook his head. "Well, we don't have time to request a replacement, but since you don't look particularly dangerous, perhaps you'll draw less attention from the wrong sort." He picked up a small package wrapped in simple brown paper. "My name is not important, Mister Worth, but this," he said, handing the package to Harry, "is vitally so."

The anonymous gentleman resumed his seat before handing Harry an envelope. "Here's a second-class ticket to Southampton for a steamer leaving tomorrow morning. Once you arrive in England, you are to deliver this package to Mister Morgan in London, at his suite in the Savoy."

Harry opened the envelope and found it stuffed with dollars and pound notes in addition to the ticket. "For expenses?" he asked.

"Indeed. Two hundred dollars and the same in pounds to get you a train ticket from the port and two nights' lodging in London. My counterpart will see to your final payment when you make delivery." He steepled his hands over the desk. "Are you armed?"

Harry opened his coat to reveal a holstered .45 revolver. "As instructed."

The man nodded approval. "That's certainly large enough to earn any man's respect. Any questions?"

"Just one, sir. What am I carrying?"

"Ah, that's the one question I can't answer. Suffice to say, you're carrying something Mister Morgan wants which others want to take from him. If there's nothing else?"

Harry hefted his mysterious cargo in one hand. A book. It was thin and, given the dimensions, probably a ledger. The Pinkerton's were being paid over two thousand dollars to hand-deliver it to one of the richest men in the world. The librarian was right; he needn't know anything more. Harry stuffed the package in a leather satchel, nodded, and was shown out the back door into the cool night air of an early New York spring.

The taxi dropped Harry off at his hotel by the harbor just as the clock struck eleven. He had enough ocean-crossings under his belt to know what needed to be done before boarding and was mentally making a checklist as he approached the hotel entrance... when he felt a gun barrel pressed into his back.

"Follow me," a man said behind him. "Someone wants to meet you. In the alley... now!"

"You're ready to shoot me here, in plain view?" Harry asked. He turned slowly to face the would-be mugger. A big man, face obscured in the dark, but a head taller and probably one hundred pounds heavier than he was.

Harry remembered his father's advice, "A man who thinks he's winning is the easiest to fool."

"The doorman's coming out now," Harry said. "You willing to kill him, too? Then all the people who'd come to the sound of the shots? I think you're overplaying your hand."

"You willing to bet your life on that?"

"Let's ask the doorman. Hey, Bill!" he cried. "I want you to meet a friend."

The man glanced over his shoulder to an empty sidewalk. When he turned back, Harry's left hand was resting gently on the barrel of his gun, pointing it slightly away, while the barrel of a large pistol was directly under the would-be robber's chin.

"I'd like to meet your friend in the alley," Harry said, "but some other time. Please send him my regrets. I'll keep your pistol as a souvenir."

When the man hesitated, Harry added, "I wasn't asking. Release your hold, or they'll have a hard time identifying you in the morgue."

"You win for now. I'm ugly enough without a bullet to the face. Here."

Harry stood back, broke the revolver open, and emptied the chambers into a storm drain. "A Smith and Wesson thirty-eight, a fine piece. Expensive. I'm flattered you'd be willing to use it on me. Since you've been so cooperative, I'll give you a chance to get it back. There you go," he said, tossing the gun down the same storm drain as the bullets.

"There's a manhole cover at the corner behind you. Find a crowbar and you can have your pistol back before morning." Harry waved his own gun barrel dismissively.

"Now go!"

The robber slunk away, and Harry entered his hotel to prepare for an early departure and nodded at the figure chatting with the night clerk.

"Evening, Mister Worth," Bill, the ancient doorman said.

"Evening, Bill," Harry said, "and thanks."

"Thanks? Thanks for what?"

Harry tipped the man a quarter. "For borrowing your name."

Harry packed quickly, then opened his window overlooking the manhole cover. As he waited, he recalled another piece of advice his father had once given him.

"Men our size need to end a fight quickly if we're to come out on top." Then he'd tapped the side of his head. "A man with brains can usually avoid violence, but if you must fight, fight to win, and win quickly."

When Harry heard the grating of heavy metal on pavement, he left by the back stairs. It wasn't until noon the next day before the highwaymen realized their prize had fled.

Chapter Four

March 29-30

Colette and Sam crouched in the bushes beneath the window to the master bedroom, both dressed in men's dark trousers, jumpers, thin black leather gloves, their forms nearly invisible by the light of a quarter moon, and soundless in their flat, rubber-soled shoes.

"Ready?" Sam asked, her voice nasal from the paraffin-soaked cotton plugs in her nostrils to protect her from the dog hair.

"For this much money?" Colette snorted. "Watch and learn," and began wailing loudly like a cat. As soon as she began, they heard baying from the upstairs window and a light came on. The head of a balding middle-aged man stuck out the window and began cursing loudly. Colette went silent until the head disappeared and the light went out, before wailing even louder than before.

The same scene played out three times before the light stayed on, followed by another in the kitchen and the two kept silent as they watched the master approach the back door, holding a leash.

"I didn't think he'd come out!" Colette whispered. "Get ready to run!"

They tensed until they saw the man tie the end of the leash to something inside before the light in the kitchen went out, shortly followed by the one in the bedroom.

Colette's teeth shone dimly as she pulled out the copy of the front door key. "Time to see how good a locksmith I am."

Sam applied a drop of oil into the keyhole before Colette tried the lock. It opened noiselessly. Between the thick carpet on the floor and the rubber-soled shoes their shadows flowed silently up the stairs to the entrance of the master bedroom. Their shoulders relaxed a tad when they heard heavy snoring coming from the other side.

Sam pulled the chloroform bottle from her pocket and applied an unhealthy amount to some cotton wadding as Colette slid the door open. Colette slipped in first and approached the wall Sam had shown her in the diagram.

She turned and waved her arms as Sam bent over the head of the snoring form. Too late.

The man struggled briefly, but his surprise only made him breath the sedative in more rapidly, and he soon wilted back onto the pillow.

"Let's go!" Colette whispered.

"Without the painting?"

Colette pointed to the empty wall. "It's gone!"

***

"What the hell happened?" Mary asked Henrietta the next morning, with Sam and Colette looking on. "Why wasn't the painting there?"

"I came by the kitchen this morning to ask the cook for her recipe for roasted goose," the maid said, "and casually asked how preparations for the young master's trip were going. It seems you were too clever by half."

"How so?" Sam asked.

"When the master heard about the secure storage coming for the painting, he thought it a capital idea, and arranged for it to be secured in a warehouse until time to load it onto the ship, whenever that is."

"Did the cook know which warehouse?"

"I doubt it. Anyways, I felt it unwise to appear too interested," she frowned, "in case the painting does go missing."

"Don't doubt me, Mum," Mary said. "I'll not let that bastard get the better of us a second time." She paused. "Is the ship still scheduled to sail on the tenth?"

"Last cook heard."

"Then we'll be in touch. Leave your address with Sam. Once we score I'll let you know, and again when we sell it to give you your cut."

After the maid left, Mary called for a table, two more chairs, and a half-dozen sheets of foolscap.

"Ladies," she said, "we need to figure out what we know, what we don't know, what we need to know, and where we can find it out. Then we reach out to some old friends and go shopping. We'll need to travel first-class so we can mingle with the rich passengers."

She paused. "We also need someone on the inside who can travel about the ship without being noticed." She bit her lip in thought. "I have a contact in Southampton where most of the White Star crew come from, but this is a new ship so no one will have sailed on her before."

"The *Titanic*'s the sister ship to the *Olympic,*" Sam pointed out, "we find someone who's sailed on the first one—"

"We get fooled by the changes. No. Not good enough."

"Well, we could hardly expect to get a blueprint of the ship now, can we?" Colette said.

Mary smiled. "And why not? Colette, you ever been to Belfast?"

***

While Colette sailed on the Irish ferry the next morning, Mary traveled to Southampton, leaving Sam behind with instructions.

"We'll need to get some money for the trip," she told Sam, handing her an address. "Visit this store with Judith and see what they keep in the display case by the salesclerks. She knows what to do."

She sighed, "I think we'll need a man along. Usually I could use you, Sam, but I need someone a bit older who can look distinguished. See if Bruno's available."

"Bruno?" Sam frowned. "You know he doesn't like taking orders from women."

"He also doesn't like being poor. It's only for the one job and he's good at what he does."

"Colette isn't going to like it."

Mary laughed. "Maybe not, but she likes being poor even less than Bruno."

She scribbled out a note with an address.

"Take this note to the Spenser art gallery in Soho and ask for Carol." She handed over the page from *The Times* she'd shown Colette earlier.

"Show her this and tell her one hundred pounds in one week." Mary winked, "like me, Carol never gets to sign her work."

"How large, then?"

"Four feet by eight, according to the paper. No external frame."

"Anything else?"

"A table with removable legs... slightly larger than four feet by eight."

***

Sally MacDonald, a retired Elephant, ran a small pub in Southampton near the waterfront that made an honest profit, and a fencing operation in the back that did rather better. The large friendly woman who bustled amongst her thirsty patrons with fists full of ale had at one time been one of the best pickpockets in London, which was saying a lot.

"I'm looking for a stewardess who'll be on the *Titanic,"* Mary explained.

"What's the job, then?" Sally asked. "If it involves throat slitting, I doubt any of them would sign on."

"Nothing so dirty. Think of this as a charity. We'll be taking from a rich man to give to the poor. Us."

Sally laughed and tossed her thick gray hair back as she lit a cigarette off Mary's cigar. "A right Robin Hood you are, eh? I've just the woman for you. She's been transferred from the *Olympic*. Been with the White Star Line twelve years and her feet are starting to give her fits. She reckons she's got maybe two more years before she has to give it up."

"Perfect. She got a name?"

Sally smiled through the escaping smoke. "Hope. Just like the diamond."

"When can we meet?"

"I'll send my boy round to her flat and leave word. Come back this evening after eight, and I'll introduce you." She patted Mary's hand, "In the back room. I expect you two will want some privacy."

***

Hope Kelleher was a pale woman with straw-colored hair and freckles. Thirty years of age, unmarried, of average height with pale blue eyes and a sturdy body, she was a woman you could pass in the street or market a dozen times and not remember. For Mary, she was as perfect as the diamond with which she shared a name.

"What are you needing me to do?" She asked, with a soft, clear voice.

"Mostly we need you to look about the ship and tell us things, like who's on duty in the cargo hold, what kinds of locks are on doors, maybe distract a seaman on watch long enough for one of us to get in or out of a secure area. We won't ask you to take anything or harm anyone. Do you have a problem with that?"

Hope shook her head. "Long's I don't get in trouble. I'm not ready to leave the sea just yet, but a girl needs to feather her own nest if she hasn't a man to do it for her." She shrugged. "How much are you paying?"

"How about twenty pounds today, and twenty more when we reach New York?"

Hope cleared her throat. "How about fifty pounds now and fifty then? I plan on having a well-feathered nest."

Mary smiled. "I like your sand, Miss, but my offer's twenty pounds. Take it or leave it."

The young woman sighed. "Can't blame a girl for looking out for herself." She grinned. "I'll take it."

Mary handed over twenty pounds and they shook on it. "I see Sally found me the right woman. Oh, one more thing. I need to know who makes your uniforms. Tomorrow if possible."

"That's easy, Mum. I've got my uniform from the *Olympic* back at my flat. Come along and you can copy down the name."

Chapter Five

March 31

COLETTE'S PASSAGE ON THE Irish ferry went well enough until a young man sat beside her, smiled, and offered her a cigarette.

"I don't smoke," she said, popping a stick of Beemans into her mouth as emphasis.

He gently placed his hand on her knee. "What vices do you have?"

She smiled up at him, fluttered her eyes, removed her hatpin, and placed the tip on the web space between his thumb and forefinger.

"Several. But stupidity isn't one of them."

The young man froze, afraid to reach for the hand holding the sharp and very long needle to his tender flesh.

"Now," Colette purred, "remove your hand and your person, or you'll see how poorly I sew."

The remainder of the crossing was unremarkable.

It was easy to find the Harland and Wulf shipyards at the entrance of Belfast Harbor, unmistakable with hulks of ships in various stages of construction. *Titanic* was in the final phase of preparation for its sea trials, and Colette was taken aback at how it loomed over everything else.

That's a grand lady, to be sure, she thought as she stood outside the shipyard gates and felt a sudden chill when she realized she'd soon be aboard this massive iron lady. It was mid-afternoon, and she had three hours before a whistle sounded the end of the day's labor for the men who twisted metal into a ship. It would also mark the start of the shift for a small army of women with buckets and brooms who prepared the offices for the next day's effort.

Colette found a tavern with rooms to let, then went downstairs to the 'snug' where only women were allowed and looked for someone dressed for work. She spied two within the fog of tobacco smoke with kerchiefs around their necks and hair tied up, sipping ales at a table in the corner.

"Evening, ladies," she said. "Can I buy you two a drink?"

"Fair enough," said one who looked to be in her late thirties, her companion not more than twenty. After Colette returned with one for each of them, the older woman asked, "Where you from? You sound French, but also a bit like a Southie. What're you doing here?"

"So many questions," Colette said as she sipped her ale. "Aye, you got the accents right enough. I grew up in Montreal but have lived in London long enough to talk a bit like the locals. We wear accents like flags on our lapels, don't we? You say three words and the other person's sor'ed you right out."

"Now," she said after she took a long pull on her ale, "my turn for questions. What would it cost me for one of you to stay here tonight and let me take her place, while the other shows me about?"

"A bit of smash and grab?" the younger woman asked, frowning. "I'll have nothing to do with it. The pay at the yard ain't grand, but it's steady."

"No, nothing like that. If I find what I'm looking for, it'll never be missed."

"Depends on what you're looking for and where you need to go," the older woman said.

Colette studied her companions. *No fools, these. Best lay my cards out on the table.*

"I'm looking for blueprints of the *Titanic.*"

The older woman smiled. "Hell, that's easy enough. We trip over the damn things all night. There's a crew going on the sea trials soon, each with their own set. I can't get you the whole ship, they've got diagrams of the toilets and the swimming pool, yes, swimming pool if you can believe it! Is there a particular blueprint you're wanting? We may be able to get it for you without you sneaking in."

"I need a general layout of the ship. Deck plans. I don't need to know where the pipes run."

The two charwomen huddled in whispered conversation for a moment, before the older one raised her head. "Name's Amanda." She nodded towards the other woman. "You can sign in as Bessie, here, and the guards won't care a fig. Pay her a pound, and me two, and I'll get you through and show you about. Fair enough?"

Colette opened her wallet and slid three quid across the table. "We have a deal."

Amanda held up her now-empty glass. "Two things. First, we could use another round."

"And second?"

"You keep your yap shut inside the shipyard, or it'll be as plain as a pig in church you're not from Belfast."

Colette nodded and looked closely at Bessie. "Before I get the next round, I think you and I need to go to the loo and change clothes."

Bessie eyed Colette's wool skirt and white cotton blouse with lace collar. "One pound, a new skirt, and a night off. Aye, I can do that."

"The clothes are only on loan, Miss. I'll want them back tomorrow morning."

Bessie winked. "After tonight, maybe you will, and maybe you won't."

***

After the change in attire and another round of ale, Colette and Amanda answered the factory whistle and trudged to the gate as the weary men made their way for home, or the nearby pubs. As it wasn't payday, home was more likely.

Colette filed through the gate behind the older woman, making her mark beside Bessie's name in the ledger. The watchman at the gate paid no mind to the women as they walked past, being occupied with inspecting workmen's lunch pails to ensure they weren't stealing from the yard.

Amanda made straight for the three-story brick building just past the entrance.

"You're in luck for here's where Bessie and I work, emptying the bins and sweeping the floors. The crew going out for the sea trials and maiden voyage are putting their kit together, so you'll have easy pickings."

They entered through the front and Colette was struck by the large rooms on both sides, all in white, with large flat worktables arranged neatly in rows. "Isn't it hard keeping this place clean?" she asked.

"You'd think so, but all this white on the walls and large windows lets the light pour in something wonderful. These are the drafting rooms, and there's not a lamp anywhere. The waste bins hold paper from drafts gone wrong, but the more experienced the draftsman, the fewer false starts."

She raised her hands and spun about. "The best in the world work here, so I mostly sweep and straighten up."

Colette was looking about for a diagram of the entire ship when a back door opened, and its light spilled across the table.

"Good evening, Mister Andrews," Amanda said, "working a bit late tonight, are we?"

The slender man appeared to be in his mid-thirties but was already slightly stooped and walked slowly with a cane. "Can't be helped, Amanda, With the *Titanic* about to get her sea legs, I need to make sure everything's in order."

He nodded, placed his bowler on his head, and made for the door. "Goodnight, ladies," he said, and the managing director of the shipyard limped his way to the gate.

"Mister Andrews? The director?" Colette said, "Why does he know your name?"

"I'm not fond of rich Prods in general, but Mister Andrews is quality. You notice the limp? He got that from walking a hundred times from stem to stern on every ship built here since he came to work as a lad. Did you get a look at his cane?" Amanda asked.

"Aye, a nice blackthorn. Why?"

"A gift from the crew of the *Olympic.* He asked them what he could do to make their lives better on board and listened."

"I see why you say *Mister* Andrews like you mean it."

Colette spied a tin cylinder about ten inches in diameter and four feet long with a leather carrying strap, propped against a drafting table. She opened it and saw it was stuffed with blueprints for the entire ship. "*Voilà*," she murmured. "It couldn't be easier."

"How do you intend on taking this out without the guard noticing?" Amanda asked. "They could care less what we takes inside, but you saw how he went through the lunch pails on the way out."

"Where do you empty your waste bins?"

"We've a wagon inside the shipyard we take them to an hour before the end of shift. A guard checks 'em before they get tossed."

Colette considered her options. "Short of jumping into the harbor with the tube and swimming to a dock, I don't see how I can take the lot. *Allor,* watch the door and I'll look for the one I need most."

"Don't dawdle! Our lunch break's in an hour and if we don't show, someone goes looking for us."

Colette spread the drafts upon the worktable. In the darkness it was difficult to tell which portion of the ship each sketch portrayed, but she finally saw one with the entire ship outline and hoping for the best, rolled it into a tight tube, bent it in half, and tied it closed with twine lying on the table. The folded tube of white paper was two feet long and three inches in diameter. Colette used more twine to tie the top and folded bottom of the tube to just above her right knee and ankle.

"Time to go, dearie!" Amanda hissed.

The charwomen took their meal break in a common room in the basement of the main building, and they found the other cleaning women huddled in small groups around long tables, some knitting while others read the paper or chatted with their mates between mouthfuls.

"And who is this fair young thing?" a stout middle-aged woman asked as Amanda and Colette took their places at her table.

"Evening, Gladys, this 'ere's Francine. Bessie wasn't feeling well tonight, so Francine's pitching in, to keep her cousin out of trouble."

"Funny," the other woman said. "Don't recall Bessie ever mentioning a cousin. Where you from, lass?"

Colette coughed, and said in a raspy voice, "Glasgow." She coughed. "Sorry," she croaked. "Too many cigarettes."

"You don't sound Scot to me," Gladys said. "Least not from Glasgow." She winked. "I can almost understand you."

Colette coughed again, deeply. "Loo," she said, and left, where she hid until it was time to return to work.

Amanda knocked on the door, "Francine, you there?"

"Aye," she said as she came out. "Let's finish the shift."

When it was time to leave the guard looked over the lunch pails and handbags before letting a woman pass through. As Colette approached the gate, she felt the knot above her knee give way, and the draft began to wobble as she walked. She pinned the top of the tube to her knee with her right hand as best she could, hoping the paper was stiff enough not to fall beneath her skirt. She began limping stiffly and Amanda gave her an odd look but said nothing as they approached the exit. When it came her turn to be examined, the guard smiled. "I've not seen you before, miss. What's your name?"

"Francine, Sir, and yours?" she said, dimpling.

"William, but you can call me Billy."

"Well, Billy, I'm new here, and I could use someone to show me around the town." She craned her face up to him and slightly parted her lips. "Do you know anyone who could do that?"

The guard doffed his cap. "We could start at the Leaping Stag pub this afternoon, say four o'clock?"

"Four it is... Billy."

As they made their way back for the clothing exchange with Bessie, Amanda turned to Colette. "Why on earth did you lead that idiot on?"

Colette reached beneath her skirt and jerked the blueprint free.

"Because I wanted him looking at my face, not my skirt."

"Trust me, Missy, he was looking everywhere."

Chapter Six

The Savoy Hotel, London

April 1-3

HARRY WAS A STUDY in brown. Brown hair and eyes, in a brown tweed suit and highly polished brown leather boots. His palms were moist as he knocked on the door to an expensive suite. The door was opened by an older man in a well-tailored dark wool suit, wearing pince-nez on the tip of his bulbous nose.

"Yes?"

"Excuse me, sir," Harry said as he produced a badge. "I'm with the Pinkertons and have a document for Mister Morgan."

"Philip Williams, personal secretary," the man said, not extending his hand. "Mister Morgan is indisposed, but I can sign for him."

The way the man looked down at him, Harry knew Mister Morgan would always be indisposed. It was against Pinkerton protocol for anyone other than the person named on the delivery to sign for it, but the wealthy didn't bother with such niceties. For a man as rich as JP Morgan, they didn't exist.

Harry handed over the small package after the secretary signed. He wondered what could be in a ledger that could provoke so much (apparently warranted), security but accepted he would never know. Such was the life of a messenger, a bringer of unknown treasures.

"It must be worth a lot," Harry said. "A man tried to rob me of it almost as soon as I left the mansion."

Mister Williams sniffed. "Which is why you were so well paid." He patted the thin package. "Someone may soon be going to prison if we find what we expect in this little book. I can understand why they didn't want Mister Morgan to have it."

The secretary gave the slightest suggestion of a smile. "As he doesn't take kindly to those who would cheat him." Then he reached into his jacket and handed Harry two envelopes. One was open and full of US currency; the second was sealed, with Harry's name written on it.

"Your agency's fee," he said, indicating the envelope overflowing with dollar bills in large denominations, "and I was asked to give you this second envelope when you arrived."

"My apologies, sir, but I cannot accept gratuities."

The man shrugged. "Good, because I'm not giving you one. It's a telegram from your agency. Good day."

The door closed firmly in Harry's face; a minor servant dismissed by a better one.

Harry opened the first envelope, grinning as he pocketed his one-thousand-dollar payment, then opened the second and his grin became wider still.

TO: HARRY WORTH
C/O: JP MORGAN, SAVOY HOTEL, LONDON
DO NOT RETURN DIRECTLY TO NEW YORK. STOP
REPORT TO J. BRUCE ISMAY, DIRECTOR, WHITE STAR LINE, LIVERPOOL FOR NEXT ASSIGNMENT STOP
PAYMENT ADVANCE FROM ISMAY STOP
PINKERTON

A message from Mister Pinkerton himself! *Guess no one else is available,* he thought. Still, a personal assignment from the head of the agency was an opportunity to get noticed.

Harry tucked the telegram into his coat pocket. *Good thing I didn't unpack.*

***

The head of the White Star Line was an easy man to find but difficult to speak to. With the *Titanic* just days from its launch, Mister Ismay's office saw a steady stream of supplicants whom his secretary deemed more important than a young Pinkerton agent, and Harry waited four hours in the outer office. By the time he was granted an audience, he'd memorized the design of the large Persian carpet in the secretary-cum-gatekeeper's domain.

The director was a slender man with a prominent handlebar mustache but otherwise not given to ostentation... nor idle words. His large, dark oak desk was meticulously neat and the window behind him looked down the street onto the larger office building belonging to Cunard, his major rival. Harry wondered if the view helped the man focus on his own company's fortunes.

"Ah, the Pinkerton agent," he said as Harry entered. "Worth, is it?" He squinted at Harry closely for a moment. "How old are you?"

Harry straightened and used his best public-school accent. "Twenty-two, sir."

"And how long have you been with the agency?"

"Two years. Almost."

"You'll forgive me, *Mister* Worth, but you seem a bit green to handle the service I've contracted your agency to provide. Will you have anyone else with you?"

Harry swallowed. "No, sir. Just me."

Ismay sat back and steepled his hands. "I need an agent to mingle amongst some of the wealthiest people in the world... to detect, and hopefully deter, any criminals who might board the *Titanic* in hopes of fleecing them. Their guard will be down as they mingle with their own kind, and I don't want my ships to become known as a hunting ground for swindlers and cardsharps. What reassurance can you give me that a man of your tender years is up to the task?"

Harry looked the man up and down. "You're from England, but you've lived abroad. America or Canada?"

"America. New York, in fact. One year, and my wife is American," Ismay confirmed.

"You are a wealthy man but wear a plain, rather well-worn silver watch. A family heirloom?"

Ismay nodded. "My father's."

"Which tells me you are not overly concerned with what others think of you. May I take a closer look?"

"Very well."

Harry walked around the desk as the director stood, and before the older man had a chance to react, Harry pulled the watch out of Ismay's waistcoat pocket. He leaned in close as he examined the back then opened it and gazed briefly at the photograph of a much younger Mrs. Ismay.

"A rich man who carries a plain silver pocket watch doesn't flash a lot of money in people's faces to impress them. Judging from the neatness of your desk, I'd hazard you know to the farthing how much money you have on you at this moment, and that it's less than twenty pounds."

Ismay snorted. "You seem very sure of yourself, young man. I'll have you know I have twenty-three pounds on me at this very moment."

"Have you now, Mister Ismay? You'll forgive me if I doubt it."

"I'll prove it to you!" he said, and reached for his wallet, only to find it missing.

Harry held the absent pocketbook aloft. "However much money is in your purse, sir, I'd wager that at this precise moment you 'possess' less than twenty pounds."

Ismay grimaced as he took the wallet back. "A clever trick, I'll grant you. Is this standard training for the Pinkertons?"

Harry made a slight bow. "No, sir, not standard at all. I had a very non-standard childhood. I was raised among thieves, safecrackers, cardsharps, and pickpockets. You've heard it takes a thief to catch a thief? I know how they operate. I know how they think, and most importantly, I know how they select their targets. I can't imagine anyone in the agency better suited to sniff out the fox amongst the chickens than I am."

"If you were raised as a criminal, how is it you're a Pinkerton man?"

"I wasn't raised to be a criminal, sir, but *by* one. My father was Adam Worth. He sold a painting to the Pinkertons they'd been pursuing twenty years, for a nice sum and a promise from Mister Pinkerton that I'd be allowed to join the agency when I came of age. At one time Father had a mansion, a stable of racehorses, and a yacht, but died nearly penniless after release from prison. His last wish was for me to avoid the path he chose." He continued in a New York accent, "And, as I've spent my formative years between England and America, I can fit in with passengers from either country."

The director patted his wallet once more to make sure it hadn't strayed during Harry's explanation.

"You may just have the cheek to pull this off. I accept your unusual résumé. Are you armed?"

"I commonly carry a revolver. A .45 when I'm a guard or courier, and a .32 when undercover. Why?"

"I don't want you carrying firearms on the ship, as I can't have you frightening the passengers. You'll be required to surrender any weapons when you board, to be returned to you when the ship reaches New York. I don't foresee any armed robberies taking place during the voyage. Where could the criminals go?"

"But..."

"No buts, young man. On this point I'm quite firm. I have two large Masters at Arms available if force need be applied, and they'll keep your firearms safe until you are released from contract. You can be the scout; let them be the infantry. Understood?"

"Quite."

"You'll need to take a traveling name—any thoughts?"

Harry paused. "Something easily forgettable, I think. How about...Philip Daniels?"

"Philip Daniels...Yes, good. As people are likely to become confused as to which is your first or last name, they'll be less apt to approach you. I'd like to keep your identity and purpose confidential, and I've instructed that no one except myself, the Masters at Arms, and the naval architect from the shipyard, Mister Andrews, should know it. I only include the architect, so he understands why you need a full tour of the ship before it sails." Ismay smiled, obviously enjoying the role of spymaster. "Now, in what business shall we list you?"

"I think 'Insurance' will do nicely, sir."

"Agreed. As a member of the board of an insurance company, I know the public perception of that profession couldn't be duller." He winked. "All the same, don't be surprised if some young lady in search of a husband doesn't declare it to be the most fascinating subject in the world. You've been warned." Ismay consulted his watch. "Report to the ship at five in the evening on Tuesday, April the ninth, the day before the ship sails. Any questions?"

"Was there a particular threat that caused you to hire the Pinkertons, sir, or are you just being cautious?"

Ismay pursed his lips. "I've learned a valuable painting will be on board, escorted by the young son of the owner. In addition, we'll be transporting a book encrusted with one thousand diamonds, as well as some rubies and emeralds. I've no idea the value, but it's got to run into the thousands of pounds."

"What's the estimated value of the painting?" Harry asked. "My father taught me a fair bit about art, it being one of his specialties."

Ismay smiled. "Yes, I can see how he'd be quite the expert. The painting is by Blondel and was just sold for one hundred thousand pounds."

Harry whistled "A Blondel! Aye, that's some serious coin."

"Add in some of the richest people in the world in one place drinking lots of champagne... I'd be surprised if one or more thieves don't turn up to look for crumbs. I want my guests to feel safe, especially on the ship's maiden voyage, so they'll sail again and tell their friends.

"I'll arrange for your steward to show you about the first-class areas, where the greatest threat will be. Mister Andrews can take you about the rest of the ship so you'll know where thieves might hide." He pointedly checked his watch. "Now, unless there's anything else?"

"There is the matter of payment."

"Ah, yes." The director scribbled out a quick note and handed it to Harry. "Give this to my man outside. Half for the voyage to New York, the remainder when we begin the return journey... if your service on the outward trip is satisfactory. Good day, Mister Worth."

Fifteen minutes later, Harry left the offices of the

White Star Line with $2,500 in his pocket. $1,500 to the agency, but the remaining $1,000 was his. Between the payment from Mister Morgan's secretary and Ismay's, he'd just earned more money than he'd ever owned in his entire life.

Now, all I have to do is stave off an army of thieves, swindlers, and cardsharps for a week on my own, and I'll have another payday like today. Ah well, he consoled himself, the passengers and miscreants would all be confined to the ship once it left port.

What could go wrong?

***

The White Star Line's newest ship was undergoing its sea trials in the waters around Belfast under the watchful eyes of Board of Trade surveyor Francis Carruthers, a man not given to smiling. He took his task seriously, and when offered tea he accepted grudgingly but declined the biscuits.

The ship's handling was monitored from eleven to twenty-one and a half knots, the latter close to her expected full speed. At eighteen knots she came to a full stop in three minutes and fifteen seconds, traveling only three times her length, which the dour Mister Carruthers had to admit was remarkable for a ship its size, and another indication of her safety.

At the end of the trials, the surveyor allowed himself a brief relaxation of his customary scowl as he signed the certificate granting the *Titanic* a standard twelve-month certificate of seaworthiness as a passenger vessel. He wished the shipbuilders, Mister Thomas Andrews among them, a good night, and a successful maiden voyage before disembarking.

The next morning, the ship steamed from its birthplace in the Belfast shipyards to its homeport, Southampton, the White Star ensign flapping proudly from its stern.

Chapter Seven

London

April 4-5

THE OLDER WOMAN AND the younger lady with the bulging belly stood quietly as the clerk displayed bejeweled rings on the black velvet tray. Although it was a cool spring day, the young woman dabbed her forehead with a lace handkerchief.

The clerk looked at her with concern. "Pardon me, madam," he said. "Would you like to sit down? I could have our boy fetch you some tea and biscuits."

She shook her head slightly before her eyes rolled upwards and she melted to the floor.

"Louise!" her companion cried. "Is it the baby?"

The young woman lay noiseless as her companion cried out to the room, "Help us, please! My daughter is due next week, but I fear the baby's coming now!"

The other customers immediately separated themselves by gender, women rushing forward, while men shrank back—all save one.

"Let me through!" a fastidious middle-aged man commanded. "I'm a physician." He knelt beside the supine woman while pulling a stethoscope out of his small black bag, then moved it around her chest, bending forward to listen intently as he took her wrist in hand, checking for a pulse.

The older woman withdrew a pace once "the doctor"

declared himself and stood against the counter; the clerk leaned over, transfixed by the convincing portrayal of Fainting Woman.

If we had a musical accompaniment, Colette thought, *it might make a decent panto.* She recalled her drama teacher at finishing school in Montreal. While she doubted he'd approve of her purpose, he couldn't fault her performance.

Meanwhile, Mary laid her substantial purse on the counter between the clerk and the ring-covered tray, and—with the skill of long practice—slipped the catch, opening a false bottom. The duplicate board holding gold- and silver-plated rings with fake gems slid smoothly out before Mary placed her bag over the real ones. She secured her booty silently, all other eyes on the drama of the young woman and her rescuer.

Not one to waste an opportunity, Mary scanned the room and focused on an older gentleman who seemed more prosperous than the rest, standing at the back of the room, as far from the scene as possible. He held a silver-headed cane and wore an impressive gold pocket watch with matching chain running across his silken waistcoat. She rushed toward him, a handkerchief to her eyes.

"Oh, sir! Please help us. I don't know what's to be done."

He instinctively reached out with his right arm to lay it across Mary's shoulders in consolation, causing his coat to gap… just enough.

Bruno Vallarsa, safecracker and occasional "doctor," exchanged glances with Mary. She nodded.

"I need to get her to hospital immediately," he said and barked at the clerk. "Fetch us a carriage. Now!"

The clerk instinctively grabbed the tray of rings on the counter and secured it before rushing out and finding an oddly convenient carriage—the driver feeding his horse a carrot—scarcely twenty yards away.

Bruno enlisted two male customers to convey the unconscious woman into the carriage, giving Mary the chance to lift their wallets. The larcenous actors were out of sight before anyone patted their jackets and noted a disturbing vacancy.

"Well-played, Colette," Bruno said as the young lady removed the stifling pillow from beneath her dress.

"Thank you, 'Doctor,'" Colette said, "but a word of caution. The heart doesn't reside in a woman's bosoms, and I'll thank you to remember that if I'm ever your 'patient' again."

"My apologies, *signorina,*" he said with a slight bow, hand over his heart. "A momentary excess of enthusiasm. But, in my defense, I was wearing gloves."

"Fondle me like that again, and I'll enthusiastically examine your *couilles* with my foot. But do not be offended, *monsieur,* I'll be wearing a boot!"

"Enough!" said Mary. "Bruno… you're only part of this job because I needed a man to play doctor. You'll get your cut but play nice with my ladies if you want me to call on you again."

Bruno's jaw clenched before his face returned to its customary smirk. He raised his hands in mock surrender before asking Mary, "How's the take?"

Mary laughed as she counted out the bills from the three purloined wallets. "Men who go shopping for jewelry don't go with meager purses." She winked. "I count seven hundred and forty pounds between the three—four hundred and fifty from the older gentleman alone." She sighed. "Pity I couldn't lift that fine cane of his. That's probably worth a hundred on its own."

Mary pulled a cigar from a small tin in her purse before cutting off the end with a small-bladed knife. She raised the cigar while looking at Bruno and he quickly produced a match and lit it. She inhaled deeply before leaning back and blowing a long slow stream of smoke into the carriage while Colette leaned out the window and popped a stick of Beemans chewing gum into her mouth.

"What a disgusting habit!" Bruno said to Colette. "Makes you look like a cow chewing its cud."

"What? How is it any worse than sucking on a burning weed? It calms me down and doesn't stink up my clothes." She shrugged, "I developed a liking for it as a young girl in Montreal and my only problem is finding it here in Britain, as you "Roast Beefs" have little taste for it."

She pulled out her hat pin and began cleaning her

nails before continuing. "I learned an important lesson early in life, sir: only have vices you can afford, so how you say? Bugger off!"

Mary blew a smoke ring and laughed at the two squabbling like an indulgent parent. "As for me, I enjoy a good smoke now and again."

"Why can't you smoke a cigarette like a normal woman?" Bruno said. "Most men are scandalized by a woman enjoying a cigar."

"Which only deepens my enjoyment. Besides, the type of man who's so easily scandalized isn't worth my time."

Colette removed the tray from Mary's purse and Bruno's focus moved to the sparkling jewelry. "How much do you believe these rings will fetch us?"

She pulled out a jeweler's loupe and, with a practiced eye studied the eighteen rings on the tray.

"Retail, together they'd probably fetch us another fifteen hundred, which means Phineas will pay us, at best, five hundred. Still, between the wallets and the rings, we've just netted well over a thousand pounds."

She turned to Mary with a raised eyebrow.

The Queen of the Elephants smiled. "I'll be traveling posh, for sure."

"While I travel second-class as your maid." Colette sighed, then brightened. "But I haven't a thing to wear!"

***

Harry was sipping ale in a pub when he saw a three-paragraph notice in *The Times* on page twelve. It mentioned a reward of five hundred pounds for any information leading to the arrest of a man and two women implicated in a recent jewelry store heist. When he read a description of how the robbery was carried out, he smiled. "Elephants," he muttered. *"No one else could pull off a heist like that in broad daylight,* he thought. *It took planning, skill, and nerve, and no one has more nerve than they."*

"What's that?" said an elderly man at the bar beside him. "Elephants in London? They escape from a circus?"

"Not real elephants, sir," Harry explained. "Just some people my father used to know."

The thought of a circus reminded him of monkeys, an organ grinder, and a day in Belgium that changed his life forever.

Belgium. He'd been eight years old when his father appointed him lookout while he and a safecracker, posing as businessmen, met with a bank officer to discuss a 'loan.' A loan they had no intention of signing for nor repaying.

Harry was a little fuzzy on the details, but knew it involved a smoke bomb and his father yelling, "Fire!" while the safecracker did his job. His father posted Harry on a street corner between the closest police station and the bank, ordering him to release a balloon if he saw any policemen heading his way. He sat on a bench watching the world go by, the image of innocence, when an organ grinder came by with a small monkey on a chain and Harry was delighted by its capers and gave it a small coin. He was so entranced he failed to notice two policemen rushing past him and only looked up when he saw his father and the other man being led out in manacles.

The grim look his father gave Harry as he trudged by was a dagger to his heart.

Chapter Eight

April 5

THE FENCE'S EYES BETRAYED him when Mary laid out their booty on a small, felt-covered table in her back room "office" in the Elephant and Castle. He brought out his own jeweler's loupe, and his hand's slight tremor told Colette, entrusted to do the bargaining, how much he wanted to do business.

"They're good quality," I admit," he said. "But they'll be hard to sell." He rubbed his chin. "I can give you five hundred pounds for the lot, tops."

"Rubbish, Phineas, and you know it!," Colette countered. "Look at the settings. Standard four prong. The stones are good quality, but not exceptional, and the styles are quite in fashion. You'll have no difficulty selling these to a jeweler of easy morals."

"Five hundred and fifty then. Naught more," his narrow eyes hard.

"Then naught it is," Colette said. "I can easily rent a table in the New Caledonian Market and sell them all in a week's time, at twice that!"

"Seven hundred pounds!" Colette exclaimed after the fence left, grumbling only slightly, as she counted the pound notes for the fifth time—just for the sheer pleasure of it. To have so much wealth slide through her fingers was as intoxicating as brandy.

"It helps having you along, Colette," Mary said. "Phineas isn't known for his charity. You being able to quote the shop price held his feet to the fire. The day I caught you trying to pick my pocket in Trafalgar Square was a good day for us both." She laughed. "And you've gotten a good bit better since; not sure I'd catch you now."

"I've been reading about the wealthy people going," Colette said. "Even an actress of the cinema! We'll be very busy. Who else is coming with us?"

"Sam for sure. She can pass for a man easily, and that gets her into the First-Class Smoking Room where she can listen in on rich men's bragging. I don't expect us to need any muscle on this trip, but if pinch comes to shove, she can handle herself."

"How's she traveling, then? As your butler? If so, she'll be second-class like me."

"Sam will travel as my son. She's a good cardsharp and has the manners of an aristocrat, having been raised in a rich man's home. She'll fit right in."

Mary patted Colette's hand, "while you, my dear, can crack a safe like it's tin and can get most men to do what you want with a bat of your eyes."

"And you, Mary, with your gift of gab could sell whisky to a Salvation Army captain." Colette sighed. "And all those wonderfully full wallets just begging to be plucked."

Mary frowned. "No pocket cleaning while we're aboard! If someone knows they've been robbed, where're we to go? No, dearie, we'll only take what's offered to us on this trip."

Mary switched from her South London accent to the voice of an upper-class matron. "While my dear son is playing at cards with other sporting gentlemen, I can intimate to someone with bad luck that I'd be happy to console him in our stateroom. The combination of intimacy with a beautiful woman," she coughed, "and revenge... is a tonic few men can refuse."

"And that's where I come in? You want me to catch you in a, how you say, a 'delicate' situation?"

"Exactly. You can threaten to denounce us both to my beloved son. The whiff of scandal will pry the man's purse open quickly enough. One well-heeled fish could pay for the entire voyage. If there's one thing the wealthy detest more than poor people, it's a poor reputation."

"How do you know so much about the rich? And your accent? How'd you learn to talk like that?"

Mary laughed. "A tale best told over a glass. Let's have a drink, on me."

They adjourned to the front of the pub, and no one gave them a second look as Colette ordered an ale for herself and gin for Mary before they sat down at a back table. The regulars didn't welcome idle curiosity, and as the Forty Elephants had operated out of the pub for well over one-hundred years, the comings and goings of unaccompanied women was hardly noticed.

"I was a lady's maid as a young girl," Mary explained. "I'd been sent to prison at age ten and had just gotten out. I may have forgotten to mention that when I was hired as a domestic, though I made good use of my time in jail. If you ever go to St Paul's Cathedral, visit the basement and pay your respects to Lord Nelson. I helped make some of the tile work on the floor beside him. It wasn't Michelangelo," she laughed, "but the Admiral never complained."

"A thief and an artist?" Colette said. "I can never say my work is on public display. If it is, I'm in trouble."

"The family weren't nobility," Mary continued, "though they put on airs like they was. I started out working for the cook, but the lady of the house liked how I did my hair, and soon I was 'er maid. I dressed her and did her *coiffure,* a word she taught me. I recall her favorite gloves had sixteen buttons on each side. It took me two minutes to do one, though I got as skilled with a buttonhook as I am with a needle.

"The lady grew fond of me and taught me my letters and numbers, though not all out of kindness. She'd have headaches and I'd read to her as she lay in bed, and she'd often send me to the shops on errands, so I had to know how to make change. She also gave me a book to read on how to be a proper lady's maid, which I had to recite by heart. If you're to play the part, you'd best listen closely."

Mary posed with her hands clasped as though reciting for a school play.

"The principal responsibility of a lady's maid is to ensure every detail of her mistress's clothing and hair are well-presented at all times." She winked. "Being of good temper and reliability are vital qualities. Your toes should point straight ahead and never out. Hips should be under you at all times, and in the same forward position that one would assume when squeezing through a narrow space, while the chest is neither thrust forward like a strutting peacock, nor caved in like a broken reed."

Colette laughed. "I can see why you left, the way you thrust out your chest... to good effect."

Mary smirked. "I was naively happy there. I had enough to eat, a roof over my head, and—when the mistress was out, and I wasn't needed to help cook—I borrowed books from their library and read them."

She took a sip of gin before continuing. "God, I love the sound of Shakespeare. I don't understand it 'alf the time, but it don't matter; it's like a priest chanting. The words have a power beyond their meaning.

"Tomorrow, and tomorrow, and tomorrow,
Creeps in this petty pace from day to day,
To the last syllable of recorded time;
And all our yesterdays have lighted fools
The way to dusty death..."

She paused, and for a moment her gaze drifted to another place and time, before shaking herself. "I get only a vague grasp of it all, but enough to make me want to cry. But I didn't quit my place with the family; I was let go. About the time I turned sixteen the family's eighteen-year-old son, Randolph Findlay, Henrietta's recent employer, visited me in my room one night... and not to borrow a book!

"I yelled and the lord and lady came running. She could see what was what right enough, but her husband refused to believe me, and I was shown the door for 'seducing' their son." Mary stared at the light reflected on her drink's surface. "I'd made a mistake, you see. I thought they saw me as a person, that they cared for me, which is why I didn't steal from them. But the moment I became an embarrassment, I was tossed aside."

"Then what happened?"

"The lady must have felt some guilt, for she gave me a letter of recommendation without saying why I left, and I soon found another family. I worked for them for three months, then robbed 'em blind and found another family. The night I was shown the door, I realized where I stood in the eyes of my 'betters,' and I never forgot.

"I worked for a time as an artist's model, and I'd charge less if they'd have someone read to me while I sat. I was still young and romantic, and I fell in love with Tennyson. My favorite is *The Lady of Shalott."*

"I remember some of it from school. It has Lancelot in it, *oui?"*

"Trust you to remember the knight. In the poem, a woman's stuck in a tower and can only see the world through a mirror. One day, she says, "Bugger it all!" She looks out the window and dies. I decided that's how I wanted to live. I'll take life as it comes and whatever the cost, it was my choice. Once I learned about the Elephants, I followed my own path. Thieves may not dine as regular as servants, but they aren't eating table scraps and don't ask anyone's permission."

Colette sipped her ale while in thought. After a moment, she said, "It's not the life I imagined as a young girl in Montreal, but I've never felt freer, not at a man's beck and call." Then she hoisted her tankard. "To the Elephants, a woman's best friend!"

The Queen of the Elephants laughed at that and echoed the toast before turning serious. "One more thing. Having a French maid is quite a distinction, so please bat your eyelashes a lot and talk with *zee Franch* accent on board the ship. You'll certainly raise my social capital."

"Mais oui, madame!" Colette said, tilting her head and playing the coquette. "Though I hope no true Frenchman is nearby. I learned proper French in school, but if I'm not careful, my *Québécois* could trip me up."

At a nod from Mary, Colette signaled the barmaid for another round before continuing. "What can you tell me about the painting?"

Mary pulled out a well-creased copy of *The Times* and pointed to a portrait of a nude woman getting out of what looked like a Roman bath. "I won't try to pronounce the French name—you'd laugh, I'm sure—but this painting is going to set me up for life."

Colette studied the picture closely. *"La Circassienne au*

Bain. It means the Circassian woman of the bath. How are you going to sneak something that large off the ship?"

"I've got some ideas, but we won't know for sure what works until we're on board. The ship leaves on the tenth and is scheduled to arrive in New York on the seventeenth, giving us six full days to sort it out, which is why we needed someone on the inside and a copy of the deck plans."

Colette returned the paper to Mary. "Have you got enough to wear for the trip?"

Mary shook her head. "Not yet. A lady in first-class is expected to wear three different outfits every day, and never the same one twice. Formal wear every night for dinner, 'cepting the first and last nights of the trip. You'll be doing a fair share of honest labor getting me in and out of clothes. Do the figures and I need nineteen outfits and a bathing suit if I want to use the pool." She smirked. "A nice way to meet a gentleman with a roving eye and an insecure wallet."

Colette turned five hundred pounds over to Mary, keeping one hundred for herself. "I still don't see why I don't get a full third of the take. I was the one lying on the ground while Bruno put his hands all over me. My breasts were sore for two days."

"Well, if you didn't show them off all the time, maybe he wouldn't think they were free for the touching."

"*Oui, madame*, I forgot. Poor Bruno."

"Besides, you know my rule. We set something aside after every job in case we need a barrister. I'm good for it."

Colette nodded. It was true, Mary had never failed to hire a barrister from the contingency fund whenever one of the gang got "nicked." Mary was firm but fair. "Very well. I'd rather pay into the pot than spend eight years in prison. I'd be quite an old woman when I got out."

"Why, you little Canadian sled dog! Old woman, you say? I'm over forty, and I still look as good as women half my age."

Colette knew Mary was, in fact, past fifty, but turned to a safer topic. "You'll certainly look good in all those dresses while I'll be in a maid's uniform the whole time. It's not fair!"

"Oh, don't pout so! I'll need your help to maintain and wear all those clothes, plus do my hair before dinner. We wouldn't have the time for you to go fishing, too." The Elephant Queen knocked back the rest of her gin. "Between what we can haul in, Sam's 'luck' at cards, and the painting, we might be able to take a holiday on the return trip and just enjoy ourselves."

She burped and put her glass down. "Dress in something smart with a full skirt. This afternoon, we'll be taking tea and a few stylish things for the cruise from Harrods." She winked, "The store that every woman knows."

***

First Officer Charles Lightoller was immaculate in his dark blue wool winter uniform when he reported to his new post. "Good afternoon, sir," the Purser said as he marked him aboard. Such trivialities were important, as Lightoller's pay did not commence until he was listed "present for duty."

"The captain has requested all officers report to his cabin as soon as they board." The deck officer said. "Will you need someone to guide you there?"

"No need. I've served aboard her sister ship. Though I notice some modifications in the *Titanic,* I doubt there'd be any major changes in the wheelhouse or officer's quarters."

Lightoller knocked respectfully once he'd climbed to the pinnacle of the ship, both geometrically and politically.

"Come," a soft voice commanded.

"First Officer Lightoller reporting, sir. What are your orders?"

Captain Smith—with his kind face and white beard—could have easily posed as Father Christmas, and his demeanor matched his appearance. The senior captain of the line, he'd been persuaded to forgo retirement long enough to make the initial round trip of the company's newest treasure, and more than one crew member who'd sailed with him before counted themselves lucky to make a crossing with him one final time.

"I've rather bad news for you, Charles," he said. "It appears you've been demoted."

"Sir? Have I done something wrong?"

Smith placed his hand on his young officer's shoulder. "Not in the slightest, but the line has chosen William Murdoch as First Officer, based upon his recent post as First aboard the *Olympia.* You're still to serve, of course, and rightly so, but as Second."

"But my uniform... I don't have time to change the stripes!"

"Not to worry, Charles. I'll make plain to the other officers what happened. Just take your orders from First Officer Murdoch as befits your position, and no one will be the wiser. Consider this as postponement only. I'm certain you'll command someday; this is but a temporary setback."

Lightoller swallowed bile along with his disappointment. "Is there anything else, sir?"

"Not at this time. I admire how you took the news. Very British of you. We have much to do to prepare, and I'm fortunate to have you as one of my officers. Carry on!"

Not the best start to a new posting, the new Second Officer thought, as he made his way to his cabin. *I suppose I'd best inform the Purser, so I don't get overpaid.*

Chapter Nine

Hoisting in the Woman's Attire Department at Harrods went smoothly. Colette would distract a salesclerk, say a request for a blue silk chemise when they only had cotton, and Mary could slide some kidskin gloves or silk stockings within the compartments beneath her skirt. After two hours Mary found it difficult to walk normally, and she signaled Colette it was time to move on.

"Oooh, what lovely hats!" cooed Colette as she lifted a shoulder-width silk creation.

"Put it down," Mary said, looking over her pince-nez lenses. "A maid would never wear such a thing." She pointed to a shelf in the back of the department. "A proper straw boater for you, as befits your station."

"As befits my role," Colette retorted.

"As you like. It would still be out of character. Your job is to make me shine." Mary patted her shoulder. "No worries, love. If this makes us as much as I think it will, I can retire and run a nice little bookshop in Soho and you'll have the field to yourself. 'Til then, just follow my lead."

"I have, Mary, ever since Trafalgar Square, and you've never led me wrong. Very well."

Colette sighed but returned the ponderous headgear to the hat stand and trudged towards the plain straw head covering "worthy" of her assumed place in society. She wrinkled her nose. "This is what an English maid would wear, but if you want an exotic 'Frenchie' like me, then you'd best let me choose something less... utilitarian."

She eyed a black felt cap slightly smaller than a beret with a single red pheasant feather and snatched it. "*Voilà*!"

Colette admired herself in the mirror, while Mary looked on.

"Very well," the older woman relented. "It does suit you. Pity I've no more room, it would fit easily in my pockets otherwise. You'll make an honest woman of me yet."

After a light lunch in the Harrods Tea Room, they stopped at the White Star Line office to book passage.

"Are there still first-class staterooms available?" Mary asked the young ticket clerk.

"Aye, madam, more's the pity. Her maiden voyage, and the *Titanic* will be about a third empty at this rate. What with the coal strike and all, people are nervous she won't make her sailing date."

"My good fortune, then," Mary said. "I require two first-class tickets for myself and my son, and one second-class for my maid," she nodded towards Colette who did a small curtsy, gritting her teeth as she did so.

"Your name, and those of your fellow passengers?"

Mary looked out the window and noticed an advertisement in a pharmacy window. "Bayer," she said. "Mrs. Mary Bayer. My son's name is Samuel, and my maid is Colette, Colette Du..." Mary saw the young woman's face tighten, "Bois. Colette DuBois.

The ticket clerk raised his head but before he could ask, "I'm widowed, sir." She sighed for effect, "these past twenty years."

"My condolences, Mrs. Bayer. I have a first-class stateroom with bunk beds available."

"That would be perfect. My son enjoys climbing."

***

Once outside the ticket office Mary squeezed Colette's shoulder. "I'm sorry, Colette, I nearly gave them your real name. I can understand you not wanting it on an official document."

Colette wiped her moist palms on her skirt. "You gave me a fright. There's small chance anyone would notice, but why take the chance at all? I can never return to Canada, but New York is close enough to put me in danger.

DuBois is a fine name, and I might even remember it."

They returned triumphant to Mary's flat and found Sam there. Hanging on the back of a chair was a small white cotton jacket, while spread upon a large antique-appearing table were the deck plans of the ship. Beside it on the floor was a case of wine and a tin cylinder four feet long with a leather carrying strap.

Propped up against the wall was a large painting of a nude, red-haired woman standing in front of a vaguely Roman background. Colette whistled. "It's grand!"

Mary inspected the artwork with a critical eye. "Carol did a good job, especially having just eight days to do it. Luckily, she had the right tints in stock, having recently done a similar work."

"Aren't we celebrating a little too soon?" Colette asked as she pulled out a bottle and studied its impressive label. "This must be grand, whatever it is. It certainly looks expensive."

Sam took the bottle from Colette's hands and replaced it. "A bottle of this vintage usually sells for ten pounds."

"What?! You spent one hundred and twenty pounds on wine?"

Mary laughed. "I spent one pound for the bottles and the case and another pound for the cheap plonk I had Sam fill them with."

"The wine is our excuse to go down to the baggage hold," Sam said, "where the painting will be stored."

She pulled a slender knife from her boot and cut a length of cord to secure the box of wine before walking over to the painting. "Carol told me it's easier to duplicate a large painting than a small one; the scope of the work makes you stand back to admire it, so variations in the brushwork are easily overlooked."

Colette narrowed her eyes. "I understand. If we simply steal the painting, it'll be discovered and there'll be a hunt until it's found."

"Not to mention the hunt for its thieves," Mary added.

Colette peered under the table. "There must be a secret compartment then. That's how you get the copy on board?"

"Exactly," Mary said. "I'll say it's a valuable antique so it'll be stored in the same area of the ship as the real painting. We'll pop the real one out of its external frame and make the exchange once the ship is underway and the staff are confident everything is secure. Putting the fake inside the real frame will make it look all the more genuine."

Sam pulled the jacket off the back of the chair and put it on. "This is an exact copy of the jackets the stewards wear on board. I'll say a passenger directed me to secure a bottle of their expensive wine from the hold, and you, my dear," she said, bowing to Colette, "as the maid... will come along to make sure I select the proper bottle, and distract any guards that might be there."

"How will we know where the real painting is being held?" Colette asked. She nodded towards the ship plans on the table. "There's more than one cargo hold. I doubt we can wander among them for very long."

"That's where our new friend, Hope, comes in," Mary said. "She'll locate the painting beforehand so we can go right to it and she can help distract any Able-Bodied Seamen assigned to the area."

"Oh, I don't need any help in distracting men, but that painting looks heavy. Sam, can you make the exchange by yourself without damaging one of them?"

"With that much money to be had? Just give me five minutes." Sam mock bowed. "And no one will be able to say for certain when the switch was made."

"Sounds simple enough," Colette said. "But afterward, how do you intend to sell it?"

"The payment scheme is my favorite part of the plan," Mary said. "Henrietta gave me the name and address of the new owner, a Mister A. C. Smith. He's an American who made his fortune in railroads and is what the wealthy call 'new money,' so he probably bought it to earn his way to respectability. Assuming no one detects the fake quickly—and they shouldn't as they won't be looking—he'll be sure to display it to impress his important friends with how sophisticated he's become. We'll give him three months after the crossing before I send him an anonymous letter telling him his prize is a copy. He'll be keen, frantic even, to ransom the real Blondel from us to protect his reputation.

"His pride will be worth even more than the painting," Mary concluded. "I'll demand a hundred thousand pounds for the original."

Colette gasped. "A hundred *thousand*?"

"And another hundred thousand... for my silence."

Colette frowned. "What's my cut?"

"Ten percent for you and the same for Sam."

"*Ten* percent?"

"Ten percent of a large sum is far better than one hundred percent of what you make in your little escapades at Harrods and Selfridges. *Twenty thousand pounds*, Colette. You'll be quite comfortable, I'm sure. I'm paying Hope, the passage, making the copy, and doing all the planning. If this goes right, I'll retire, and you'll never see me again," she winked, "unless you want to buy a book."

"And how do we live until the owner ransoms the painting? Three months is a long time to wait."

"Oh, we shall not be idle aboard the ship. Never fear. But nothing we do should jeopardize the heist as we don't want to draw the wrong kind of attention to ourselves. Remember, *no pick pocketing*. I know it's a game to you, but if I see someone patting their pockets after you pass them, I'll cut your share in half, understand?"

"*Oui, madame*! Now, if you'll excuse me, I need to practice walking without thrusting out my chest."

"She's very animated," Sam said once Colette had gone, her chest protruding. "What was that about chest thrusting?"

"A long story," Mary laughed. "She reminds me of myself at her age, a mix of dirt and dreams."

"She seems an odd fit for the Elephants," Sam said. "Most grew up on the streets in London; she's educated and has proper manners when she chooses to use them."

"Which is why she could pose as well-to-do for the jewel heist back at the store. I'm lucky I found her when I did. She'd just arrived in England from Canada the week before; the poor thing was near starving."

"I suspect she worked in a jewelry store and stole from her employer. That would explain why she's here in

England and knows so much about gems."

"You're half right, Sam. She did work in a jewelry store, her father's."

"She stole from her own father?"

"Yes, after she killed him."

Chapter Ten

April 9

HARRY ARRIVED AT THE harbor in Southampton just before five p.m. Had he been blindfolded, he'd still have known his location by the smell of the ocean, sound of the gull cries, and rumble of the mighty engines powering the vessel as she idled pier side. He paid the cab driver and turned to look at the ship awaiting her maiden voyage. Though no naval expert, he admired the clean lines of his temporary home. Freshly painted, the dark black hull was majestic, its sharp white lines above bright and hopeful like the future the ship heralded.

Harry's head craned up, and up, then up some more. He had sailed a half-dozen times before between Britain and America, so was accustomed to the size of modern passenger ships, but while he'd read in the papers the dimensions of this behemoth, it was one thing to recall numbers, to recite them in his head: eight hundred and eighty-two feet long, ninety-two feet across, and *ten* stories above the surface. But this seagoing palace was more than a ship; it was a vast floating city. On that cool spring afternoon Harry had every reason to be awed, for the vessel floating before him was the largest moving object ever created.

Laborers were scurrying madly across various gangplanks, carrying furniture, art fixtures, and food. Four sweating men were wheeling a grand piano. As Harry approached the vessel, he noticed a truck arrive, its bed overflowing with flowers. The driver no sooner halted before stewards descended like locusts, leaving the truck barren in the blink of an eye. The Star newspaper had named the ship "The Millionaires' Special." For once, it was not journalistic hyperbole.

Harry introduced himself to the officer guarding the main gangplank as Mister Daniels, a special guest of Director Ismay. The man, in his spotless blue winter uniform, looked at a clipboard, checked off Harry's name, then frowned.

"My apologies, sir," he said, "but I have a note to summon a Master at Arms to meet you here when you come aboard. Would you please stand to the side until one can arrive?"

There being no passengers to supervise, the Masters at Arms were mostly unengaged, and thus a burly uniformed man soon arrived. In his hand was a heavy canvas bag with a lockable opening, like those used to carry bank notes.

"Ah, Mister Daniels, I believe?" the burly man said, displaying a thick Scottish brogue.

"Correct, Mister...?"

"King, sir. Just King." He opened the bag. "I believe you know what this is for?"

Harry produced his .45 and .32 caliber revolvers.

"Are they loaded, sir?"

"Aye. An unloaded weapon does me little good."

"Unload them, please, and keep the bullets. We don't store loaded firearms in the office."

Harry did as instructed under the widened eyes of the officer of the deck, removing the bullets before placing the revolvers inside the bag, and King locked it.

"They'll be kept in our office until you leave the ship. My mate or I can return them then."

Harry nodded, feeling undressed without the comforting weight of the .45 against his chest.

"Well, I'm off. I'll see you shortly in the Gentleman's Smoking Room."

The burly man tugged his cap and was gone.

The deck officer directed a nearby steward to take the handcart with Harry's single suitcase and lead him to his room. Harry followed the man to the first-class reception area. Once past the entrance, the steward swerved to the left around a descending staircase to the elevators. Harry was struck by the smell of fresh paint, varnish, and the glare of polished brass fittings.

The ship was like a grand young debutante—a royal one, almost—dressed in her finest to impress. And impressed Harry was.

***

"Nice canister, Colette," Mary said as she smoothed out the deck plans in the back room of Sally Farthing's pub.

"I saw that's how the draftsmen carried them and got one to keep the plans clean and dry," she laughed, "as I'm not going back for another. I broke a young man's heart getting these."

"Lifts!" Sam said. "They've got lifts fore and aft."

***

The three elevators were spaced neatly side by side, with a small sofa in the back of each and an arched top somehow reminiscent of a dog's house. Harry's stateroom was one deck below, on C Deck, on the starboard side and forward of midships, next to the surgery.

The standard for first-class cabins was to be equal to the Ritz hotel, so Harry was surprised to learn he'd have to share the common toilets and bathing suites with other first-class passengers. Only the ship's captain and deluxe staterooms had their own facilities. The steward, who introduced himself as Littlejohn, told Harry that reservations for the bath could be made through him.

Harry shrugged. As he'd never stayed at the Ritz, he couldn't compare, though the bunk bed (he chose the lower berth) seemed more than adequate, and the armoire had ample space for his meager luggage. A small desk also served as a bedside table, and a washbasin in the corner below a mirror completed the furnishings.

"It's not very large," he said.

"Sorry, sir," Littlejohn replied, "but this stateroom is the lowest standard for first-class. It was designed for a business traveler who preferred the luxury this class affords. We have several unclaimed staterooms of a higher standard if you'd prefer. I could get you in touch with the Purser to arrange other accommodations."

"No, thank you, steward. This cabin suits my budget nicely."

Once the luggage was stowed, the steward bowed slightly. "I've been instructed to give you a tour of the first-class areas of the ship between here and the Smoking Room, where Mister Ismay will meet you." His eyebrows lifted slightly. "A most unusual request, but then so is boarding a passenger the day before departure."

The steward looked at Harry, but the detective said nothing. He'd learned the power of silence from watching senior agents interrogate criminals. Most people can't stand it for more than a moment, so if one kept quiet long enough in a conversation, the other person felt compelled to speak. When the steward saw Harry would offer no explanation, he left the handcart in the passageway, and led Harry back to the elevators.

"I'd like to take the stairs," Harry said, "so that I know all their twists and turns."

"Good enough, sir," the steward said. "What business did you say you're in?"

"I didn't, but it's insurance."

"Well, you're a thorough man, Mister Daniels. Let's get to it then. Mister Ismay is expecting us at six."

"There's naught for you to concern yourself with forward," the steward said, after they'd ascended to B Deck. "The most expensive staterooms are there, and you'll have no need to visit them 'less you get invited to a game of cards on Sunday."

"Why Sunday," Harry asked, "and not any other night?"

"Cards aren't allowed in the public areas on Sundays, but we don't police what folks do in their cabins. Still," he said, pointing towards the aft staterooms, "if someone in that part of the ship invites you to play, I'd recommend you decline." The steward looked at Harry's plain wool suit. "They can play for higher stakes than you or me."

They reached the aft staircase and reception area that

surrounded it. Wicker chairs lined the wall on three sides, and a passageway led aft to a restaurant. Harry looked past the entrance and saw an impressive dining area with tables set with bone china and sparkling crystal.

"There's a restaurant in addition to a dining area?"

"Aye, sir. Some passengers prefer dining alone at a time of their choosing or something more exotic than what's offered by the ship's kitchen." He hesitated. "Not that there's anything wrong with ship fare, mind you."

"I'm sure there's not, Mister Littlejohn."

The steward led on, resigned to the mysterious passenger having more questions than answers, and guided Harry aft to a little café on the starboard side named the Café Parisian. "Judging from my time on the *Olympic*, you'll find younger passengers here late at night drinking and playing bridge or meeting up with someone of the opposite gender. After we sail, the ship will list all the first-class passengers in the ship's daily bulletin." He winked. "Mothers with marriageable daughters use that list like a menu to select unattached men of the 'proper' class to introduce to their young ladies. Sometimes the stewards take bets on how these meetings will turn out." He froze, then stammered, "All in honest fun, of course."

"Of course," Harry said, smiling—in part to reassure him and in part because the steward's comment had reminded him of Jane Austen's famous opening line: *It is universally acknowledged that a single man in possession of good fortune must be in want of a wife.*

Pride and prejudice, indeed.

As they made their way back to the stairs, the steward noted Harry wrinkling his nose as they passed a group of laborers applying varnish to a wooden floor.

"Sorry for the smell, sir. The delivery of the ship was delayed, and we've been scrambling to finish her in time. You may have noticed the large shipment of flowers just as you arrived? They're to be placed all over the ship to cover the smell of paint and lacquer. It should fade away in a couple of days."

On A Deck, Littlejohn directed Harry aft once more. "Only staterooms forward from here." They passed through a revolving door into a narrow passageway with windows on the starboard side, looking out onto the First-Class Promenade. The passageway was dark, framed in black, but the decking on the promenade was a bright yellow pine, making it easier to navigate in dim light.

Littlejohn noticed Harry's gaze. "Here's where you'll find most of the ladies between breakfast and luncheon to lessen the effect of seven-course dinners. Those who don't take the air soon need their stewardess to adjust their corset stays."

They continued aft until they reached the Reading and Writing Room, a large yet welcoming space filled with writing desks and small tables. A perfect place for a young lady to read an indiscreet note from a young man and to write her reply. Harry estimated the room could comfortably seat around forty women as the steward dryly noted that men rarely entered this room on its sister ship unless they were seeking their wife.

They proceeded down the port side to the First-Class Lounge, the largest single room within the ship after the dining area. The room spanned the width of the ship and was well appointed with a fake fireplace and a full bookcase.

Looking about, Harry estimated the room could accommodate over one hundred standing guests. This was the social heart of the first-class world, where the peacocks would preen and, given the flourish of feathers adorning women's hats, there would be actual plumage in abundance. Harry could almost hear the rustle of silk and see the sparkle of champagne glasses as the elite of polite society congratulated one another on being wealthy.

After admiring the glistening "public square" of the First-Class Reception Room, Steward Littlejohn led him through a revolving door on the far side and down an enclosed passageway. Harry had traveled from the world of women in the Reading Room to the mixed-gender environment of the Reception Room. Next stop: the male bastion of the Smoking Room, where the managing director of the Line awaited.

The saloon contained the only working fireplace on the ship. There were small boxes of coal on both sides while the mantel extended arms out in a welcoming embrace, making for a small alcove in the middle. Before the fireplace was a small dark oaken table with four heavy leather chairs. Seated at the table was Mister Ismay, sitting beside a slender middle-aged man with an open face and keen brown eyes, holding a blackthorn walking stick.

Standing on both sides of the table was a Master at Arms, each in a dark blue jacket and white pants, with broad shoulders, and one with a crooked nose, indicating a rougher life before his current posting on a luxury liner. Their large hands were clasped before them, and they gave the impression of bored mastiffs.

Ismay nodded towards the man sitting beside him, who stood as Harry approached. "Thomas Andrews, the ship's designer and midwife. He's overseen every detail of the ship, from drawing the design to the construction. There's not a rivet on this vessel he hasn't personally inspected."

Andrews took Harry's hand and muttered, "Pleasure," before resuming his seat.

Ismay turned to the steward. "I'm sure you've already puzzled out that Mister Daniels is not a typical passenger."

The man nodded, saying nothing.

"He is on short-term contract with the Line, consulting on security issues."

Littlejohn looked at Harry with newfound respect. "He did mention he's in the insurance business. If you don't mind me asking, Mister Ismay, why tell me?"

"Because I'd like you to pass him any gossip you hear from the other stewards that sounds suspicious. As the staff are often ignored by our passengers, you and your colleagues may notice something he misses. If so, please share what you hear with him."

Littlejohn shrugged. "As you wish, sir. I'm no spy, but I'll pass along whatever smells off. Is there anything else? I've still much to do to prepare for tomorrow."

Ismay shook his head. "You're dismissed, but please keep Mister Daniel's true purpose to yourself."

"Aye, sir," Littlejohn replied, giving Harry a final look before departing.

Ismay gestured to the burly statues standing silent beside him. "You've met Mister King already," Ismay said, indicating the man to his right, "and this is his colleague, Mister Donachie." The man on Ismay's left with the broken nose nodded briefly. "Their major occupation is to enforce proper behavior below decks, but if you need muscle, they'll assist you."

"Is there someplace we could secure a prisoner?" Harry asked.

Mister Andrews cleared his throat. "When I designed the ship, I gave no thought to a brig, as we've never had one on any of our other vessels, but I've identified a third-class cabin where we could place an external lock. I had the holes drilled for the lock and hasp before filling them in with putty and painting over them. They can be quickly installed if necessary. The Masters at Arms have a lock ready to emplace and the cabin is on E Deck, the same as their office, so it would be easy to tend to a prisoner without attracting attention."

Ismay turned to the Master of Arms to his right. "You're both free to go. I wanted you to see Mister Daniels, so you'd know he's acting under my authority. Give him your full cooperation."

The two statues nodded, demonstrating they were fully animate, and left without speaking. *Apparently,* Harry thought, *they weren't hired for their conversational skills.*

"I expect to be notified as soon as possible should you detain a passenger," Ismay said, handing Harry a thick folder. "Here's a brief biography—some with photographs—of our wealthier guests, the ones I deem at highest risk. I expect you to study this file closely and to pay particular attention to young Mauritz Findlay, as he'll be accompanying the Blondel to its new owner in America. Such biographical information is common knowledge amongst the 'Four Hundred,' and it will allow you to blend in with the Americans."

"The 'Four Hundred?'" Harry asked.

"The elite of New York Society, which coincides with the capacity of the ballroom in the Astor mansion."

"Good Lord, they have a metric for everything!" Harry said, then remembered his place. "Thank you, sir, I'll study it tonight. Anything else?"

"I've asked Mister Andrews to complete your tour, including below decks, in case you need to pursue a suspect. Good hunting!"

Andrews stood, leaning slightly on his cane, "If you'll follow me, please, Mister Worth."

Andrews guided Harry to the rear of the Smoking Room and through a revolving door leading to a glass-enclosed room sporting potted palm trees, rattan chairs, and settees. In the center was another elevator.

"Here's the veranda and Palm Court," the architect said. "A popular place for young ladies and gentlemen to meet up."

"Based upon what Steward Littlejohn told me, that seems to be a major preoccupation onboard ship."

Andrews shrugged. "The passengers spend a week together in forced idleness. It would be more remarkable if young, healthy people didn't preen and strut to attract a mate when they are denied other distractions."

"Ah," Harry said. "It sounds as though you're a devotee of Professor Darwin."

"Well, you'll certainly see some odd specimens here."

They made their way forward to the Grand Staircase then went down to D Deck and the reception area. There being no other first-class public areas on this deck, they halted.

Andrews gestured to the stairway. "You'll find the Swimming Bath and the Squash and Racquet Courts on F Deck, as well as the Hot and Steam Rooms, the Shampoo Rooms, and the Temperate Room for the patrons to cool off. Unless you're willing to put on a bathing suit, you'd stand out. I doubt you could hide a set of manacles there."

"As I didn't pack the proper attire, I'll forgo the pleasure."

"Well then, that concludes the public, first-class areas. Now to see the sinews of this fine lady and see what makes this ship something more than a floating hotel."

They took the stairway, no longer so grand, and—after reaching E Deck—turned right. Andrews pointed up and down a long corridor. "This is called Scotland Road, and it runs the length of the ship. If you ever need to get from one end to the other quickly while below decks, this is the route to take. Let's go forward, and I'll show you where your colleagues have their office."

"You mean the Masters at Arms?" Harry straightened his cuffs. "I think I'm something more than a trained guard dog."

"Are you now, Mister Worth? From my perspective, you're just another hound with a fancier pedigree." He frowned. "Your agency's reputation as strike breakers hardly qualifies you for sainthood. To me you're little more than a private policeman, paid to exact private justice for those who can afford it, against those who can't."

"I've never been involved in strike breaking, Mister Andrews."

"Lack of opportunity isn't the same thing as virtue. If your employer sent you to bash a man's head for wanting a decent wage, I reckon you'd do it readily enough. Never mind, we both have work to do, let's be about it."

Andrews turned and headed off, while Harry, gritting his teeth, followed in silence. Becoming a private detective sounded grand when you read about it in the cheap novels called 'shilling shockers' in England, but Mister Andrews had the right of it, Harry admitted.

I thought I was on the side of Justice, he thought. *Turns out I'm mostly paid to protect the rich from the poor.*

Chapter Eleven

ONCE THEY REACHED AN open area at the end of the corridor, they turned right and crossed another long hallway before reaching the office of the Masters at Arms, finding Mister King in residence.

"Checking on your weapons?" the burly man asked. He pointed to a locked gun cabinet with a glass front fastened to the wall where Harry saw his pistols neatly stowed in racks alongside two others. "A couple of the ship's officers keep firearms here but no others at present. No need to repel boarders on this ship."

"Do passengers give you much trouble?" Harry asked.

"Not much on a liner as fine as this, but we've also got to keep our eyes on the crew." He winked. "On other ships, I've caught a steward dressed in his finest pretending to be a passenger after striking up a friendship with a young lady. If a lifeboat's rocking during a calm sea, I've a pretty good idea what I'll find."

"You don't mind having me aboard?"

"I gets paid the same, and I could never pass for a 'gentleman' amongst the crowd you'll be rubbing elbows with. Be careful, lad." He wagged his finger. "They may dress finer than the folks in third-class, but their teeth are all the sharper for it. You're welcome to 'em. Give me a drunken bricklayer from London who's raising a ruckus, and him and me will likely become mates before the evening's done. A wealthy banker who punches a lawyer?

Best I can do is help the man up, but not to worry. Whispers over champagne glasses will do the banker more harm than I ever could."

"From what I've seen," Harry said, "I must agree. The rich have their own code, and their own way of enforcing it."

Andrews pulled out his pocket watch. "I have a busy night ahead of me, Mister Worth. And we've still two more decks to walk."

"Quite." Harry turned to King. "Hope to see you during the voyage."

"If'n you do, sir, it's bad news for us both."

Andrews increased his pace as they descended to F Deck, and he breezily conducted Harry past the squash court, swimming pool, and Turkish bath, arriving finally at a dining area with long tables.

"Mister Ismay takes offense when someone refers to the third-class passengers as 'steerage.' They have a selection to choose from at meals, a steward to serve them, and cabins for families and single passengers, separated by sex, of course."

"That's very generous of the Line."

"Not at all. They know the first thing an immigrant does after arriving in America is write their family in the Old Country. A letter saying how well they were treated makes it likely the next lot will sail with them, too."

When they descended to G Deck, Andrews pointed out an office where several clerks sorted through mailbags.

"We are designated RMS *Titanic*, as we are chartered as a mail ship, hence Royal Mail Ship, though you'll find two of the clerks are with the American postal service."

"You mean I could post a letter to the United States from here with American stamps and seals?"

"Certainly. Money orders as well."

"This entire ship is a mixture of two countries."

"More than you realize. Although the White Star Line is a British concern, it's entirely owned by the American, JP Morgan."

Harry felt his throat constrict. "Will he be aboard as well?"

Andrews shook his head. “He was considering it, but other matters required his attention at the last minute. Something concerning a financial scandal, I believe.”

Harry remembered the mysterious package that brought him over to London, but said nothing. Guarding secrets was another part of a courier’s job.

“You’ll be spared from guarding *his* purse, at least,” Andrews continued. “Now, if you’ll follow me, we can complete our tour before you attend to the files Mister Ismay gave you.”

After passing through the fireman’s quarters to the boiler room, Harry saw the den of the dragon that drove the ship, and those who fed it.

The architect paused outside the watertight door. “I doubt you’d ever need to go in here for your job, but I wish every passenger could see what it takes to power this floating pleasure palace. It’ll only take a moment, and we won’t go far past the door, but I’d like you to remember there are men down here every hour of the day and night flinging coal into the boilers to make sure the champagne is cold, steaks hot, and this mass of iron can travel the world.”

Harry nodded, struck silent by the man’s intensity, and braced himself before stepping through. The heat of an Arabian desert nearly blasted him back out as he gazed at the sweating, coal-streaked men serving boilers arranged in ranks from fore to aft. Though the blazing fires reminded him of Dante’s Inferno, he noted an order to the process.

“Welcome to the home of the Black Gang!” Andrews shouted, over the roar of the furnaces. He pointed to the men flinging coal into the red, hungry mouths of the boilers. “Those are the firemen. After the engineers, they’re the top of the pyramid at the bottom of the ship.”

“What could be a lower job than that?” Harry croaked, the dry heat stealing the moisture from his mouth as soon as he opened it.

The architect pointed to men carrying coal about in baskets. “The trimmers, so-called because, as the ship consumes fuel, they trim the bunkers to keep the ship on an even keel. They lug coal to the firemen and carry off the ash and 'clinkers' that don't burn."

Andrews wiped the perspiration quickly forming on his forehead. "Due to the coal strike, which gave the miners a living wage by the way, we had to offload fuel from other White Star ships so we could depart on time, and some of it's poor quality. Between that and the fire in bunker number one—"

"There's a fire onboard?!"

Andrews gave a rueful smile. "More of a smolder, but your reaction is precisely why we don't want it to become common knowledge, so keep it to yourself. We're dousing it with water regularly and one fireman is digging it out. We'll need to go to Belfast once we return to England to inspect for damage, but we're in no danger. The ship is double hulled beneath the water line, so even in the unlikely event it caused a breach in the inner hull, we would maintain integrity.

"Then there's the watertight doors between compartments." He pointed to a passageway at the aft end of the compartment. "We have the boilers divided into six compartments linked by doors that can be closed from the captain's bridge, by the crew here in the boiler room, or automatically—if rising water triggers the float mechanism. Add the other doors in the ship and it's divided into sixteen compartments along its length."

He pointed to a ladder. "Each compartment has an escape hatch should a crew member not get out before the door closes. I also put in watertight doors along Scotland Road, but those are operated manually to prevent trapping people between them, as there is no other way out of the corridor except along it."

"You've thought of everything."

"As much as is humanly possible. This ship could stay afloat with as many as four flooded compartments. Between that and her double hull, she's as unsinkable as I could make her."

Harry looked at the men feeding the fires, singing as they flung coal into the infernos. He imagined what it must be like to work there as the deck lurched during a heavy storm and was certain it wasn't a job he'd sign up for.

"I'll take you back to Deck C, Agent Worth, where you should be safe to wander on your own. Then I, like you, have a full night ahead of me in preparation for tomorrow."

They parted ways on the Grand Staircase just as Harry saw his steward, Littlejohn, walk by with his arms full of towels.

"Is there anything you require for the night, sir? My apologies, but we're not staffed for passengers tonight, so this'll be the only time I have for you until tomorrow."

Harry hefted the folder Ismay had given him. "I've got my work cut out for me to memorize some of the notables, so if you could bring a sandwich and a beer to my cabin, I'd best get to it."

The steward nodded and left, intent on retrieving the meager dinner before setting his assigned rooms to rights. Tomorrow would be a madhouse for them both. Tonight would be Littlejohn's last good night's sleep until they reached New York.

Chapter Twelve

AFTER THE DECK PLANS had been thoroughly reviewed, they were stowed and Sally brought them dinner in their room above her pub.

"You won't get a meal like this on the *Titanic*," she said. "It'll be all quail eggs and foie gras. No solid food for people who work for their bread."

Mary laughed. "I haven't worked for a living in years, but it's time to study the situation. I'll clear the table, then we can go over our possibilities. We can't afford to lose an opportunity because we don't recognize someone. Thank you, Sally, for doing the research for us. We're all ears."

The tavern owner brought a small cardboard box to the table and pulled out a sheaf of newspaper clippings and a magnifying glass.

"Let's start with the richest first," she said, and laid down a newspaper article with a photograph of a bespectacled, slender, middle-aged man wearing a straw boater hat. "Here's the prize catch, John J Astor IV, one of the richest men in the world. He served in the Spanish American War in an artillery unit he paid for himself, so if you call him 'Colonel,' he'll like you immediately."

"Weak points?" Mary asked, studying the picture closely.

"He's a shrewd businessman, so I don't think he'll be interested in fake Australian mining stocks, and he's not fond of cards, but not to worry. His Achilles heel will be boarding alongside him."

She laid a picture of a young woman next to Astor's.

"This young lady, the second Mrs. Astor, has yet to reach her twentieth year and is great with child. She is the apple of his eye, and he cannot deny her anything. The way to his rather enormous wallet is through this little woman."

"And what are her weaknesses?" Colette asked. "Since she's pregnant, I doubt she'll be easy to engage socially."

"I suspect that, like many women who are not born to riches," Sally said, "she craves the approval of the elite to feel she belongs, just like the man who bought the painting you're after. There was a great scandal when Astor married her due to her age, and several ministers refused to officiate their wedding. She'll feel judged in the presence of old money."

"And what role will you play, Mrs. Bayer?" Colette asked Mary. "Old or new?"

"I can't pretend to be aristocracy, not English anyway. Someone would know the person I was pretending to be. I don't speak any foreign languages, so can't be a *Contessa.* I'll explain the name, Bayer, as the name of my deceased husband who was related to the family that founded the company. I guess that makes me 'established' money, if not old."

"Established," Sam chuckled. "So, I'm your established son? Sounds better than bastard, anyway."

"I'll try to make friends with her," Mary said, "and see where that leads us. Any other passengers we should consider? There are a lot of wealthy Americans returning from Europe and the closer they get to New York, the more careless they'll become."

***

Harry studied the next newspaper clipping from the overflowing folder, containing a photo of a robust middle-aged woman.

"Mrs. Margaret Brown," Ismay's note read, "a well-to-do divorcee. Her husband made a fortune mining in Colorado. Close friend with Mister and Missus Astor."

Ismay's notes said she had a reputation as a shrewd

businesswoman, though generous to charity, having come from poverty, and a fierce supporter of Woman's Suffrage.

If I were a conman, Harry thought, *I'd approach her with a fake charity. I'll need to look out for someone posing as a missionary. Not many missionaries can afford to travel first-class on a ship like this.*

***

"Sounds like Missus Brown would respond better to another woman than to you, my son," Mary said, winking at Sam. "I'll see what gossip I can pick up over tea."

Sam frowned. "Do Americans even drink tea?"

"When in Rome, my dear," Sally said. "She's well-traveled and should know how to behave amongst the British."

"That's a relief! Anyone else?"

"There's an elderly couple, Isidore and Ida Straus..."

***

Harry studied the photo of the elderly couple. The notes listed Isidore's brief stint as a blockade runner for the Confederacy during the Civil War before becoming a Congressman. Afterwards Straus focused on his lucrative business life as co-owner with his brother, Nathan, of Macy's Department Store. The couple's devotion to one another was the source of envious gossip amongst the elite of New York society.

A man who is settled in life and enjoying the fruits of his labors, Harry thought. *Unless he has a fondness for cards, he'd make a poor target for a swindler.*

***

"I want to hear about the movie actress!" Colette interrupted. "What do you know about her?"

Sally laid another photo on the table, this time of a young woman with dark, curly hair and dimples. "Dorothy Gibson. Not the best target you have."

"Why not?" Mary asked. "Too well-known?"

"Actresses are more famous than wealthy. Oh, she's not poor, not by any means, but compared to the old money on this voyage, she's almost a pauper. Besides, she's so popular it'll be difficult to get an audience with her."

Mary laughed. "More famous than wealthy? Sounds like she belongs with the Elephants!"

Chapter Thirteen

April 10, Boarding Day

HARRY WOKE TO A rap on his door promptly at seven a.m. He fumbled for the light switch and opened the door to see Steward Littlejohn holding a tray.

"Sorry to wake you, sir," Littlejohn said, "but the kitchen's only making food for the crew this morning. I was able to get you a pot of tea and a scone with a rasher of bacon. Luncheon will be ready at one, so I hope this'll tide you over till then."

Harry rubbed his eyes, the names of the wealthy guests blurring together. He'd been up until two a.m. studying the list of notables Director Ismay had thrust upon him, and wished he'd specified coffee as his morning crutch. No matter. Time to face the day and the gauntlet of the privileged he'd have to guard, hopefully without their knowledge.

"Thank you, Mister Littlejohn. What time does boarding begin?"

"Nine-thirty for the third-class passengers, the rest to follow soon after. But I need to go stand muster now, so there'll be no crew to tend to you 'til that's completed. With all the to-do of boarding, I doubt I'll be free again until we leave port."

"Stand muster?"

"Aye, the doctor's got to pronounce us all fit, and we lower a couple of lifeboats while someone from the Board of Trade looks on. Thankfully, it's a one-time nonsense."

Harry raised his cup of tea and wished the man well before returning to his folder for a final review. It seemed the steward had a far more demanding day ahead of him.

After his tea and spartan breakfast, he wandered up on deck and saw a long black tent erected on the dock by the aft, third-class entrance and a line of people, many with small children in tow, lining up for their medical examination. It was a cloudy, cool day, and many emigrants seemed to be wearing every stitch of clothing they owned.

Adjacent to the line was a large crowd of onlookers, many of them women crying into handkerchiefs. Harry had never sailed on a ship carrying so many emigrants, and he suddenly realized that—for the bulk of the passengers making the crossing—it would be a one-way journey.

Those arriving by train, which constituted the bulk of first- and second-class, could use a stairway from the rail platform that took them level to their entrances on B Deck at the end opposite of the lower-class boarding area. Third-class had a direct entryway at dock level to facilitate entry once they passed the final gatekeeper, a doctor armed with a buttonhook. When a passenger approached the physician on the gangway, he would carefully turn over the edge of their eyelid and examine it for signs of trachoma—a highly infectious eye disease—and once cleared they would be directed to step onto the plain wooden bridge that led to a new world.

Harry's gaze lingered a moment longer, before he turned his eyes to the first-class entrance. Odd. While third-class was a steady stream, the other two gangways were sparsely occupied. He went inside and, passing by the white-paneled first-class reception area, found the stewards with anxious faces clustered in small groups.

Littlejohn shook his head as he came over. "Train's delayed. It's going to be tight if we're to make our departure on time. The passengers will be rushed and in a foul mood for sure."

Harry took a position beside the Grand Staircase so he could observe the arrivals and overhear the greeting as passengers passed through the gauntlet of ship officers and stewards. He held a small notebook to jot down first impressions. Harry looked at his pocket watch: forty-five minutes to departure, and no rail arrivals yet. If the ship missed high tide, it would be several hours until they could safely leave harbor, and the maiden voyage of the *Titanic* would be off to a very bad start indeed.

***

Sam, dressed in a man's tweed suit and a flat cap, fidgeted as porters wrestled steamer trunks aboard the boat train. She checked her watch for the third time in five minutes as Mary patiently observed the young woman's intensity.

"We're in the hands of the Fates, Sam. Please keep a stiff upper lip."

"I know. I just wish the fates would move faster!"

"Would the ship leave without us?" Colette asked. "Look at all the others on the train. Surely, they wouldn't sail with so many first-class passengers still on shore."

"They'd wait, if not for us," Mary said. "Though having the ship sail late on its first voyage would look bad in the press, stranding so many prominent people ashore would look worse. As long as we're with the bulk of the other passengers, we should be fine."

When the train arrived beside the ship with a noisy fanfare, the station's porters sprang like soldiers assaulting a fortress, emerging through clouds of steam to form a line of bearers swiftly handing off the luggage to ship stewards before sprinting back to the platform to repeat the process. In a matter of moments all the trunks, valises, bags, and boxes were either on the ship or stacked beside the gangways while well-dressed women demanded *their* bags be made a priority.

As they climbed the stairs to the first-class entrance, Mary turned to Colette. "Enjoy the masquerade."

"But in a masquerade, everyone wears a mask, do they not? Not only the actors."

"My dear, everyone in first-class will be wearing a mask. That's why we'll fit right in. To quote Polonius in Hamlet, we must: 'by indirections, find directions out.'"

Mary was serene amid the chaos, a queen observing the labors of her minions with quiet satisfaction, while Sam waved her hands and shouted instructions that were, for the most part, ignored. Her one victory—the wine crate was marked for the first-class storage area "to be called for later."

***

Harry noted the movie actress, Dorothy Gibson, and her retinue right away. She was impossible to miss, given her beauty and the train of flower boxes accompanying her.

Dorothy Gibson, he wrote in his notebook, *low risk. Too many hangers-on around her.*

Next came two men traveling together who were not on Ismay's list. Harry studied them, wary of their blandly smiling faces and unblinking, reptilian eyes. Something told him he'd soon find them in the Smoking Room, looking for a card game to "pass the time." He'd heard professional gamblers who frequented liners were called "boat men," and listed them as probable members of that seagoing species of card sharp.

Tweedle Dum and Tweedle Dee. Find out from Littlejohn which cabin they share. Observe at cards. Have a quiet chat if necessary.

Harry would rather not spoil his cover in case they had confederates on board. Well, he'd learned a few tricks while growing up in his father's household, having gambled for matchsticks as early as five. Perhaps he could scare these gentlemen off by beating them at their own game? He smiled. Card winnings wouldn't be deducted from his commission.

Next came an elderly couple who had to be Ida and Isidore Straus and although they were among the wealthiest people on board, Harry placed them into the low-risk category. Those on the rise are greedy for more; those in decline desperate to regain what they've lost. Those securely at the top are the most difficult to con as they fear loss more than hunger for more.

Then a large, loud woman arrived holding a bored-looking Pekingese, followed by a mountain of luggage and a small, sad woman of indeterminate age, dressed in a maid's uniform. It seemed the maid's mistress only spoke with exclamation marks as she barked out orders to a squad of stewards who grappled with her avalanche of steamer trunks, most marked for stowage below... "to be called for later." Even so, it took the maid and two men, Littlejohn among them, to tote away those items required to sustain her until the next day.

Harry referred to his notes from Ismay and easily picked her out. Charlotte Cardeza of Pennsylvania, who'd been banned from other lines for her mistreatment of staff and effect on the morale of her fellow passengers. Not as wealthy as she let on.

Cardeza, Harry wrote, *high risk. No friends, so anyone who can play upon her large ego will find her easy to sway. Maid with no influence on her mistress but may be motivated to assist a con artist for coin and revenge.*

Harry easily identified Lady Duff-Gordon by her enormous hat with a taxidermied swallow impaled atop the crown. No one else, Harry reckoned, could wear a hat like that and make it work.

She and her husband arrived fashionably late, which was no surprise, as fashion was her world. Lady Gordon owned salons in London, Paris, New York, and Chicago, and Harry had smiled the night before when he read Ismay's note: *Men around the world are grateful to her for introducing slit skirts and low necklines.*

Though she and her husband, Cosmo, were traveling under an alias, her office had informed Ismay she'd be aboard, thus safeguarding her from adoring fans while ensuring her demands were met promptly. Her business acumen was legendary, but her husband was less well-known. Harry would do his best to keep him away from the boat men in the Smoking Room, and should it look like they were stalking him, he'd intervene.

Following the Duff-Gordons was the Countess of Rothes who was remotely related to the British Crown. Harry read her bio at 2 a.m., but his recollection of her exact relationship to the King was uncertain. The Countess was in her late twenties and in vigorous good health, the blush to her cheek unaided by cosmetics. She was traveling with her cousin by marriage, Gladys, and her parents who would be getting off in Cherbourg. The Countess managed a great deal of the family's combined estates and was known as a hard bargainer. She was traveling to America to join her husband in California who was evaluating investment opportunities in that remote land.

After seeing how easily she carried herself, he put her in the same category as the Straus couple; a person comfortable with who she was and what she had. *Low Risk,* he penciled in. *Not seeking to impress anyone.*

Harry next noticed a middle-aged woman and a young man, presumably her son, traveling with a young maid who were not on his list of notables. The woman was still a striking beauty, while her son was wearing a tweed suit which fit him well. He seemed anxious, understandable given the train's late arrival, but the woman calmly observed the chaos of a rushed boarding with a slight—almost Mona Lisa—smile.

An oddly appropriate observation, as the painting had been stolen from the Louvre the year before and was still missing.

The young maid wore a small black cap with a red feather and walked with a confidence unusual for a woman in her position. She gave Harry a brief but piercing glance with her sea green eyes as she passed.

As they were not on his list he put them out of mind when the final passenger strutted aboard. His pomaded dark hair shone in the morning light and Harry easily identified the young dandy as Mauritz Findlay, the son of the Blondel's owner and courier to its buyer in America. Harry noted the slight limp as the man approached the captain,and surmised it was due to his new shoes. His red silk Ascot was faded, however, and Harry noted that most British men of his age and class would be wearing their school tie as a mark of belonging to the upper echelons of polite society.

A family come upon hard times, he noted, *trying to hide it, Low risk of swindle, he has nothing to offer, and the painting is already sold. I may need to watch out for him if he's on the return voyage with his payment.*

He put away his notebook. This was but round one; several wealthy passengers were scheduled to board in Cherbourg that afternoon. His day was just beginning.

Chapter Fourteen

WHEN THEY ARRIVED INSIDE the reception area, Mrs. Bayer and her son, Samuel, along with their maid, Colette, were checked off the passenger manifest by the junior purser. Beside him stood the captain, who shook Mary and Sam's hand before turning them over to their stewardess, a young woman named Violet Jessup.

After introductions, she turned to Colette. "I see you've been given a second-class cabin. If you come along with me, you'll see where your mistress's stateroom is, then I'll attend to you." She turned to Mary and Sam. "If you'll follow me, please."

As Miss Jessup led them to the elevator Mary noticed a short man making entries in a notebook. He seemed familiar, yet she couldn't recall meeting him. Or could she...?

An art gallery... A short man who'd paid her to distract a guard while he inspected a painting...

Her pulse quickened, but her smile never faltered. The man she recalled was long dead, but the similarity was too strong to be a coincidence. Her grip on Sam's arm tightened as she nodded towards the young man. "Notice the man by the stairs. We may have some competition."

"Begging your pardon, Mrs. Bayer," Miss Jessup said as they waited for the elevator. "I can't help but admire the ruby pendant you're wearing."

"Thank you. A gift from my late husband."

"If you'd like to secured in the Purser's Office when it's not required, I could take you and your maid there, so you could authorize Miss Colette to sign for it, then you won't have to go in-person for the rest of the crossing."

Sam and Mary exchanged glances. "Perhaps we should all go," Sam said, "just to reassure my mother the security is adequate."

"Of course," the stewardess said. "I'm sure the Purser would be pleased to give you a brief tour."

"You're too kind."

Their stateroom was one of the smaller of its class, but Mary relished the fittings and patina of elegance that overlaid everything, oohing over the rich brocade of the wallpaper and velvet bed curtains. She felt like she belonged here, not as a serving girl but as the mistress of a household.

Finally.

"Is this a telephone?" Mary asked, pointing to a black enameled device on a small writing desk.

"Indeed, Madam. You can ring up the Purser whenever you like. Though the servings in the dining saloon are generous, you can request something be brought to your stateroom at any time."

Mary turned to Sam, smiling. "I may never get off!"

"Now as you've your own maid, mum," the stewardess said once a brief tour of the cabin was done, "I'll leave it to you as to what services you'd like of me or prefer to have done by your maid. Bed turndown, for example?"

"Colette will do for me, Miss Jessup. I treasure my privacy, so if I require anything from you, I'll have Colette inform you. Thank you."

The stewardess curtsied and turned to Colette. "If you'll follow me, I'll show you to your cabin."

After the stewardess left, Colette in tow, Mary found an envelope on the writing table with her traveling name on the outside. Inside was a brief note.

Dear Mrs. Bayer,

I'll be quite busy with my own passengers until around nine P.M. after which I'll drop by and see how I can help make your journey more profitable.

With kind regards,

Hope

Once they were out of earshot of their "betters," Miss Jessup became less formal. "As a second-class passenger, you'll have access to that dining area, but in my experience your duties will make it difficult to have regular hours. After I get you to your cabin, I'll take you by the pantry for maids and butlers. You can eat there as you like."

"We have our own dining area?"

Violet laughed. "Yes, and you'll even have a chair! On other ships, the serving staff stand while they eat, but this ship's architect, Mister Andrews, asked the crew what he could do to make our lives easier. I have my own wardrobe in the glory hole for the first time in the four years I've been at sea!"

"Excuse me, Miss Jessup, but English is not my first language. What is a 'glory hole?' It sounds rather... well... unpleasant."

The stewardess laughed. "And you'd usually be right. The glory hole is where the victualing staff are quartered, and on other ships it's usually the foulest portion of the vessel. We were so grateful to Mister Andrews we had a small reception for him yesterday evening to express our thanks."

Violet led Colette down to her cabin on D Deck, just forward of the Second-Class Dining Saloon. She opened the cabin and handed Colette her key. "I think you'll be quite comfortable here."

Colette noticed the bunk beds and turned to her guide. "There's two beds here, will I...?"

Violet laughed. "No, Miss. Not to worry, you have the room to yourself."

It took just a glance to survey her living quarters. Plain, but comfortable. While not the luxury she'd dreamed of, compared to her flat in South London, this was still a well-feathered nest. She wouldn't spend much time here anyways. It would more than do.

"I'm sure I'll grow to love it," she said. "It's a bit more than I have, and I've my own armoire. That's paradise to me!"

"Excellent! Now, to the victualing staff dining area. We'll need to pass through the Second-Class Saloon to reach the pantry but as long as you're in your maid's uniform no one will challenge you."

As they made their way amidships past the long tables in the saloon, Colette tried to get her bearings for this new world, both social and nautical, that she'd inhabit for the next few days.

"Is it difficult, serving so many passengers who each think you work for them?"

Violet shrugged. "I do work for them, all of them, but only for as long as the crossing takes. Some are kind, some less so, but in the end, we are only together for a few days before life and the ocean sends us on our separate ways. Once I'm ashore, my life and money are my own, and no man can command me. How many other women can say the same?"

"A woman with money of her own, answerable to no man? That makes you one of the wealthiest women I've ever known. Someday, I hope to be mistress of my own fate as you are. Still, I imagine some passengers can be quite trying."

"Well, I won't tell tales out of school," Violet said, "but whenever a passenger begins the voyage by telling me they are a personal friend of the Line Director, I know it's going to be a rough passage between us."

She chuckled. "I reckon either most of them are lying, or poor Mister Ismay has a large circle of disagreeable friends."

They finished their journey through the saloon and entered the kitchen area. Violet led them to a door directly ahead on the left side of the narrow passageway opening into a room with a table in the center long enough for twelve to a side and two on each end.

"This is our pantry. Our refuge." Violet checked the watch she wore as a broach. "Now I must see to my other passengers. I look forward to chatting with you here."

"Thank you… Violet. What should I do now, before my mistress requires me for luncheon?"

"You should go to the promenade deck. We'll be casting the lines in a few moments, and you shouldn't miss a ship leaving on its maiden voyage. You can go to the First-Class Promenade deck dressed as you are, and no one will bat an eye. The view's best there."

***

While Violet introduced Colette to her new world at sea, Mary and Samantha were having a more serious discussion in their stateroom.

"That man by the staircase. Why did you point him out?" Sam asked. "He seemed very ordinary to me."

"He reminds me of someone... someone I worked with on a couple of jobs. Unless I'm mistaken, our young man with the notebook is the son of Adam Worth. The family resemblance is too strong to ignore."

"The art thief and bank robber?"

"The consulting criminal. In his prime, people would have Adam plan their jobs for a percentage of the take. If anyone put the lie to the old saw that 'crime doesn't pay,' it was him."

"So, if this man is his son...?"

"He's got to be on board to steal the painting. Anything less wouldn't interest a man like that."

***

Harry tucked his notebook away and wandered to the promenade to watch the ship's departure. All the first-class passengers were wandering the ship or unpacking, and his work would soon begin. The ship would make for Cherbourg next, where a contingent of wealthy Americans awaited, and Harry's life would get even more complicated. Best to take this moment of relative calm before the social whirl began in earnest.

The various gangways were being detached, and the last few third-class passengers were hustling onto the ship when a taxi pulled up alongside and a rear door flew open. A red-faced, matronly woman burst out, dragging a young girl in a plain blue dress as she made straight for the third-class gangway where a Master at Arms awaited. Harry couldn't hear what was said, but the woman waved her arms, a sheet of paper fluttering in her right hand, before the man took the form and signed it. The woman handed him an envelope and the girl's hand. As she turned to leave, the girl kicked her hard in the shins before breaking free of the Master's grip and dashing aboard.

Harry couldn't hear what the woman shouted, but from her tone he could make an educated guess. The Master laughed, tucked the envelope into his coat pocket, and followed the young assailant aboard as the final attachment to England was severed.

The cables were cast off, the ship's horn sounded, and the crowd along the docks—primarily family members of the emigrating third-class passengers—waved handkerchiefs and, in many instances, wept. Harry turned and saw many from first-class had joined him. Even if no one was there to see them off, watching this grand lady make her first official departure from her homeport on a cool April day was an experience to remember for a lifetime.

The ship eased away from the dock and once free of the tugboats, began her slow passage down the River Test towards the open water of the Channel. Harry was about to turn away from the railing when he heard a loud *snap*! The *SS New York*, caught by the suction of the larger ship's propellers, had broken free of its mooring on the stern and was drifting towards them. No smoke came from its funnels, telling Harry it was powerless to react. The *Titanic*, while moving at low-speed and in a narrow space, had no chance of avoiding the wayward ship and collision seemed inevitable. Harry gripped the railing as the two ships drew closer. A large crowd had boarded the docked vessel to view *Titanic*'s departure, and he could see the onlookers cringing as the *New York*'s stern drifted perilously close. Crew members aboard the wayward ship scurried about like ants to no discernible effect, while *Titanic*'s horns blew loud and long to warn of the impending disaster clear to all.

While Harry's eyes were locked on the scene before him, he sensed the crowd around him growing, as powerless as the *New York* before them. The two ships were now so near he could see the fear in the eyes of the other crew as they prepared to collide. It seemed the great ship would begin its maiden voyage in disgrace before she'd even left harbor, and Harry braced for the impact, frozen at the rail.

Just as it appeared all was lost, a passing tugboat veered at full speed towards the drifting vessel, and a sailor flung a line as it drew near. The tug's propellers churned the water to a white froth as the line strained, and Harry feared this cable would also fail, but the *New York* paused just as Harry felt he could leap from one to the other, then it reluctantly eased back to dockside, the tug reminding Harry of a small dog herding a bull back into its pen.

Harry let out a sigh—realizing he'd been holding his breath—when he felt a soft touch in his right rear pocket. He clapped his hand onto a smaller one and spun around to find a young girl in a plain blue dress squirming to break free.

"Don't kick me or run," he said, "and I'll let you go." He gestured with his left hand. "There's no place to go, anyway."

Her blue eyes studied his brown for a moment, then she nodded. "What are you going to do with me?"

Harry considered. He wasn't on board to deal with such a small criminal (in stature or degree of larceny). By rights, he should turn her over to the Masters at Arms, but he recalled a time when he could have been this child.

"Do you know what a contract is?" He asked.

She nodded, her blonde pigtails swaying. "One bloke agrees to do sumpin' and the other agrees how much to pay." She looked up at him. "What do you want me to do, then, and how much will you pay?"

Harry reached into his pocket. "Clever girl. I watched you board." He chuckled. "That was a fair kick you gave the matron who drug you to the ship. I'm guessing emigrating to America wasn't your idea?"

She put her hands on her hips. "You guess right. I'm being shipped to my aunt in New York. Me da died and no one else will take me in. I can't have Da's money 'cause I'm a child. I reckon my aunt just wants the money and free help in her man's store." She cocked her head. "You gonna hire me or throw me in the brig?"

Harry laughed. "You're in luck. No brig on this ship. I either toss you overboard or set you free, but I'll make you a deal." He pulled out a one-dollar bill. "This is American money. It's not quite one shilling, but it'll buy you all the ice cream you could eat for a week. I'm willing to pay you one dollar now and, if you behave yourself, another when we reach New York." He extended his hand. "But first… I don't do business with people I don't know. I'm Mister Daniels. Tell me your name and shake my hand, and we have a contract. What do you say?"

She chewed her lower lip for a moment, then stuck out her hand. "Jenny. Jenny Farthing. We have a contract." She shrugged. "I can't swim, or I'd let you toss me over."

"Now, Jenny, I'd ask you to return to the third-class passenger area. Give me your cabin number and I'll see to your second payment before we reach New York."

"I don't know it; I went straight topside. But I reckon the big man in the blue suit can tell me. He signed for me, after all."

"Ah, the Masters at Arms. Very well, we have a deal. I'll look you up the night before we dock after I ask the Master if you've been a good girl."

"My word's good," Jenny huffed, and she went below decks without a backward glance.

Harry watched her go while he considered how his life might have been had his father not exchanged his son's future for a painting.

He'd been twelve when his father got out of prison, destitute and coughing. He'd never been a large man, but the time behind bars had shrunk Adam Worth even more.

The night his father returned from America he called Harry to his room.

"I've made arrangements, Harry," he said. "For you."

"Another school? I like the one I'm at!"

"And you'll remain there if you like, though I can now afford a better one."

"So, if it's not a new school, what is it?"

"I've arranged for you to take a different path than mine. I never want you to spend a day in prison. I know it was hard on you. Your mother told me how the other boys would taunt you." His father brushed a bruise on Harry's cheek. "They like to bully you, don't they? Small men like us try to blend in so we don't attract notice." Harry's father sighed. "But it doesn't always work."

"But it was my fault! No one's smarter than you, Dad! You'd have never got nicked if it wasn't for me."

His father hugged him. "I should never have put you in that position. The fault is mine. I've been a thief of one sort or another most of my life, but I hope for better for you. That's the reason for this new arrangement."

"What kind of arrangement?"

Adam Worth pulled a letter out of his coat pocket. "I'll give you this when the time is right. It's a letter from Mister Pinkerton himself, guaranteeing you a job with his agency when you've come of age."

"You want me to become a policeman? To put people in prison so I can stay out?"

"I want you to become a man who doesn't spend his life ducking every time a policeman walks by. I want you to protect others against people like me. It's for the best."

Harry stared ahead as the ship crept past the near disaster. A heavyset man in a gray overcoat approached him at the rail. "That was a near thing," the man said, wiping his brow.

"Yes, it was," Harry replied, "closer than you know."

Harry headed for the dining area to learn where and with whom he'd be eating and was so busy in his thoughts he didn't notice a young maid who'd seen the episode between him and the young pickpocket. The maid had no notebook of her own, but if she had, she'd have inscribed: *Daniels. Interesting. Not rich but can afford a first-class cabin. Short, no taller than me. Handsome... and kind.*

Chapter Fifteen

A BUGLER CALLED THE passengers to luncheon, playing "The Roast Beef of Old England."

Looking at the well-fed patrons heading to the dining saloon, Sam whispered to Mary, "That bugle reminds me of a horse race. If this were a buffet, the starting gate would be crowded!"

Harry's table companions, two middle-aged couples, were pleasant but instantly forgettable. Mrs. Hargrave of Philadelphia, however, one of Harry's mealtime companions, had a friend aboard with a daughter perilously close to spinsterhood, and his various qualities as a potential husband were soon the topic of serious discussion in the Reading Room. Harry was unaware of it yet, but his bachelorhood was about to come under siege.

After luncheon, Sam made her way to the Smoking Room, where she found two well-dressed gentlemen with soft, clever hands dealing cards as their pile of chips slowly grew. Finding no other games ongoing, she sat in for a few rounds but found that, at best, she could hold her own and when she excused herself to use the loo (avoiding an awkward moment as there was only the Gents), one of the two card players excused himself as well.

Once they were alone, the man glanced quickly beneath the stalls before turning to Sam. "Look here, lad," he said, his public-school accent put aside for the moment. "Me and George are White Star regulars, and we ain't seen you before. You a Cunard man? If so, then bugger off and go to them. This here's our ship, and we got no room for another."

"I have no idea what you're talking about," Sam bluffed. "I may have some skill picked up during my time at university, but I play purely for pleasure."

"Have it your way, then. Just take your pleasure someplace else, or we'll mention to the paying customers how we think you're a little too lucky for coincidence. Once word gets out no one will want to play—or even speak—to you. You got some other dodge going on, that's none of our business, but leave the pigeons in the Smoking Room to us. Got it?"

"Got it," she said, and her glare made him take a step back. Those unblinking eyes made him think of a hungry cat.

Sam considered the man's words. The ship would be a small town for the coming days, and she'd not get within twenty feet of the painting's owner if word was out she was a professional. She considered her options. "Would you object to me hosting a private game?"

The boat man relaxed. "Don't know how we could stop you. Sundays, there's no card-playing in public anyways. If you find someone who still has money to lose by then, go right ahead."

The gambler smiled. "Welcome aboard."

***

After lunch, Harry made a slow perambulation through the various public areas, observing how the passengers behaved and looking for anyone a bit too friendly with his principals. He paused for an ice and coffee in the Palm Court before making his way to the Smoking Room. Every hunter knows a watering hole is the best place to await your prey, especially if you're hunting predators.

The Smoking Room was well attended. As dinner on embarkation night did not require formal attire, many male passengers had made for the place as soon as they unpacked, hoping to see old acquaintances or make new ones.

Harry meandered past a card table and noted it was fully occupied, then he recognized the man dealing the cards as one of the two suspected 'boat men' he'd noticed during boarding. Harry leaned against a wall and watched as the cards flowed through the man's hands like water and felt his own hands twitch as he observed the game unfolding. He'd been trained by the best, and when a seat came open, he took it.

Harry sat through two rounds of seven-card draw, folding early each time before the deck passed to him. He considered how to proceed and decided to show he was no amateur. He fanned the cards out on the table, flipped them, scooped them up, then bent the deck and shot the cards from one hand to the other. He shuffled three times in less than three seconds and offered them to the player to his right to cut, who declined.

"Five card stud," he declared, and won the hand with three jacks. The man who'd been dealing when Harry came in gave the slightest of nods, a swordsman raising his weapon in salute to a worthy opponent. Harry was twenty pounds ahead when he checked his watch and decided they must be approaching Cherbourg. As he rose, the card sharp excused himself also and took Harry by the elbow. "A word, if you please?"

"Delighted," Harry replied.

They went to the promenade deck, and Harry was surprised when the second boat man joined them. He wondered if he'd regret turning in his revolvers.

"Now see here, mate," the second man said, "I've already warned one bloke this is our ship. The Smoking Room's not big enough for anyone else, 'specially with so few passengers on this trip."

"Another man?" Harry said, holding his own cards close to his vest. "And who might that be?"

"A young blonde chap we've never seen before, maybe twenty-two. Face like a statue, you can't tell what he's thinking or what cards he's holding."

"Well, gentlemen," Harry said, producing his Pinkerton badge, "I'll make you a deal. I won't play anymore... if you don't."

Their faces tightened. "I don't see any harm in a friendly game of cards between gentlemen," the man who'd been dealing said.

"And if you wore an eye patch and had only three fingers on your right hand, it might be a fair game," Harry answered. "I won't ask you to return your winnings, but no more, or I'll have words with the Chief Purser and have you banned from the White Star Line for good. Understand?"

They looked at each other, then nodded. "Have it your way, then, Pink. We'll behave."

"Good. Oh, and if you've ideas, I'll be on the return trip as well. Thank you for the tip about the young man, by the way. I'll keep an eye out for him."

The boat men deflated even further at the mention of Harry's planned return trip, and he smiled as he left. He was a good card player but was glad the men hadn't called his bluff about getting them banned from the Line. He had no idea if he could make his threat good.

After Harry left, the two gamblers considered their situation. "Think we should tell that blonde bugger about the Pinkerton man?" one asked the other.

"Nah, sod 'im. Might be fun to watch him get his knuckles rapped proper." He snorted. "Teach him something he didn't learn at university."

***

Colette was invited to dine with Violet and the other stewardesses in their pantry while their betters were at luncheon.

"Your lady won't have to change for dinner tonight, this being embarkation day, so this will likely be your easiest day of the crossing," Violet advised. "Take the time to rest, dear. If we have rough weather, your mistress will be after you to tend to her while you try to mind your own stomach."

The secluded refuge for the staff was presided over by the pantryman, who also saw to food service requests by the first-class passengers. Colette had finished her meal and was chatting with the other girls about life at sea when a young stewardess rushed in, all red-faced. "Mister Hudgens!" she cried. "One of my lady passengers overslept and will miss luncheon. She's requested a meal to her room."

"Missed her first meal?" the portly man asked. "Well,

not to worry. We've some fine onion soup, a capon, mashed potatoes, and some rolls I can reheat. Run off to see if she'd like some of that."

The stewardess ran off but returned five minutes later, redder than ever. "She said she would NOT accept reheated food and demanded we make something fresh for her."

"You told her I was going to reheat it?" the pantryman demanded. "What kind of idiot does that?" He prepared a tray with all the food he'd suggested and placed it on a warming tray. "Tell her she'll have a newly prepared meal in twenty minutes. Anything less and she'll suspect something's amiss."

The girl departed on her mission, while Colette stayed to see how the man was going to pull off his deception. Once the timer sounded, he took a small pan of melted butter and poured it sparingly over the capon and potatoes.

He then turned to the hapless stewardess, bowed, and said, "Luncheon is served. Now take it and remember to never tell a passenger we're reheating something."

Violet nudged Colette in the ribs. "We expect you to keep our secrets here below decks where they belong. If the passengers knew half of what we do to pander to their whims, they'd be even more insufferable than they are now."

***

The ship arrived in Cherbourg harbor at 6:30, an hour behind time, and though the shadows were long, there was still ample sunlight for the tender, the harbor craft that ferried passengers, to make its way through a heavy chop. There were two harbor craft, the *Nomadic,* for first- and second-class passengers, and the *Traffic,* for third.

Boarding at sea was a bit trickier than in port—a gangplank erected from the upper-deck of the tender to the second-class entrance on E Deck in the aft, starboard side. One woman in first-class, the widowed Mrs. Ella White, turned her ankle on the swaying wooden bridge despite its being braced by seamen on both vessels. The heiress to a fortune in electricity production, she became the talk of first-class later that night when she limped about the ship with a cane containing a small electric light.

Harry resumed his post at the back of the reception area and, as before, made notes on the embarking passengers. Leading the way was "Colonel" John Jacob Astor in top hat and overcoat, his young—obviously pregnant—teenaged bride following meekly and somewhat unsteadily behind. He stood erect and replied courteously to the ship's officers as they greeted him, while she hung her head, not making eye contact with any of the other passengers or crew. Harry didn't hear her utter a word before the couple, with their maid and butler, were escorted briskly away.

Astors. Low risk. He's too smart and she'll keep to herself. Keep an eye on the maid. She's the only way someone could get to her mistress.

They were followed by Mrs. Margaret Brown. Mrs. Brown was born into a large, poor family, and mixed easily with all strata of society. Harry soon learned she was a favorite among the crew as a woman who treated them as fully human. He noted her firm handshake with the ship's officers and her direct gaze at all who addressed her.

Brown. Capable of managing her affairs. Given her background, knows the value of money but not enslaved by it. You might be able to steal from her but never swindle. Medium risk.

She glanced Harry's way and, seeing him scribbling in his notebook, made straight for him.

"Excuse me, young man, but which paper do you represent?"

"Madam? I don't know what you mean."

"I couldn't help but notice you taking notes as I boarded. If you're wanting an interview, the answer is no. My reasons for traveling are my own, and there is nothing new about myself or my family you could possibly include in a news story."

"I assure you, Mrs. Brown, I'm not a journalist."

"Ah, so you do know who I am, though we have never met. Well then young man, your reasons for documenting my arrival are even less clear. I'll thank you to give me a wide berth while we're aboard. Good day."

After she strode off, Harry made a quick addendum to his journal.

Very observant. Zero risk.

Harry was late to dinner, preoccupied with what the card sharps had told him of another of their kind aboard, or else he might have taken more notice when a friend of Mrs. Hargraves "happened" by their table. She seemed enthralled by Harry's/Mr. Daniels' burgeoning career as an insurance branch manager in Chicago.

Later that night, as Mister Littlejohn came to "do" for him before retiring, Harry asked, "Did you hear anything of interest?"

"No, sir, but I was going flat-out all day. Then there was Mrs. Cardeza." He sighed. "Mrs. Cardeza..."

"I saw you were shanghaied to help carry her luggage when she boarded."

"Aye, and a terrible lot that was, too. But that wasn't the worst of it—not by a mile! Once we'd stacked everything where she wanted, she decided the furniture arrangement didn't suit 'er, and damned if we weren't ordered to rearrange everything before we could go."

Littlejohn rubbed his neck in remembrance.

"I pity Miss Jessup, her stewardess. I heard the lady order her to bring six mirrors, as if she were good to look at. The woman's poor maid looked like her soul had been drained clean out of her. Next to her, Mister Daniels, you're a right saint!"

Harry laughed. "Well, I hope I'm at least on the side of the angels. Once you catch your breath, though, I'd appreciate anything you see or hear that makes you think any of our passengers are up to no good."

"I'll do my best. If I might suggest something? Miss Jessup has been with the Line for four years, and as she tends to the female passengers, she has the chance to look in on those I know nothing about. You might consider letting her in on your purpose. I could vouch for you, if you like."

"Can she keep a secret?"

Littlejohn chuckled. "'Course she can. It's the most important part of our job."

Harry nodded. "When do you think we could talk?"

"Best time's when the passengers are at breakfast. No one misses a meal. She can't come to your room alone, however. I can bring her by once everyone's gone to eat, and that way I can tell her it's on the up-and-up. Will that do?"

"Perfect. Say 8:15 tomorrow?"

"We'll be there."

***

The trio were in Mary's stateroom at nine PM when Hope arrived, red-faced from her busy day.

"What can you tell us?" Mary asked.

"If I help you steal something else, will I get a larger payout?"

"You mean in addition to the painting? Is it more valuable?"

"I couldn't say, but it's worth a fair bit and a lot smaller, so easier to carry."

Mary bit her lip. "I'm not squeamish, but I don't want to risk the big fish for a smaller one. Tell me what you got, and if I decide to go for it, I'll pay you another twenty pounds. Is that fair?"

The stewardess nodded. "It's a book."

"Unless it's a Gutenberg Bible," Mary said, shaking her head, "I doubt it's worth the risk."

"Oh, it's not the book that's so valuable, it's an illustrated copy of Omar Khayyám's *The Rubaiyat.* It's what's on it." Hope paused, "One thousand diamond chips, and a few emeralds and rubies thrown in for good measure."

"Who does it belong to? If they're keeping it in the Purser's safe, it'll be tough to get to."

"It doesn't belong to anyone on board. It's in the cargo hold on the way to someone in New York who bought it at auction. No one will check on it until we reach harbor."

"I think it's worth going for," Sam said, "don't you agree, Colette?"

"So many diamonds would be of low quality, but easier to sell in bulk and harder to identify, so *oui,* I think it is a good opportunity."

Mary pulled out her purse. "Very well, Hope, like the

diamond. Ten pounds now for the information. If we take it, there'll be another twenty."

The stewardess stuffed the bills into her bodice and continued. "As for the painting, I've rather bad news for you."

"Go on."

"Your wine will be with the first-class baggage adjacent to the mail room on deck G. The Purser decided that the painting, because of its size and value, would be stored in a more secure hold, forward of the baggage compartment on the same deck."

Colette pulled the deck plan out of the cylinder stored in Mary's stateroom.

"Show us."

"How'd you get a copy of this?" Hope asked.

Colette smirked. "I lent someone a change of clothes."

The stewardess laughed. "I think there's more to your story than that, but I can tell when I'm being told to bugger off," and returned to studying the blueprint. She pointed out the mailroom and the more forward cargo hold, and Colette made a slight mark on both.

"You're right, Hope," Mary said. "Not good news, but better to know now than sorting through the hold when it isn't there, especially if there's mail clerks about." She paused in thought. "I'll sleep on it. Can you come by tomorrow night around the same time?"

"Depends on my passengers and the sea. If we get some waves, I may be playing nursemaid, but if not then nine or as soon as I can after," Hope said, and left.

That night, as Colette put up Mary's hair before retiring, Mary mentioned the young man with the notebook. "I'm not certain, but he might be the son of a man I did a couple of jobs with some years back."

"Think he's on board for the same reason as us?"

"Perhaps. We'll see. He's short, with brown hair and eyes, and carries a notebook."

"Indeed? I may have seen him this afternoon as we left harbor. A young girl tried to pick his pocket but he caught her, and rather than turn her in paid her a dollar to behave."

"Not what you'd expect from a man rich enough to sail

first-class. I think he bears close watching."

Colette colored slightly. "I think I can do that."

Mary smiled. "I've noticed you have no difficulty in watching handsome young men."

Chapter Sixteen

April 11

MARY WAS SURPRISED TO find a passenger manifest of first-class and second-class passengers under her door as she prepared for the new day. "Look at this, Sam! They couldn't possibly make this any easier."

The young woman looked down the list like a starving beggar at a buffet. "We'll never have enough time to meet them all, but we should save this list. Perhaps later we can look up someone and use our shared journey as a means of striking up an acquaintance."

"Good idea," Mary said, "people never admit to not remembering someone who claims they've met before."

Sam turned to the back of the manifest and began to laugh. She cleared her throat and read the final paragraph aloud,

"Certain persons, believed to be professional gamblers, are in the habit of traveling to and fro in Atlantic steamships, blah blah, we discourage Games of Chance, etcetera, etcetera."

"It seems we've been expected," Mary said. "Let's make sure they didn't go to all that bother for nothing."

***

Steward Littlejohn was as good as his word, knocking at Harry's door promptly at eight-fifteen, accompanied by a prim young lady in a stewardess uniform.

"Violet," the steward said, "this is Mister Daniels, but

he's not really a passenger. He's working direct for Mister Ismay."

"How so?"

"Insurance," Harry said.

Miss Jessup studied Harry's face closely before nodding. "Right. You want to know about my guests; the middle-aged woman with her son and their maid."

"Why do you think that?"

"I can tell they've never traveled in first-class before."

"That's hardly a crime, what makes you suspicious of them?"

"They didn't know about the Purser's Office, for one. I took them 'round so the mother could sign for her maid to pick up her jewelry, and they looked at the safe like it was a roast pig. They just feel off. Out of place. I've been doing this for a while now and you get a feeling about your passengers."

"What about the maid?"

Violet shrugged. "She seems a pleasant sort. She and her mistress get along well enough, though she seems new in service. Careful in how she walks, like she's on eggs."

Harry turned to his steward. "Please ask one of the dining room attendants where the woman and her son sit at dinner. I'd like to get a good look at them tonight."

"'Course, sir."

"Anything else, Sir?" Miss Jessup asked. "I only get thirty minutes for breakfast, and you've taken half of it."

"My apologies, Miss." He handed her a five-dollar bill. "For your trouble."

She tucked it into her apron and as she turned, said, "Guess the insurance business doesn't pay very well. Good day."

***

Miss Temperance Williams was twenty-two, unmarried, and tired of the looks she got from other women when she was a friend's bridesmaid. When the list of first-class passengers was distributed to the staterooms, more than one mother of a single daughter studied the census of unattached male travelers with the focus of a medical student preparing for an examination. If such men could afford the top level of accommodation, the mothers reasoned, they had the resources to support a bride.

Therefore, when Madam Williams learned from her friend, Mrs. Hargrave, of a young, single man dining with her in first-class, she made it a point to meet him without 'meeting' him, to get ahead of the competition. What she saw pleased her. Short, well-kept, quiet, early twenties, and no band upon his ring finger. Battle plans were soon drawn with him as the prize and like any great general, Madam Williams devised her plan of operations with great precision. After slipping one pound to her steward to inquire as to Mister Daniel's habits, she chose the site for her first assault.

"He likes to take a coffee in the Palm Court. Alone. I'll arrange for some of my friends to surround an empty table so you can ask to join him once he's sat down."

"You said he's short?" Temperance said. "How short? I'm five foot five, and I'd look ridiculous towering over my husband. People would stare."

"More than they stare at you now, as an unmarried woman? Honestly, Temperance, you'll be twenty-three soon. Twenty-three! I'd look at this as an opportunity. Short men don't need to be told they lack physical stature; society reminds them all the time. But if you can make him feel six feet tall, he'll never look at another woman."

"Is he handsome otherwise? I'd hate to wake up next to a man with a hideous scar or pockmarked face."

"My dear Temperance, I'm asking you to take tea with the man. Once. You can have coffee, for all I care. Spend a few pleasant moments with him and if you like what you see, we can proceed from there. Based upon the passenger list, I have three other possibilities, but he's the closest to your age. The longer a man's been a bachelor, the more he sees that as the natural order of things, and the harder it is to get them to consider a change in their station."

"The youngest, you say? That's encouraging."

"No, not the youngest. There's the son of a wealthy American banker who's nineteen, but people do tend to look askance at the woman being the older of the two. It's unfair, I know. Men are always looking for young brides but if it were up to me, they should only be wed to a woman mature enough to guide them properly."

Mrs. Williams sighed. "Only queens have that prerogative," she said, turning to the wardrobe. "Now we must select the proper attire to make you attractive without appearing forced."

"Yes, mother, I understand." Temperance rolled her yes. "You want me to look casually devastating."

"No need to get testy, but yes."

"So, what kind of business is this Mister Daniels engaged in?"

"Insurance."

"And where does he reside?"

"Chicago."

"An insurance man in Chicago? An uncivilized outpost in the freezing center of America... why, I'd be bored to death! I could hardly be more remote from culture or proper society if I were in Alaska married to a gold miner." She paused. "No, I take that back. Being married to a gold miner would be far more interesting."

"And the income from an insurance executive would be far more reliable. Here, I think this will do," she said as she laid out an ensemble on the bed.

"A corset! No one wears a corset in the morning. Civilization is more advanced than in your day, Mother."

"And when you are the mistress of the Daniels' household, you can forsake them for the rest of your life."

***

The plan of attack finalized, the troops briefed, Madam Williams' friends readily agreed to assist Cupid in the 'accidental' meeting of the future Mister and Missus Daniels, soon to be of Chicago. More than one early riser made for the empty table amidst the occupied ones, but the stares they received from the romantic conspirators surrounding it caused an abrupt change in direction.

Harry, unaware of the trap laid for him, sat in the one unoccupied table with his morning coffee and was planning his activities when a young lady materialized beside him.

"I beg your pardon, sir," she said, looking around the

room, “but all the other tables are occupied. Would you mind if I sat with you?”

Harry told himself his job required him to mingle amongst the guests, so sitting with a pleasant young woman could be considered in the line of duty. “I wouldn’t mind. Shall I order you something? A coffee? Tea?”

“A pot of tea would be lovely,” she said. “If you’d care to share, you could ask for two cups.”

Harry raised his coffee cup. “No, thank you. As I’ve lived in America as well as Britain, I’m a man of mixed heritage, so I split the difference. Coffee for mornings, tea in the afternoon.”

“Ah, that would explain your distinctive accent,” she said. “You strike me as a man of mystery.” She extended her hand. “My name’s Temperance. Temperance Williams.”

Harry stood and briefly took her hand. “Daniels. Philip Daniels.”

“Do people confuse your first and last names?”

“Frequently.”

She briefly stuck out her lower lip as her mother had instructed. “How tiresome that must be for you. And what do you do, Mister Daniels?”

At that moment, the café attendant happened by, and Harry, grateful for the interruption, ordered a pot of tea after consulting with Temperance over her particulars regarding leaf and anything to go with. She declined a scone to avoid looking gluttonous. Once the complexities of tea had been addressed and the waiter left, Temperance moved to the next stage.

“Your being a man from two worlds intrigues me, Mister Daniels. May I call you Philip?”

Harry nodded weakly; increasingly suspicious this was no chance meeting. There had been plenty of empty tables in the café yesterday, which was why he’d chosen this time and venue. Had his identity been compromised? Was she part of a gang, feeling him out as a potential mark?

“Certainly, Miss Williams.”

“Oh! And you must call me Temperance. I insist!”

“As you like.”

"And what do you do in Chicago, Philip?" she effused, forgetting he'd not mentioned where he came from.

Harry smiled at her faux pas. A professional criminal would be unlikely to make such a mistake when staging a 'chance' meeting. He recalled Mister Ismay's warning about women with marriageable daughters.

"I'm in insurance, Temperance."

She batted her eyes and sighed. "How interesting!"

Just then, Colette passed by and saw Harry in conversation with a young woman, a young woman who was significantly overdressed for this time of day. His eyes scanned the room as she spoke, showing he was not engrossed in whatever she was saying, and Colette felt sorry for him.

Feeling charitable, she stopped at their table and curtsied. "Pardon, *Monsieur,* but I couldn't help but notice your kindness towards the young girl yesterday as we sailed from Southampton. It was very, how you say? Gallant."

Temperance glared at this pretty, young interloper. "Is Mister Daniels your employer, Miss?" she asked with icy precision.

"No, *mademoiselle,* I merely wanted to comment on his generous nature and to wish him well."

"I'd advise you to remember your place, miss. Servants shouldn't speak with anyone above their station unless spoken to first. I'll ask you to leave now, or I shall speak with your mistress about your flagrant disregard of etiquette."

Colette's ears burned, and before Harry could speak a word, she spun around and stomped off.

Harry sat there, stunned by what he'd just witnessed. A kind young woman complimenting him on a simple act of charity being ruthlessly humiliated by this... harridan.

He rose. "Excuse me, Temperance, but I have a pressing engagement elsewhere."

"But our tea hasn't arrived!" she sputtered.

"*Your* tea, Miss Williams. Which I'm sure you can enjoy without my presence. Good day."

As Harry left the café, Madam Williams dryly remarked from an adjacent table, "Cruelty towards animals or servants does not befit a lady, Temperance. There's no point in pursuing this gentleman any further." She sighed. "Ah, well. We've three more possibilities and five more days." She rose and addressed her friends at the adjoining tables. "The path to love is rarely smooth, and that to marriage even less so. Thank you for your help."

***

Harry strode out of the café in the direction the young woman had gone. Given how flushed she was when she left, he expected he'd find her outdoors, seeking fresh air to cool her anger.

Sure enough, he found her on the promenade amidships just outside the First-Class Lounge gripping the railing, her posture stiff as a store mannequin.

He stood six feet to her left in case she should explode. You could never be sure about women, and Harry was even less so about a French one, so was doubly cautious.

"I'm sorry for what happened, *mademoiselle.* I assure you, the young woman whom I just met this morning does not speak for me."

She turned to him and, seeing the pain in his eyes, swallowed the retort she'd been practicing during her percussive retreat from the *petite chienne.* If she didn't control her temper, she'd be barred from public spaces in the first-class areas except when accompanying Mary, limiting her usefulness.

"Your courtesy says much about you, *monsieur,* and I confess my anger towards you was foolish. I could tell you were not enjoying the company of the… woman you were with. I thought perhaps I might give you an avenue of escape." She laughed. "It appears I was successful, though not as I planned. Very well, you have made your apology, and I accept. If you wish to return to her now, I understand. If you are under some sort of obligation, I pity you, for I think she will prove a difficult companion."

"I am under no compulsion to return and find the idea repugnant. I don't believe wealth makes one superior to another. That is a question of character."

"Indeed? And what would you say about my character? A maid, bound in service to a wealthy woman? My lot in life is to array her hair, change her clothes three times a day, and fulfill her every whim. Is that a life for a person of character?"

"Why not? A famous stoic philosopher, Epictetus, was once a slave."

She looked closer at this quiet, short man with deep brown eyes and saw a sincerity she'd not seen since fleeing Montreal. He seemed a man comfortable in his own skin with nothing to hide.

She glanced through the large windows of the First-Class Lounge. Inside, a string ensemble played while a dozen young couples were having a dance lesson. "Look at them," she said, "dancing without a care in the world."

"While below a hundred men shovel coal to keep this floating extravagance moving, the lights on, and the food cooking."

"You've been in the boiler room? I didn't know passengers were allowed to go there."

"I, uh, I've met the architect of the ship, Mister Andrews. He gave me a personal tour."

Colette noted the hesitation. He'd made a slip. Perhaps Mister Daniels wasn't quite the open book after all? How did he merit a personal tour of the ship? Mary was right about one thing. This man merited close watching.

She turned to the window again. "They're waltzing, an elegant way for two people to learn to trust each other... at least on the dance floor."

"My father insisted I take dance lessons while I was in preparatory school, saying it was an essential social skill, but I never was very good at it." He shrugged. "I guess I never had the proper instructor."

Colette turned back to him and smiled. "Truly? And what do you have planned for the next twenty minutes?"

"What? You mean... here? Now?"

"Of course. All we ever have is now." She winked. "What did your philosophers say about that?"

"Carpe diem," Harry admitted. "Seize the day."

"Then let's Carpe waltz." She showed Harry the proper stance, and he didn't resist when she led. He was sure-footed and moved gracefully, but more like a boxer than a dancer, and soon they were flowing around the promenade like two fighters in an arena locked in intimate combat.

Colette glanced at their reflection in the glass and was warmed by the image of the two of them gliding back and forth on the polished pine deck to music only they could hear. When at last they finished, with their faces inches apart, both yearned to cross that small divide between their lips. Neither was ready to release their grasp until they were surprised by the sound of applause. Looking into the lounge they saw several of the couples clapping for their performance, making them blush and step back.

"I think that's enough for today," Colette said, shorter of breath then she should be.

"Y-yes," Harry said. "I believe we quite "carp-ed" this particular diem. Thank you, Miss...?"

"DuBois, *monsieur,* but after such a dance that seems awkwardly formal. You may call me Colette."

He bowed. "My name is Philip Daniels, but please call me Philip."

"*Merci, Phillipe.*" Colette looked at his eyes again. A kind man. A gentle man. Yet one with secrets of his own, perhaps? She would have much to share with Mary when she returned to her stateroom, and to ponder alone in her bed that night.

Soon, the green shores and hills of Ireland came into view, and the ship arrived in Queenstown for its final stop before New York. The harbor was too shallow for the ship to enter, so—as in Cherbourg—the boarding of passengers and supplies was conducted by tenders. Scarcely more than one hundred additional souls joined, nearly all in third-class.

The small number of passengers didn't merit the stop, but the ship was chartered as a mail carrier and, as such, was fulfilling its contractual obligations to earn the 'M' in RMS *Titanic.* The boarding was faster than in Southampton, the tearful farewells having been already conducted on dry land, and the ship was off again by 1:30 p.m. Passengers enjoyed the view of the shrinking green island from the aft veranda for the next three hours. Once the sight of land faded away there was nothing but open sea between the ship and New York.

As the ship left the harbor, Harry wandered towards the aft promenade and overheard the sound of Irish—or uilleann—pipes being played somewhere below on the Poop Deck, in third-class territory. He recognized one tune, called "Erin's Lament," a song about Ireland's thirst for independence that was sharply critical of the landed gentry. The wealthy passengers in the Verandah Café above, however, were behind closed doors and windows, and heard nothing.

Chapter Seventeen

THIS BEING *TITANIC*'S FIRST full day at sea, the ship's dress code was now in effect, and Colette found herself spending an hour before each meal fussing over Mary so she could properly see and be seen in the public areas. That evening as the young woman carefully worked her buttonhook up the back of Mary's dress, she mentioned her unexpected dancing lesson on the promenade. "Oh, Mary," she gushed, "he is *trés gallant!"* The horrible young woman he was with was so cruel to me that he rushed to apologize after I stormed off, and I'm sure he will never see her again. I could see the pain in his eyes as he spoke to me." She sighed. "We waltzed as though we'd known each other for years."

"Really?" Mary turned around, her dress half-fastened. "How interesting. Did you learn anything useful about him? His name, at least."

Colette blushed. "Oh, yes. It is *Phillipe* Daniels."

"Daniels, you say? Did he mention why he was traveling?"

"*Non,* Mary, but he is a kind man. I'm sure we have nothing to fear from him. He is the man I saw yesterday catch a young girl trying to pick his pocket and what did he do? Instead of turning her over to the *securité,* he gave her one dollar if she promised not to do it again during the crossing, with another dollar when we reach New York."

"He's got to be Worth's son," Mary said. "Adam's heart

was as good as his brains."

"You think you recognize him? Why didn't you tell me before?"

"It's only a guess, but he looks too much like his father to be anyone else. I met his son once as a boy. I'm sure he doesn't remember me."

"What can you tell me of his father? You say you worked with him years ago?"

"Adam Worth was the smartest man I ever knew. He once paid me to distract a guard while he examined the fastening of a painting in a London art gallery, the *Duchess of Devonshire.* I was scarce seventeen at the time, but I was woman enough to keep the guard smiling while Adam poked about. He nicked the painting right enough and paid me well for my small part. A gentleman thief if ever there was one."

"So *this Phillipe* Daniels must be...?"

"Harry Worth. It looks like your kindly dance partner is here on the same business as us." Mary paced the stateroom, the upper part of her unfastened gown fluttering as she walked. "I'll need you to chat some more with 'Mister Daniels', see what you can learn of his movements. It'd be embarrassing if we ran into him down in the hold. Anything else you can tell me about him?"

Colette frowned at the thought this small, kind man could be a thief. She'd become so out of necessity. Perhaps being born into that society was the same? Colette should have remembered a normal life would never be possible for her again, and a single, kind criminal was the best she could ever hope for. "He mentioned the ship's architect gave him a personal tour."

Mary whistled. "Then he's as charming as he is smart, which is saying a lot, as Adam had the brains of ten men."

"Perhaps we could partner with him? It's a lot of money, even divided four ways."

"You may be right, but we don't know enough yet. 'Til then, stay as close to him as you can." Mary turned so Colette could complete the buttons. Once this was done, Mary said what Colette already knew. "This changes everything."

***

Mary had asked to be assigned to a large table in the dining room to make as many contacts as possible through shared meals. Breaking bread together was a powerful social lubricant, especially when the bread was covered in caviar and washed down with champagne.

Mary reminded herself she was no longer a serving girl but that she, at least for the moment, 'belonged' to this gathering of elegantly dressed men and women. She felt more kinship with those catering to the whims of the wealthy than with these upper-class travelers intent on flaunting their status, and their smugness only increased her desire to pick every one of their pockets clean.

Ship's officers were sometimes detailed to dine with the first-class passengers, and on that night Second Officer Charles Lightoller was at their table, trying his best to be charming and patient.

"I'm sure a great ship such as this must have some valuable cargo aboard," Sam said.

"There are one or two unusual items I had to store with special care," Lightoller said. "Perhaps the oddest is a jewel-encrusted copy of Omar Khayyám's *Rubaiyat*. I haven't viewed it personally, but the man from Sotheby's who brought it told me it's encrusted with over one thousand jewels. I saw to its storage personally."

"I would imagine such a valuable treasure would be secured in the Purser's Office?" Sam said.

Lightoller shook his head. "The safe has limited space, so we only use it for valuables our passengers might desire during the voyage. Say, at dinner. No, the book is secured below decks."

"Beside the painting by Blondel, I suppose?" Mary asked. "It was in all the papers. It's a pity we won't be able to view it while we're at sea."

Lightoller paused, "Perhaps I could introduce you to the young man carrying it to America for his father? It would be an easy matter for you to see it if he agrees, as he decided to keep it in his stateroom after we'd stored it below."

Mary pounded Sam vigorously on the back as she choked on a piece of bread, before turning back to the officer.

"Indeed," Mary gushed. "I flatter myself as being something of an art lover, and I would love to stand in the presence of such beauty. Wouldn't you, Sam?"

"Indeed," Sam croaked, after clearing her throat. "Please introduce us. We would consider it a great honor."

The officer stood and surveyed the room before spying Mauritz Findlay and, after pulling out Mary's chair with a flourish, Lightoller conducted them to a nearby table. He tapped a blond man in his early twenties on his shoulder. The man rose and frowned when he saw who'd approached him.

"Is there a problem, sir?"

"No, no problem, Mister Findlay. May I present Mrs. Mary Bayer and her son Samuel?"

Mary swallowed, struck for the second time in two days by the similarity between a father and his son. She forced a smile and raised her hand, palm-down, bending just enough to give the young man a full view of her generous cleavage.

"Of course. A pleasure to meet you, Mrs. Bayer," Mauritz said, as he shook Sam's hand before bending slightly to kiss Mary's, "Charmed, I'm sure." He slowly released his grasp, his gaze lingering.

While the ship's officer excused himself, Mary took the opportunity to press her advantage. "Officer Lightoller was telling us of the marvelous Blondel you're transporting to America. You might find it hard to believe," she said, striking a pose, "but I often served as an artist's model before I met my late husband, and he made an honest woman of me."

Mauritz smiled. "A great loss to the world of art, Madam, if I may say. I'd be pleased to show it to you sometime before we arrive in New York."

"How thoughtful. Yes, let's exchange stateroom numbers and we'll send you a note proposing a time. Is that acceptable?"

"I look forward to it." Mauritz said.

"Excellent!" said Sam.

Cabin numbers exchanged, Sam escorted Mary back to their table just as the dessert tray made the rounds. Between the proximity of the painting and the apparent effect she'd just made on a strapping young man, Mary's chocolate truffle had never tasted better.

I've still got it, she thought. She considered their next move as she savored the slow transit of the dark chocolate across her palate. Seducing the young man probably wouldn't be necessary but it would be a revenge of sort upon his father. *I should have taken up art theft before now,* she mused.

***

Harry's dining room steward met him as Harry approached his table and pointed out Mrs. Bayer and her son at a table on the far side of the room. "I was told to let you know where they sat, sir. That's them over there."

"Thank you, steward," Harry whispered as he slipped a five-dollar bill into the man's hand. Harry was fortunate his chair sat facing them. He vaguely recalled them from boarding day. Then he recalled they had a maid. A young woman with a black felt cap… with a red feather, and thought back to his dance partner.

There's no way she could know I'm with the Pinkertons, he thought. *So, either she's evaluating me as a target, or she's just toying with me.*

He looked back on their dance lesson with a new perspective. He'd have to be more careful with her. Still, the moment in her arms remained a pleasant memory.

He had never understood the fascination birdwatchers had for their hobby, but tonight felt a kinship as he observed the habits of the *Widow falsus* and its brood, taking particular interest when the ship's officer escorted them to Mauritz Findlay at a table near him. He couldn't overhear their conversation over the constant murmur of the voices around him, but the effort the couple made to strike up an acquaintance with the painting's owner was obvious.

Curiouser and curiouser, he thought.

After dinner, Harry made for the ship's officer who'd done the introductions.

"Pardon me, sir," he said to Lightoller as the room emptied, "but I couldn't help notice you speaking with a young man during dinner. He looked familiar. May I ask his name?"

"Certainly, sir. He's Mauritz Findlay."

"He and the couple you took over to him seemed quite animated. Old friends of his family?"

"Not as far as I know. They asked about a painting the young man is bringing with him to America. It's quite the prize, apparently, though I know little of such things."

"Ah yes, the Blondel."

"Indeed. I feel quite the barbarian. Everyone aboard seems to know more about it than I do."

Harry thanked the Second Officer and wished him good night then retired to the café to allow this bit of intelligence to digest, along with a most excellent *créme brûlée.*

***

After dinner Mary found Colette waiting for her, and Mary shared what they'd learned over dinner.

"The bad news is the painting's not in the hold, it's in the young man's room."

"Which sounds like good news to me," Colette said. "Pity all our preparation to get into the hold will go to waste."

"About that," Sam said, smiling.

There was a knock at the door, and the stewardess, Hope, joined them.

"Tell me about the security in the first-class holding area," Mary told her.

"Once the ship's left harbor, there's only one seaman on duty with a visitor's log to record anyone who enters or leaves. It's considered light duty and given to the younger sailors who have less experience. Are you going after the painting tomorrow, or the book?"

"The painting is in the stateroom of the idiot son," Mary said. "He's practically begging us to steal it. An invitation I won't refuse."

"So the painting, then."

"Exactly." Sam said. "When's the best time to try for the book?"

Hope shrugged. "No time like the present. The new crew are still finding their way about the ship and don't know each other."

"Good." Mary said, turning to Sam. "Put on your steward jacket so you and Colette can make a brief withdrawal from the library." She nodded to the stewardess. "Hope can lead you."

Colette laughed. "I've profited much from reading, but never before from the book itself."

As Sam changed, Mary recited a line from Hamlet apt for those who ply their trade in darkness. "Tis now the very witching time of night, when churchyards yawn and hell breathes itself out."

Chapter Eighteen

HOPE LED THEM DOWN to the steel door outside the baggage area. "Good luck," she said. "I'd best be seen elsewhere."

The seaman manning the entrance looked briefly at the storage check for the wine in Colette's hand, gazed at her a little longer, then gave Sam a hard stare.

"I ain't seen you before."

"I was hired last-minute in Southampton" Sam said, "Is that a problem?"

"No, no problem. I just don't remember seeing you at muster is all, but it's not like I know every Jack or Jill on the crew. Just curious." He tipped his hat to Colette. "If you'll follow me, Miss, I'll help you find your wine."

They walked past an assortment of trunks and a touring car before finally, atop a large wooden box, they spied the wine crate. Sam and Colette exchanged a look, and she began phase two of their plan.

"Oooh, these iz such a large space! How can you find what you are looking for?"

"We've got it all laid out quite logical like. Care for a tour?"

"*Mais oui!* You must be very clever to know your way around."

The sailor winked at Sam. "Think you can find your way out, mate?"

"Oh yes, I think so. I, too, am very clever," she said,

nodding at the man before making for the exit, a bottle of wine in each hand.

Once they were out of view, Sam placed the wine bottle in her right hand beneath her left arm before continuing. Her search pattern was simple—stay away from Colette's voice as she kept up a steady stream of commentary. Colette was halfway through her guided tour of the hold and Sam was getting anxious when she spied a small, locked cabinet of steel mesh, with a wooden box inside it. She peered through the grating and smiled when she saw Sotheby's name on the shipping label.

Sam put the wine bottles on the deck, pulled out her picks, and began testing the lock. She flinched as the voices came closer and she saw the seaman approaching, Colette on his arm. Sam gritted her teeth before replacing the picks into her jacket.

She picked up the wine and stumbled towards the door. "There it is!" she cried.

"What's this then?" the seaman came up to the fake steward, frowning as he did so.

"Sorry, mate. I've never been on such a big ship before and got turned around."

The seaman looked Sam over once more, giving a close inspection of the pockets in her jacket. "Right, then. Bugger off, but I'll be watching you. I can't have you wandering around the hold now, can I?"

He turned and gave a slight bow to Colette. "But you, lady, are welcome anytime. I'll be back on duty tomorrow morning at eight, should you find yourself free."

Once outside the hold, Sam whispered to Colette. "I found the box, and if you'd kept him busy another minute, I could have made off with it!"

"That's hardly my fault," Colette said as they reached the stairs. "But you heard the man. I have an open invitation to return tomorrow."

"Too early in the day to return for more wine, so we'll need another time, and a less-suspicious guardian."

Colette accepted a bottle of wine before they began the climb. "I'm sure you'll think of something, Sam. Time to show Mary you're as clever as you think you are."

Sam gritted her teeth. *When I take over from Mary,*

you'll use a different tone, she thought, *or out you go.*

***

Harry inquired at the Masters office about his young pickpocket, Jenny, and learned she was in a two-person cabin at the other end of Scotland Road, past the galley. Harry went to the head of the long passageway and looked down it. The deck swayed just enough to be noticeable. The further he gazed down the hallway the more it seemed the walls narrowed, and he felt his chest tighten. When it came time to pay the girl the final installment, he'd approach her cabin from the other end of the ship.

As he turned to go, he saw Colette with a steward climbing the stairs, each bearing a bottle of wine. As he approached, she turned to the steward, "I can take the wine from here, thank you," and relieved him of the second bottle. The man nodded and continued up the stairs, looking away as if in deep thought.

"Your mistress must have a powerful thirst to want two bottles this late at night," Harry said. He looked at the labels. "I know this vintage. Those two bottles represent over a week's wages... for most men, I mean."

"Meaning they are not for you, *Monsieur?"* Colette asked. "How fortunate to be you."

"I... uh... I didn't mean to imply..." he stammered, red-faced, surprised how this young woman left him tongue-tied.

She smiled at the effect she'd made. "It is late, and I am perhaps over-harsh when I become tired. Take no notice. But you, too, are up late."

Harry's face cooled as the conversation moved to a safer topic. "You recall I promised our young miscreant a second payment for good behavior. I was just checking with the Master of Arms to learn her cabin number."

"Then you are a man of your word, despite your mysteries. Never fear, *Philipe,* I shall decipher you before we reach New York. You have become my little... how you say? *Passe-temps.* My hobby. I warn you, *Monsieur,* I am relentless." She yawned. "But I must bring my mistress her wine before going to bed. Tomorrow promises to be a busy day."

"Then I shall be on my guard, Colette. *Bon nuit!"*

He half-bowed as she disappeared up the stairs, leaving him with a cryptic smile. He checked his watch and surprised himself when he began calculating how many hours until he'd be in the café, waiting to see her. Hopefully, she'd be less distracted then.

***

Sam said nothing back in the stateroom until Colette set the bottles down, then she grabbed Colette's arm and spun her around. "The young man seemed very happy to see you. This is no time for games."

"Mary wanted me to keep an eye on him," she snapped, jerking her arm free. "That's easier to do if he doesn't despise me."

"What's this all about?" Mary asked, an unlit cigar in the corner of her mouth. "Did you find the book?"

"I did, no thanks to this empty-headed magpie. She had the sailor eating out of her hand and if she hadn't been so distracted by a handsome face, she'd have kept him busy long enough for me to get away with it."

"And no one would notice you walking about the ship with a locked box?" Colette retorted. "I thought we weren't supposed to draw attention to ourselves."

Mary nodded. "She's right, Sam. You don't want someone to remember you in a steward's jacket and you won't have time to remove the diamonds while you're in the hold. We'll have to get it here unobserved, then return it. After we've removed the jewels, of course."

Sam glared at Mary, then exhaled slowly. "Very well." Sam picked up one of the bottles and took it to the sink, opened it, and poured herself a generous glass. She smiled as she peered through the blood-colored liquid in the low light. "I think I have the answer."

"What is it?" Mary asked.

"Surely, Mary, with your love of the classics, you've heard of the Trojan horse."

Chapter Nineteen

Ship's Gymnasium

April 12, Friday

HARRY WAS WORKING UP a good sweat on the rowing machine when Margaret Brown entered, wearing an exercise dress over a gym suit. He nodded to her and she grudgingly returned his silent greeting before turning to the gymnasium steward who, to Harry's surprise, placed a pair of boxing gloves on her and laced them up.

She followed the steward to the heavy punching ball and began banging away at it with a skill that spoke of long hours of practice.

"Well-struck, Madam!" the steward said. "You never disappoint. I should pay you to watch you work."

"Thank you, Mister McCawley," she said, pausing to push a stray lock of hair out of her face. "I just imagine the bag is the manager at the dry goods store I worked at in Leadville, before marrying Mister Brown." She slammed her innocent target with conviction. "He was a man who couldn't keep his opinion, nor his hands, to himself. Imagining his face on the bag brings out my best."

She glanced over to Harry before resuming her assault and he applied himself to rowing with increased enthusiasm. If he'd had his notebook handy at the moment, he'd have amended the entry he'd made when she boarded: *High risk, to whoever tries to rob her.*

***

Colette was barred from the males-only Smoking Room and not allowed to sit in any of the public areas in the first-class section of the ship when not with her mistress, so keeping an eye on Harry proved difficult. Striding about as though she were on an errand was only good for one traverse of the ship and she despaired when she passed through the Palm Court and spied him standing just as a young woman approached his table.

By now, Harry was keenly aware he was the object of study for more than one unmarried young woman and was quick to shift location whenever any approached. The current stalker's smile faded as he beat a hasty retreat, leaving his coffee cup half-full.

Colette crafted a plan to remove him from female harassment while 'keeping an eye' on him at the same time. She walked beside him as he headed for the promenade deck. "It seems you are very popular with the young ladies, *Monsieur.* I am fortunate to have gotten a dance with you while I could."

"I feel like a hunted criminal," Harry said, wiping his forehead. "They're relentless. Everywhere I turn, I find another young woman who wants to take tea with me or ask me some inane question about the ship to start a conversation."

"In their eyes, you are a criminal. A well-off bachelor who refuses matrimony. They feel you have a duty to society to share your good fortune with a woman suitable to your station."

"And what, exactly, is my station?"

Colette spread her arms to encompass the promenade deck and the well-dressed ladies walking off breakfast. "First-class. Posh. Smoking jackets and champagne. The world you entered when you came onboard."

"And what would you say if I told you I no more belong here than you?"

Colette felt her pulse increase. Was he truly a thief, like her? The thought of spending time with him as an equal was… not unpleasant.

"I would say it makes no difference to the man you truly are." He was hiding something, that much was clear.

Best let him tell her on his own time.

They found themselves standing by the rail where the dance lesson happened the day before. "I see we've returned to the scene of the crime," Harry joked.

"Oh?" Colette said, batting her eyes. "Did *Monsieur* find my dancing criminal? If so, then you must take me into custody."

"I'll let you go if you promise to behave from now on."

Colette laughed. "A dangerous decision." Then she sobered up and turned to the railing, gazing at the reflection of the great ship in the water below. *Is anyone as they seem?* she wondered. She shook herself and forced a smile. "Perhaps I can help cool the ardor of the young ladies pursuing you?"

"And how could you do that?"

"By making them think we're having an affair." She winked. "A shame you cannot take my arm while we walk the promenade. If we did, imagine how the fans would flutter in the Reading Room with the gossip! If the ship had sails, the men in the boiler room could lay aside their shovels for the day."

Harry bowed slightly, offered his arm, and Colette accepted. "Let the tempest begin!" he said.

As they strolled, Harry saw the young woman who'd first approached him in the café—Temperance?—walking towards them with a dazed young man on her arm. She was chattering away while her captive nodded weakly with a look of desperation on his pale face. Temperance glanced up at their approach and without breaking stride wheeled the two of them around and continued in the opposite direction.

Harry had to admire her coolness under fire and felt sure she'd make a formidable card player. He and Colette exchanged glances and choked down their laughter as best they could.

"I see she has survived your rejection, *Phillipe*." She giggled.

"She should do fine, she's fast on her feet!"

As they approached the front of the promenade, they heard the happy squealing of children and laughter of adults, mixed with cheering.

"Look, *Phillipe*! A sack race!"

They cheered on the young athletes hopping madly down the forty-foot course, the winners adorned with large red paper badges.

They watched three heats and joined the throng in congratulating the grand champion. Once the paper crown was placed atop the head of a grinning ten-year-old girl, the steward began gathering the sacks when Colette turned to Harry.

"I challenge you to a race."

"What? Here? Now?"

She punched him lightly in the arm. "You forgot to ask why."

"OK, why?"

"I'll make you a wager."

"What are the stakes?"

"If I win, you must answer my questions."

"And if I win?"

She tossed her head. "You won't, but if you do, I'll answer yours."

"It's hardly a fair contest, Colette. I'm larger, stronger, and a man."

"In other words, you're saying you're afraid you'll lose."

Harry went to the steward. "Pardon me, sir, but the lady and I have a wager. Would you loan us two sacks and give the start command?"

The steward smiled as he handed over two burlap bags. "As you like, sir." He looked over at Colette. "I'd say you've got your work cut out for you, Miss. Good luck!"

The two contestants lined up at the starting line and crouched as the steward counted down, "Three... two... one... GO!"

On the command of GO! Colette crashed into Harry's back, sending him sprawling as she hopped to the finish line, unopposed.

"I win!" she crowed. "Pay up!"

The steward, laughing, retrieved the bags, tipped his hat, and returned to other, less enjoyable duties.

"It doesn't count!" Harry cried. "You cheated!"

"I play to win, *Phillipe*" She touched him lightly on the

nose. "You should remember that."

They resumed their walk along the promenade before she spoke again.

"I warned you I would discover your secrets. Surely, a man of the world such as yourself knows secrets are like catnip to women. Are you ready for my interrogation?"

"Such a strong word on such a lovely day," he teased. "What would Inspector Colette wish to know of her suspect?"

"Are you really in the insurance business?"

"Yes, and before you ask, it's as dull as you think and I'd rather not discuss it further. Do I get to ask you anything in return?"

Colette cocked her head. "What would you wish to know?"

"The wine I saw you carrying last night. Was your mistress having a late party in her quarters?"

"What my mistress does in her stateroom with her wine is none of my business, *monsieur,* as I hope you appreciate. Why your sudden interest?"

"Surely you noticed the warning in the pamphlet left in our rooms about unsavory characters aboard ship?" He paused and cleared his throat. "I wouldn't want your mistress to be taken advantage of if she was entertaining any. .."

"Any what?"

"Unsavory characters. Anyone with the ability to travel first class is a potential victim to such people."

Colette was grateful Harry wasn't holding her hand as it turned ice-cold. "What kind of insurance do you manage, *Phillipe?*"

"All kinds, Colette. Life. Property. Fire... theft."

She looked out to sea so he couldn't read her face. "I see." After she'd composed herself, she turned to him. "I shall certainly warn my mistress about these unsavory people, but now you must excuse me. I think I've damaged your good standing enough for one day."

Just before she went inside, she paused to look back at him. He'd hoped for a smile, but her forlorn look told him his hunch about her employer, and her, were probably correct.

It's a shame, he thought, *that I have to be so suspicious, and so often with good reason. Hopefully, they can take the hint, and reconsider their designs on the painting.*

***

Colette held her head erect as she walked towards the First Class stateroom, despite the emotions flooding through her.

He's a thief, just as Mary predicted. Only another thief would try to warn her off so they could have the way clear for themselves. You little fool! A normal man with a normal life is not for you. Accept your fate.

Colette thought back to a snarling, drunken face advancing towards her as she stood between her father and her younger sister's room, a revolver in her shaking hand.

Non. I am a criminal—or would be, to a jury of twelve men. My life is not my own.

Her face was hard, and only once she was safely inside the stateroom did the tears burst through. *Bon. If I am to be a thief, then finding a kind man to hide within the shadows is the best I can hope for.*

Harry Worth may be a criminal, like her, but he was a kind criminal, and she desired kindness more than respectability.

Mary returned to prepare for luncheon soon after, and found her protégé on a chair, drying her tears. "What is it, Colette? Did you find Master Worth flirting with another woman?"

"Do not tease me, Mary! *Non.* He practically confessed he is a criminal. He asked me about you and warned me about thieves aboard ship. I said nothing, of course, but when I asked what kind of insurance he managed, he mentioned 'theft.' He must be here after the painting, the same as we!"

Mary nodded. "Not surprising, but still good to be sure. I wonder how he found us out, I thought we'd been very careful. Perhaps I should approach him and lay our cards down and ask him to throw in with us."

"Do you think Sam would go along with it?"

"She might not like a smaller share, but she knows I'm in charge. If Mister Worth trusts me to handle the ransom on the piece, he might settle for a smaller take... it'd still be a lot of money to go around."

"Would you like me to talk with him?"

"No, dear. You can bat your eyes at him while I conduct business. Trust me, it's better that way."

Sam returned as Colette was dressing Mary for lunch and wasn't happy when told they had a rival. "What exactly did he say?"

"Only that we should be wary of thieves and that his 'insurance' company covered theft."

"Maybe he was just trying to sell you insurance," said Sam. She paused to give it some more thought. "Or you're right and he is a thief after the painting and it was his way of warning us off. That's what I'd do in his position."

"Don't jump to conclusions," Mary said. "I think I need to have a heart-to-heart with young Mister Worth, so we don't step on each other's toes in case he really is here for the same reason as us. Once we clear the air, we can plot the way ahead."

"All right," said Sam. "But please wait until we have the jewels from the book before you meet with him. I see no reason to include the gems in any agreement. I'd like something of our own to tide us over until we ransom the painting."

"Agreed," she said. "Colette, continue to play the sweet young maid and keep him talking until I meet with him." She turned to Sam. "The sooner we get the jewels, the sooner we can make our final plans for the painting. I'll make an appointment to visit Mauritz's stateroom so I can see what we're up against."

***

Mary wasted no time. During lunch, she passed by Findlay to remind him of his promise. "I'm all aflutter to see your painting, Mauritz. Would this afternoon be acceptable? Say three o'clock?"

"I'd be delighted, Mrs. Bayer! I shall ensure my cabin and the lady are both prepared for your visit." He stooped to kiss her hand. "Will your son be accompanying you?"

"No." She let her hand linger in his grasp just long enough. "He isn't much for art appreciation."

"Then I shall have to be on my best behavior. Until three, Madam."

Mary returned to her seat and answered Sam's unspoken question with a nod. *Best find Colette right after luncheon. We'll have an hour to make me irresistible.*

***

Harry noticed the brief conversation between the mysterious Mrs. Bayer and the Blondel's owner and felt like he was at the theater observing a masterfully staged play. The woman's subtle flirtation was skillfully paced. However the encounter fit in her scheme, he knew it had gone well. Apparently, his subtle warning to Colette had no effect on their plan, and he'd have to prepare for their next move. It was time to give them his particular attention.

Chapter Twenty

April 12, 2:30 pm

Colette returned with hair coloring in time to brush it through Mary's hair before her three o'clock appointment with a painting—and the young man standing between the thieves and the prize. Mary placed a drop of belladonna extract into each eye, causing the pupils to dilate, creating what was commonly referred to as 'bedroom eyes," hence the name for the plant, Belladonna or "lovely woman." Colette felt like a squire preparing their knight for battle as she lit a match and let it burn down before blowing it out and applying the charred wood to darken her mistress's eyelashes. As a final touch, Mary placed two drops of perfume strategically on her bosom. If she was able to lure Mauritz close enough to smell it, she knew the rest of the journey to his bed should go swiftly.

Sam laughed. "He won't know what hit him." She handed Mary a small tin box, in which one might carry lozenges. "If you can make a wax impression of his key, then we won't have to pick the lock." Sam held up her own. "I can form it from mine, then ask the stewardess for a new one. I'll just say I lost the original."

"Excellent idea, Sam. Now, if you two want to be useful, you can go fetch me that book. No reason I should have all the fun."

Mary gave Colette a peck on the cheek before shaking herself. "Once more into the breach, dear friends!"

"Or breeches," Sam said, opening the door for her. "I hope you enjoy your art appreciation."

Once Mary was gone, Sam turned to Colette. "Mary's right about going for the book now. Once she sees the security of the painting, we'll want to move quickly on swapping it out for the fake."

"Very well," Colette said. "In for a penny, in for a pound."

"For thousands of pounds, I hope."

***

Mary waited until ten past three, not wanting to appear too eager. Mauritz was all smiles when she entered. The painting was displayed on a nightstand across the room from the double bunk and was even more impressive than she'd expected, portraying a naked, red-haired woman standing between two Roman columns. Only after taking in the painting did she notice another young man rising from the chair beneath the porthole as she came in.

Mauritz waved his hand towards the other gentleman. "Allow me to introduce you to my friend and cabinmate, Hugh Woolner."

Mary's smile faded briefly, before she took the other man's proffered hand. "Delighted," she said.

She turned to study the painting from a slightly different angle and decided that in her day she'd have outshone the woman depicted. *In my day,* she thought, finding that phrase a bitter pill to swallow.

Beside the painting was a mirror, and Mary was drawn to it, comparing herself to the woman Blondel had so skillfully portrayed. Mary noticed her thinning hair, crow's feet at the corner of her eyes, and other marks of time no cosmetic can hide forever, and felt foolish.

"It is a marvelous thing, in art," her host said, "that in all societies throughout time, men have found the female form to be the highest standard of beauty." He bowed slightly. "Perhaps someday I might see what impression you made upon the canvas, and the artist."

Mary swallowed the hard truth the painting and mirror had just shown her. "I had my moment in the sun, Mister Findlay. As do we all." She studied the young woman's likeness more closely this time and was no longer sure how the two of them would have compared. It suddenly seemed a very long time ago when artists clamored for Mary to shed her clothes for their private viewing. *Memories are lies we tell ourselves,* she thought.

"Thank you for this moment of beauty, Mister Findlay" she said. "Now, I must be off to bore my long-suffering son with my rendition of this beautiful lady, and the kind man who shared her with me. Good day."

She floated out the door, her face a smiling mask, but within her mind the reflection she saw beside the flawless young woman in the painting had revealed how she must appear to the young, vibrant men behind her.

Idiot! Vain old idiot!

She couldn't return to the stateroom. Not yet. Instead, she sought the one refuge available to every woman in first-class and headed for the Reading Room.

It being midafternoon, the room was well-subscribed, and Mary found one seat available adjacent to the teenaged and very pregnant Mrs. Astor, being served tea by her maid. Mary gave the young woman a smile, which was returned shyly. Mary noticed the others in the room were ignoring the mother-to-be and understood why a smile from a stranger was so welcome.

At the opposite side of the room sat a large woman clinging to a Pekingese as though the poor thing might sprout wings and fly away at any moment. A woman in a maid's uniform stood listlessly at her elbow, silently awaiting the next outburst from her mistress with the fatalism of a soldier under siege. The woman slurped her tea before pronouncing loudly, to no one in particular, "I don't know what the White Star Line is coming to, allowing pregnant children into first-class as though they belong here."

Mary saw Mrs. Astor's knuckles pale as she clutched her cup tightly, her chin up, fighting tears. Mary paused, remembering a night long ago when she'd been shown the door for the sin of being a woman. She rose without thinking and strode across the room until she loomed over the dog's owner.

"Mary Bayer," she said, not offering her hand, "and

you are?"

"Mrs. Cardeza of Pennsylvania. A pleasure, I'm sure. A pity we haven't met before." The woman's face twitched into what she must have thought was a smile.

"Pity? I see little pity in a woman who berates another for following her heart. A woman struggling to bring a child into the world when all around despise her. No, Mrs. Cardeza of Pennsylvania. When you speak of pity, you might as well speak of comets or eclipses, things I'm sure you know no more about than tolerance, kindness, or basic humanity. I think you owe this young woman an apology. No! The room is owed an apology, madam, for all of us have been soiled by your vulgar display of arrogance."

The woman rose, glared at Mary for a moment, then she thrust her dog into her maid's arms and snarled, "Come, Josephine! Apparently first-class means nothing anymore." Missus Cardeza stalked out of the room without a second glance, but when her maid reached the door, the young woman looked back at Mary and nodded, saying with her eyes what she dared not speak.

Once Mrs. Cardeza was out of sight, there was a long, awkward silence. Then one, then another, then all the women in the room began to applaud, and Mrs. Astor looked at her champion with shining eyes. She gestured to Mary. "Please, Mrs. Bayer, would you sit with me a while? This has been a lonely crossing thus far."

"A pleasure, Mrs. Astor."

"Oh, do call me Maddie! My friends call me Maddie, but no one has dared to since John and I were married."

"As you wish, Maddie."

The young woman turned to her maid. "Please bring another pot and cup for Mrs. Bayer. I think I'll be here a while longer."

***

Harry knocked on the door to Mister Ismay's private stateroom and was quickly admitted, the butler apparently apprised of his Pinkerton connection. "I need to update you on a serious matter, sir," Harry said as the director rose from a leather sofa.

"By all means," Ismay said. He pointed to an adjacent

seat before turning to his butler, "A whiskey and soda for me. Agent Worth?"

Harry shook his head before continuing. "It appears we have a trio of art thieves going after the Blondel."

"Are you sure?" Ismay said, regaining his seat. "How could they hope to get something that large off the ship without being caught?"

"I can think of two or three ways, especially if they have a steward as an associate."

"We chose our crew mostly from those who've served elsewhere."

"Mostly, you say?"

"Well..." Ismay rubbed his chin. "I don't personally see to the hiring of every member of the victualing department. We may have had one or two last minute vacancies filled with locals in Southampton."

"I saw one of the thieves late last night with a steward, the two of them carrying wine bottles. I thought it odd at the time, but now I suspect the steward is in on whatever plan they have."

"Well done, Agent Worth. I'm impressed."

Harry paused, not used to being taken so seriously by a wealthy man. "Thank you, Director. I'll make sure they don't succeed, and that there's as little scandal as possible."

Ismay smiled. "Scandal? I'm not sure I'd use that word. If a gang of thieves are caught trying to steal from one of our passengers, publicizing it will serve to scare miscreants away while reassuring our clientele we look after them throughout the voyage. No, Mister Worth, I'd like to see their pictures in the paper being paraded down the gangway in New York. The more publicly we humiliate them, the better!"

Harry thought of Colette in manacles, photographed for all the world to see and felt his chest tighten. "I work for you, sir." He swallowed. "As you wish."

He turned to go, then stopped. "There are three of them and only one of me."

"I have no one available to assist you, Mister Worth, at least until you are ready to place them into custody."

"I know, sir, but I was thinking of another possibility.

Are you familiar with Sherlock Holmes?"

Ismay laughed. "What Englishman isn't?"

"Then you'll have heard of the Baker Street Irregulars."

***

"You look quite dashing in your white jacket," Colette said, as she watched Sam convert from the soft-spoken son of a wealthy woman to an anonymous steward aboard a vast, impersonal ship.

"And you look adorable in your maid's attire," Sam said. "It galls me to play the servant. It reminds me of my childhood."

"You were... what, a waitress?"

"Among other things. I was a servant girl in my father's house. Oh, he made sure I received a proper education so I wouldn't embarrass him, but my status was never in doubt. He wanted a son and well, he got me. I was groomed to be his secretary, a loyal hound trained to obey. To live in his shadow in a world where I would never truly belong... at his elbow, but never by his side." Sam removed her cufflinks and rolled up her sleeves enough that the jacket hid them when she put it on.

"A servant in your father's house? I don't understand."

Sam carefully knotted her tie before responding. "My father was a wealthy man. My mother was one of the servant girls, and they never married, so... yes, before you say it, I was—and I am—illegitimate."

She completed her inspection in the mirror before turning around.

"We have a lot in common, Colette."

"What could we possibly have in common?"

Sam bowed before opening the door. "Both of us killed a father, though I was gentler... I used a pillow."

Chapter Twenty-One

April 12, 4 pm

THE SAILOR ON DUTY was allowed a chair at the entrance to the hold and was dozing in it when Sam stuck her head in. "Pardon" she said gently, and the man jerked awake. She held up the claim check. "I'm here for this." She turned as Colette entered. "The young lady already knows where it is. We don't require an escort."

"I can't have you wandering about the hold, regardless." He winked at Colette. "I can't have something happen to such a fine a young lady while I'm on watch."

"Oh, *Monsieur,*" Colette cooed. "You are so sweet. How do you stay safe in here during a storm?"

"We make sure everything is tied down proper, Miss. Care for me to show you?"

"Oh, *oui!* I remember the beautiful touring car I passed last time I was here. Please show me how you secure it without damage. I've always dreamed of riding in such a magnificent automobile."

The seaman offered his arm. "There's lots of ropes you could trip on. Come with me and I'll show it to you. Care to sit inside?"

Sam huffed, "I've more things to do than escort a young lady around sightseeing. I'll tend to my business and be on my way."

The seaman nodded absently, "As you like, mate. Now, Miss, let's show you that grand car. The seat's a fine leather." He chuckled, "I admit I've sat behind the wheel meself. Follow me."

Sam made for the locker as Colette kept up a steady stream of chatter, the seaman leading her deeper into the darkened hold. The Chubb padlock in the hasp was new so the grease on the tumblers was fresh but the springs were stiff, and she went through three picks before finding one thin but strong enough to hold the pins in place. Finally, after a dozen tries and a few muttered curse words, she felt the give of the lock's surrender, and its body slid noiselessly down. The thief smiled in the dark as she removed the Sotheby's box and headed for the wine crate.

Sam pried off the lid and removed the packing between the space left by the two bottles she'd taken earlier, but the box holding the book was too wide! She cursed softly, unsure what to do when she heard the door to the automobile close and voices headed towards her. She removed another bottle from the crate and shoved the box inside before replacing the lid.

They were almost upon her, and Sam had no idea how to explain why she'd carry one bottle of wine outside the crate. Then she smiled and loosened the crate's lid so it was partly open before lifting the superfluous bottle high and dropping it to the metal deck. The sound of the shattering glass drew the seaman immediately.

"What the hell are you doing?" he asked.

Sam spread her hands and turned to Colette. "I was trying to find the specific bottle your mistress asked for, and in my clumsiness, I dropped this one."

"She will be furious!" Colette said, taking her cue. "Since I do not know which of the remaining bottles she'd prefer, I insist you carry the entire crate up so she can choose for herself."

Sam sighed before lifting the crate after she secured the lid. "As you like, Miss. It's the least I can do."

"It certainly is." Then Colette turned to her guide. "My apologies for the mess, *Monsieur.* I hope the smell of wine doesn't cause you grief with your superiors."

The seaman's face paled. "Damn, you're right! I could be accused of drinking it myself. I've got to clean this mess up before the change in watch." He pointed his finger at the fake steward. "Don't show your face here again, mate, or we'll have more than words."

"As you like," Sam said, then wordlessly followed Colette out of the hold. Despite the added weight in the box, it seemed light as a feather.

***

The duo walked in silence as they made their way to the stairs up to C Deck, then walked down the corridor past several passengers and crew. The passageway had never seemed so long, and Colette feared Harry might appear at any moment. She knew if she saw him, her face would give her away. She walked as meekly as the maid's handbook had instructed, demure, chest not thrust out, eyes down. Thankfully, no one gave a second glance to a maid escorting a steward bearing a crate in first-class territory. No one, that is, until they passed a large woman with a Pekingese clutched to her ample bosom.

"Steward, come here!" she commanded.

Sam froze, then—sighing— obeyed. "Yes, Madam. How may I serve you?"

"My worthless stewardess has failed to bring fresh flowers to my stateroom today. I shall speak with Mister Ismay about the degradation of service in the White Star Line before I disembark, but for the moment, you need to see to it that my floral arrangement is refreshed before I retire. I am Mrs. Cardeza. The Purser can direct you to my quarters once you have secured the bouquet, and I expect them in a fresh vase!" She sniffed. "Did you understand me? Did I speak too quickly for you?"

Sam smiled as she considered what this pompous woman could do with her vase of flowers and only with great difficulty resisted the urge to tug her forelock. "Oh indeed, Madam. Right away!"

"Finally," she sniffed. "Someone who understands respect for one's betters. Carry on then, don't just stand there like a statue!"

Sam nodded her head before resuming the voyage to her stateroom. Colette had never felt more kindly disposed towards Sam when she heard her mutter, "If only I could find a bouquet of nightshade."

Once the door was safely closed behind them, they looked at each other as they began breathing normally.

"We did it!" Colette said, and they laughed together.

"I feel sorry for the next steward she sees," Sam said. "No. I pity anyone forced to be in her company."

She brandished her boot knife and, after considering other uses, turned to the box containing the book and pried the bottom off in an instant. "This way the seals on the top are pristine," she explained. "Few would think to inspect the bottom."

She placed the box upon a side table and drew out a package wrapped in green wax paper. Within was an oaken case containing a book bound in dark, engraved Moroccan leather studded with so many small glittering diamonds as to rival the night sky, as well as a scattering of rubies, topazes, and emeralds.

"Bloody hell!" Sam said. "This must be worth a fortune!"

Colette whistled, then pulled out a stick of gum to calm her nerves before studying their booty.

"How much do you think?" Sam asked.

"How many gems or how much money?"

"Money! That's all that matters."

"Let's get 'em off the book and let me do a proper count before I make up some figure because I know you'll tell Mary whatever I say, and I don't want to steer her wrong."

"But the number will be in the thousands, yes?"

"I don't need a scratchpad to tell you that. Yes, it'll be in the thousands."

Colette pulled out her jeweler's loupe and was happily occupied for the next two hours. Every jewel plucked free from the book was another step closer to true freedom, the freedom from want. At the end, she counted fifteen rubies, fifteen emeralds, twenty topazes, and exactly one thousand small, low-quality diamonds, heaped together like grains of sand upon a crystalline beach.

She didn't have nearly enough fake gems to replace all taken from the book, but carefully fastened a dozen on the cover so that at least on a first glance the theft wouldn't be obvious.

Mary came in as Colette was assessing the jewels and froze, then whistled when she saw the sparkling mound upon the linen napkin where Colette had placed their treasure. "It's plain your day has gone better than mine. What's the take?"

"I'd reckon the diamonds are worth about four pounds each," Colette said, "so four thousand for them, then another two thousand for the other gems, makes for six thousand altogether." She sat back, marveling at how so much wealth could occupy such a small space. "Since these are low-grade, no one could prove they were stolen, and we might do best going to Amsterdam and selling two hundred at a time on the open market. That way, we'd get closer to true value than what a fence would give us."

Mary placed her hand on the young woman's shoulder as she savored the glittering booty. "Well done."

"I like your idea of selling the diamonds in Amsterdam," Sam said. "So many stones trade hands there every day that two hundred more will go unnoticed, and we'll get an honest price."

"So, honesty is important to you after all?" Mary teased. "How refreshing."

She shrugged. "Honesty has its place. But how did your afternoon go? Your clothing looks undisturbed."

"Mauritz has a cabin-mate, who was in attendance when I visited, as was the painting. It appears he found me quite resistible, a fact I'd forgotten until you reminded me." She scowled. "Sorry to disappoint you."

Unsure how to respond, Sam shifted to another topic. "The roommate complicates matters. We'll need a new plan."

"Now that we have the gems," Colette said, "perhaps it's time we approached Harry to see if he'll join us for the painting? I'm getting tired of the charade."

"You're right," Mary said. "Tell him he and I have much to discuss."

***

At dinner that evening, Harry had a difficult time not looking at Mrs. Bayer and her son across the room—nearly as much trouble as they had not to look at him. The couple parted after dessert and Harry followed the son to the Smoking Room where in one corner a card game was already in progress. Harry was pleased neither of the two boat men were at the table, but he tensed when Sam passed by the card table and after asking permission, took an empty chair.

Harry noted Mauritz Findlay was also in the game, and Harry ordered a whiskey and soda as he sat at the bar and watched Bayer slowly but steadily lose around forty pounds to Mauritz. There was some laughter between them, and Harry overheard something about "winning back my own" as Bayer rose and bid the table a good night.

Harry hesitated. Should he follow the man about? Surely a professional like him in the small confines of the ship would notice sooner or later. He rose and walked to the vacant seat, and after a receiving the blessing of the other players, sat in.

I'll have to pretend I'm Goldilocks, and make sure I don't win or lose too much, he thought. *This is just a social call.*

Introductions were made all around, and once Mauritz announced his name, Harry smiled.

"I read about your painting," he said. "A pity it's locked away in storage. I'd love to see it."

"Odd," the young man answered. "You're the second person to ask about it. I should start charging, I suppose, but if you'd like I could arrange for you to come by my stateroom to see it."

It was a good thing Harry wasn't dealing when he understood the Blondel was only secured by a stateroom key, else he'd have spilled the cards.

***

Mary went to the Reading Room to check up on her new friend, Maddie Astor. Sure enough, the young woman was in her usual spot drinking tea and Mary noted the other women in the room often smiling at her and asking after her health. Mrs. Cardeza was noticeably absent, which could account for the more convivial atmosphere, and Mary noticed several grateful glances towards her when she entered.

Maddie lit up when she saw Mary and waved towards an empty seat beside her. "People have been ever so kind since this afternoon, Mrs. Bayer. Thank you again!"

"My pleasure, Maddie. I've suffered from people like that woman before, and it felt good to take her down a notch or two."

Mrs. Astor laughed. "I can't imagine anyone treating you like that!"

"Oh Maddie, the tales I could tell, but it was a very long time ago. Let's talk about something more pleasant."

As they chatted about the concerns of the mother-to-be, Mary listened patiently, understanding the young woman hadn't had anyone to confide in for some time. As they talked, she noticed a young girl in a white apron and a blue smock carrying a silver tray with what Mary assumed was a message. The girl walked slowly about the room before leaving, and Mary thought no more about it until shortly after the girl returned with two vases of flowers and placed them on opposite sides of the room and began carefully arranging one, then the other, while glancing about. Finally, after about ten minutes per vase, she left.

Mary wasn't surprised when—later, after bidding her companion good night—she passed by a window looking out over the promenade and saw the young girl carrying a tray in the window's reflection.

The game is afoot! She thought to herself, quoting her favorite author. Mary saw a certain irony in her enjoyment of the writings of Sir Arthur Conan Doyle.

Chapter Twenty-Two

April 13, Thursday

THE NEXT MORNING, THE trio was in the stateroom as Sam and Colette prepared to return the book before it was missed. Sam was in the steward's jacket, while the wine crate containing the book—now stripped of real jewels—rested on the floor.

"I'm starting to become known by the sailors," she said as she inspected her reflection in the mirror. "Good thing this will be my last time in this role. If they see the resemblance with Mister Bayer, the jig is up."

"Those sailors would never have a reason to come to the first-class area of the ship," Mary said, as she helped knot Sam's tie. "Besides, the clothes make the man. When you're wearing this, all anyone else sees is a steward, not a person."

Colette laughed. "Just ask Mrs. Cardeza of Pennsylvania!"

Sam winced. "If she recognizes me, there'll be hell to pay. I wonder if she ever got her fresh flowers?"

"I know the... person you speak of," Mary said. "I can see you've had a run-in with her as well. I'll go first to the stairs, and if she sees me, she'll probably flee to another corner of the ship and cede you safe passage."

"Why would she run from you?" Colette asked.

"Because she's a bully, and like all bullies, she ran as soon as she met a stronger one."

Sam raised her hand in a mock toast. "Long rule Mary

Carr, Queen of the Forty Elephants!"

"And don't you forget it!" Mary said, winking before she opened the door and sauntered towards the stairs, prepared to clear the way for her confederates—a human minesweeper.

As most passengers were at breakfast the way was largely empty, save for the occasional ship's officer. After the dowager from Pennsylvania, Sam most feared being seen by an actual steward, but their timing was good; the victualing staff were enjoying their own breakfast while the passengers dined.

Once at the stairs, Mary left Colette and Sam to complete the transfer. "I've no reason to go just to return a wine crate," she said. "The rest is up to you."

Sam gripped the crate tightly to her chest as she approached the hold, Colette right behind. She'd need one minute alone to pick the lock and return the book box to the locker. One minute. She knew what to do; it was up to Colette to keep the seaman distracted. She thought Colette's floral perfume couldn't hurt.

Colette went in first; Sam taking a deep breath before following.

"You again!" said the seaman Sam had distracted with the broken bottle. "I thought I told you to bugger off!"

"Really, sir!" Colette blushed, "Such language in front of a lady!"

"Begging your pardon, ma'am," the seaman said, his own face now bright red. "My mother did raise me better."

"I should hope so!" she said, giving him a slight smile. She turned to Sam. "You know where the crate goes, steward. Restore it to its proper place—carefully this time, or my mistress will have words with the Chief Purser."

Sam nodded and scuttled off before the seaman could engage her in further conversation.

Colette popped a stick of Beemans into her mouth and offered one to the hold's guardian.

"Never tried it," he said.

"It leaves your breath fresh," she said, leaning close to demonstrate and giggling as she did so.

"Then I don't mind if I do," he said, taking the offered chewing gum and sniffing it before giving it a taste."

"Not bad. Not bad at all," he said, leaning close and breathing into her face.

"What do you think?"

While Colette was giving chewing gum lessons to the sailor, Sam put the crate back before slipping the book box out and making for the locker. Having picked it before, she had the lock open in less than half the time of the first attempt.

She made it back to the entrance just as the seaman was trying to convince Colette how fresh his breath was, and Colette gave Sam a grateful look when she reappeared.

"It's done, miss. Would you care to see for yourself, or are you satisfied?"

"Quite satisfied," Colette said as she leaned back from the amorous sailor.

"Maybe you could come back later with another stick?" he asked. "I'm getting quite a taste for it."

"I think you already had that taste, *monsieur,*" she replied. "But perhaps I shall return. The crossing's not over yet. Who knows where the winds and the sea shall take us?"

And with that, the two confederates left. There was a joy in a theft well done, and bliss in knowing you could never be held to account for it.

***

Once free from the hold, Colette turned toward the pantry and breakfast, while Sam made a beeline to her stateroom, and soon the dutiful son of Mrs. Bayer, aspirin heiress, was at their table. Mary raised an eyebrow, Sam nodded, and Mary toasted her accomplice silently with her tea.

***

Back in the pantry, Violet Jessup made room for Colette beside her at the table.

"You can't imagine the screaming I got from Mrs. Cardeza last night," Violet said as she buttered her toast. "Something about me and a steward both failing to bring her flowers." She rolled her eyes. "That woman's getting forgetful but will never admit it, so anything she believes she said or did becomes fact."

"I'm so sorry," Colette said sincerely. "What did you do?"

Violet laughed. "One of the good things about being a stewardess is the rich tend not to see us. I've served her on two other crossings, and she no more remembers me than a doorman at a hotel, and she goes through maids so often she's had a different one every time she comes aboard. I knew from a prior voyage she's allergic to nasturtiums, so I slipped a few petals into her pillowcase. Her eyes were so puffy this morning she had a breakfast tray brought to her room. I doubt we'll see her for the rest of the trip."

Colette's jaw dropped at the image, and Violet was surprised how long and hard the young maid giggled at her story.

***

Harry was at his usual spot by nine-thirty. His stomach bothered him as he waited for Colette to appear. The smart move would be to continue to let her think she'd duped him and see where that led. He could pounce on the trio as soon as he had proof of their chicanery.

Yes, that would be very clever, but the image of Colette being paraded down the gangplank for all the world to see troubled him; her delicate wrists were never meant for manacles. She was a thief, true, but she hadn't harmed anyone. Much like his father, she was stealing from the rich, using brains instead of violence. Harry's heart ached at how she'd played him, but that was all part of the game. He'd been a fool to think a vivacious young woman could find a man like him of any interest, and he couldn't blame her for his naiveté.

Harry was deep in thought when he looked up, and there she was, and his heart skipped a beat.

Even with all I know, he thought, *she still affects me.*

He smiled out of habit and rose. "Let's go to the promenade. We have much to discuss."

She nodded, subdued by his tone. "Always happy to help preserve your bad reputation," she said, trying to lighten the mood. He didn't smile, nor did he offer his arm, and she shivered as though a cloud had just passed over the sun.

Once on the promenade and away from casual listeners, Colette began. "I've talked a lot about you to my employers, and they'd like to meet. They have a business proposition they want to discuss."

"A proposition? Please, tell me more."

She swallowed. "We know who you are. Who your father was. Mary, Mrs. Bayer, is actually Mary Carr, Queen of the Forty Elephants. She recognized you as soon as she boarded as she once worked with your father."

Harry leaned against the rail, looking out to sea as Colette continued.

"We reckon you're on board for the same thing we are."

"The painting? The Blondel?" Harry said, hating himself for leading her on.

"Yes."

"You have a plan then?"

"We did, until we learned the painting's in the stateroom. Sam, Mary's 'son,' is sorting that out."

"This Sam, are they...?"

"A woman. We sometimes work with men, but Mary wanted a job this large to stay in the family, so to speak."

"I see. No boys allowed, and yet you're now willing to work with me?"

"There's enough to go around for all of us, and from what Mary says, your father was a brilliant man, so we'd be willing to hear your thoughts."

Harry saw the pinched expression and lines on her forehead. *This is hard for her. I suspect she came to crime later in life, wasn't born into it like I was.*

"So, all this flirtation? The dance? It was all to feel me out? Nothing more?"

Colette looked into his eyes and saw the pain hidden within his question. "I wasn't looking for a handsome thief to steal my heart, Harry, and we have only just met... but it did... does mean something." She wrung her hands. "I'd like to know you better once this is over and we can both stop pretending to be someone we aren't. Then I can answer your question better than I can now."

"I see." Harry felt the ship's roll as his heart tightened in his chest. "I don't know what to say about us, Colette. Not yet. When and where would Mary like for us to meet?"

"Two o'clock, in her stateroom, number—"

"I know where it is."

Colette froze. "You've been following me?"

"Not you, the, so-called 'son.'" He suddenly didn't know what to do with his hands and put them in his pockets so they wouldn't flap about.

"So, you've been deceiving me! You knew why I was aboard and were playing with me the whole time!"

"I didn't suspect until after our dance lesson. Your employers' interest in the owner of the Blondel raised my suspicions, but after what I know now, I'm not sure we should continue our... flirtation."

"Indeed! How could I want to spend time with a man who lies to me?" She stomped her foot. "You must think me very stupid, *monsieur.* I will not be toyed with. I hope we can still find a way to cooperate on the theft, but once that job is done, it will be *au Dieu* forever."

Colette's flushed face and fiery eyes melted Harry's heart, and he imagined her with head bent as she was marched down the gangplank straight to jail. *Damn Ismay! I can choose how to do my job myself.*

"I'm afraid I can't accept Mary's generous offer," Harry said as he reached for his wallet and produced his badge. "My employer wouldn't take kindly to that."

Colette saw the badge as a one-way ticket back to Montreal. Once she was arrested, the police would look to see if she was wanted elsewhere and life in prison would be the best she could hope for—otherwise, the gallows. Juries find it hard to sympathize with women who kill their fathers, no matter the reason.

"You're a detective, not a thief? But your father..."

"My father was everything Mary said he was. Late in life, he bargained with William Pinkerton for my future, wanting me to avoid the life he'd led. I was hired to protect the wealthy passengers aboard *Titanic* from people like you and your companions."

"Then why are you telling me this now?"

"Mister Ismay, the line director, wants me to catch you in the act and have you paraded in shackles before the press. He wants to make the three of you into an example to scare away others."

Harry put his badge away before continuing.

"I have discretion in how I perform my duties and... uh... I've never arrested a dance partner before. I wanted to give you a chance to step away. Let the painting go, enjoy the rest of the crossing, and I'll have no reason to turn you over to the authorities in New York."

Colette had wanted them to put away their masks and to know each other as they truly were. The bitter taste in her mouth reminded her to be careful what you wish for. She saw the truth in his eyes. He cared. She also saw the hard truth in his badge. If Harry discovered she was a wanted murderess, he'd be duty-bound to turn her in.

If only he was simply the thief I thought he was.

She sighed. "*Bon,* Agent Worth. By your leave, I'll inform my employers you must decline their proposition due to a prior obligation. If there is nothing else...?"

Harry stood mute.

"Then I bid you a good day," she said stiffly. "*Adieu.*"

The sight of Colette trudging away pained him. His French was far from perfect, but even he knew the difference between *au revoir,* and *adieu,* the later lacking a promise of ever meeting again.

This time when she got to the exit for the stairway, Colette didn't look back.

Chapter Twenty-Three

April 13-14

MARY AND MADDIE WERE now fast friends, though the young Mrs. Astor had become popular with the other ladies, too, many wanting to share their own stories of giving birth. Mary had to advise her that for every horror story there were a dozen women who delivered within half a day.

Mary was returning to her stateroom for Colette's report on her meeting with Harry Worth when she noticed the same young girl in the blue smock enter, armed as before with two full flower vases. She settled back and asked for another cup of tea.

This should be entertaining, Mary thought.

The girl rearranged the first vase in almost every variation possible before shambling past Mary to attend to the second. Mary waited until the girl was on her third attempt before she excused herself, kissing Maddie on the cheek as she rose and strode out of the Reading Room. She walked briskly through the First-Class Lounge and outside onto the promenade, standing just around the corner from the door.

Sure enough, the girl crept carefully out into the sunshine, scanning the deck. Mary stepped forward and placed her hand on the girl's shoulder.

"Looking for me?"

The girl spun around and gasped in surprise. "Begging your pardon, Missus. I was looking to deliver a message to someone. It ain't you."

Mary laughed. "You can tell Mister Worth I got his message loud and clear all the same." She stopped. "You wouldn't be the girl who tried to pick his pocket, would you?"

Jenny's eyes widened. "How'd you know 'bout that?" she said. "Wait, who's Mister Worth?"

"The man who doesn't like his pocket picked." She shrugged. "His real name is Worth, but that's no never mind. As for knowing about your straying hands, I, too, have spies. What's he paying you? Maybe I could double it and have you tell me a few things about him?"

She shook her head, pigtails flying. "I'd never turn on 'im!"

"So you do work for him, or you couldn't very well tell me about him. What's your name, girl?"

"Jenny," she sighed. "Please don't tell him you found me out! He's been fair to me, and I haven't gotten a square deal from anyone since me da died."

"I see. And how long has that been?"

"Five months now. I'm being sent to an aunt in New York I've never seen. The Purser has a check for my da's estate, and she gets paid all of it to take me in. I'm told it's almost five hundred pounds!"

"That's enough money to make anyone love you," Mary said, winking. "Were you a pickpocket before your father died?"

"No, Missus, not before, but I wasn't given any money after he passed from consumption, and I got placed in an orphanage 'til I was sor'ed. The police found a letter from my aunt, so the court decided to ship me off to 'er." The girl crossed her arms.

"I don't wanna go, and I'm coming back to London soon's I can. They talk funny in America, and I hear they eat nothing but buffalo."

Mary laughed. "You might like hot dogs once you try one."

Jenny's eyes bulged out. "They eat dogs, too!"

"It's their name for sausages on a roll. As far as I know, they don't eat dogs, and people I've met from there never mentioned bison. I think you'll adapt."

Mary considered the young spy for a moment.

"Can you read, Jenny?"

She drew herself up. "I knows me letters right enough. I used to read to me da when he first got ill."

"Then I'll have to get you a book. That'll be more profitable for you than following me around. Charles Dickens, I think. You'd enjoy *Oliver Twist,* since you're a female Artful Dodger."

"Artful Dodger? That's a grand name. Well, if you do as you say, I promise to read it."

Mary stuck out her hand. "Then we have a contract?"

"Aye Missus, we do. I knows all about 'em!"

"Excellent. Now, run along to Mister Worth and tell him if he has any questions, he can come speak with me himself and not send a... young lady to spy on me. Agreed?"

"Yes, Missus. Do I get paid for this contract, too?"

"You are an Artful Dodger! Very well, here's half a crown" Mary took them out of her pocket and handed over the coins. "You can get it changed in New York. Now off with you!"

Jenny curtsied and was gone in a blink of an eye.

Mary smiled as she watched her go. With that spirit, she'd have a life of adventure ahead of her, whatever continent she chose. A love of reading might do young Jenny more good than anything Mary could teach her.

She considered what she'd learned for a half crown. Harry had spotted her and Sam, and probably Colette, too. He was likely using Colette to learn about them. It was all part of the game, but she felt protective of the little Québécois she'd adopted into the gang. If Harry hurt her, he'd answer for it. Best have a chat with Colette and Sam before their meeting with Mister Worth.

***

The trio met in the stateroom at noon to prepare Mary for lunch and to hear Colette's report. Mary was telling Sam about her encounter with the young pickpocket when Colette entered.

"Your Mister Worth is a very resourceful man, Colette," Mary teased. "He hired a young girl to follow me about the ship. I'm sure he's convinced I'm trying to pick Mister Astor's pocket through his wife. The poor dear is as meek as a kitten, and I befriended Mrs. Astor as much out of charity as for the pleasure it gave me to banish an obnoxious American to her cabin. If there were elections for mayor of the Reading Room, I'd be able to run unopposed."

Colette didn't respond, her face tight as she chewed gum in silence.

"What's wrong, dear?" Mary asked. "Did he accept our offer for a parley?"

"*Non,* no parley. No truce. He isn't here to steal the painting." She sniffed. "He's here to protect it and anything else of value. He showed me his badge, Mary. He's a Pinkerton agent." She stomped her foot. "He's played me for the fool!"

There was a long silence as this was digested.

"Why would he tell you this, Colette?" Mary asked. "If he wanted to catch us in the act, he'd pretend to go along."

"He said the director, a man named Ismay, wants to make us a spectacle, to march us off the ship in manacles so no one else will attempt such a theft again." A tear ran down one of Colette's cheeks. "He doesn't want to see me like that. He told me so we wouldn't go any further." She grabbed Mary's hand. "We won't try now, will we? If I am arrested, I'd be delivered to the police in New York, and you know what would happen next. I can't risk it!"

"So close." Sam said. "So close to our dreams coming true." She turned to Mary. "He could be pretending to be a Pinkerton man just to scare us off and have the painting to himself, but even if he's for real, we can't stop now!"

"I tend to agree with Colette, Sam. It's risky for all of us, but for her most of all. Unless you've got a fool-proof plan, I say we call it off."

"I have an idea." Sam smiled. "If he's really with the agency, he can help us. And if Mister Worth is the gentleman Colette says, she'll have no reason to fear. All right?"

Mary cleared her throat. "Alright, Sam, let's hear it. It'd better be good. Very, very good."

"Non," Colette said. "It must be *parfaite.*"

***

Mrs. Bayer and her son nodded to Harry across the room as they entered the dining room for lunch, and he nodded back. The charade was over; the battle lines drawn. Harry saw by their stride they would not be deterred. With Jenny found out, Harry had surrendered his only other advantage by revealing himself.

If they attempt a heist right under my nose, he thought, *I won't regret what happens after. My charity is at an end.*

Harry followed Sam to the Smoking Room after the meal and was surprised when she went straight to the gaming table, sitting across from young Mauritz. There was another seat open, so Harry took it, nodding to all around.

After an hour of Sam losing steadily, she stood, frowning. "My compliments, Mauritz. My luck against you is no better than before. Would you be willing to give me an opportunity tomorrow in your stateroom? My mother told me so much about the painting, but I'd love to see it for myself, while losing more money to you, of course!"

"Sadly, I lack a proper table for the game, though you'd be welcome to see the Blondel regardless."

"Ah, but I have just the thing. We're conveying an antique table from our manor house in England to an apartment my mother owns in New York. Would you object to my having it sent to your cabin for the game?"

"Splendid. After dinner, then? Say nine pm?"

"Perfect, Mauritz. We'll be looking forward to it."

Harry couldn't believe his ears, *She's baiting me, daring me to do or say something.*

Harry's mind spun as he considered his next move when Sam nodded to him. "This other gentleman... Mister Daniels, I believe?" she said, smiling. "You seem interested as well. Care to join us, if Mauritz agrees?"

"Of course," Harry managed to say. "I wouldn't miss it."

"Delighted!" Mauritz said, "I'll have a couple of bottles of champagne brought to the room." He winked, "it wouldn't do to break the Sabbath half-heartedly."

"I can have our maid tend to the drinks while mother admires the painting, if not my skill at cards." Sam chuckled. "Better to be lucky in love, anyway."

Sam and Harry retired to their respective staterooms while Harry tried to make sense of what he'd just witnessed. The thieves knew he was there to catch them and, rather than forsake their plot, were making him a witness.

***

"We're in!" Sam said once back in their stateroom. "You should have seen the look on the Pinkerton man's face when I invited him to the game! He doesn't know what to expect, just like I'd planned."

"Don't count your chickens too early, Sam," Mary said, "even if we pull this off, we won't arrive until next Wednesday, the seventeenth. We've got to be so smooth Worth doesn't have second thoughts."

Sam grinned. "You need to be smooth. I need to be clumsy… just clumsy enough." She turned to Colette, who was pacing the room while chewing her Beemans furiously. "And you, my dear… make sure to save a stick for tomorrow."

***

Harry's job was simple now. The gamblers had been cowed, and no other passengers—save for the mothers with unattached daughters—seemed to have any other purpose than to travel from Europe to America in as enjoyable a fashion as possible. Colette had even done Harry one favor he appreciated; after being seen with her on the promenade, no marriageable woman would have anything to do with him.

Jenny had been embarrassed at being found out, but Harry assured her the woman was an old hand at the game and that he'd learned a great deal from Jenny's encounter. He'd even given her five dollars in severance pay to salve her pride and lent her a collection of Dickens from the ship's library.

He was sipping tea in the café when Mary approached him. "Good afternoon, Mister… Daniels. Mind if I join you?"

He stood, pulled out a chair, and bowed as she took it. "This is most unexpected, as was my invitation to a private card game tomorrow. It seems we are done with playing at charades, madam. What's your game?"

"You are so like your father, Harry. Polite but direct. I can tell by your lack of reaction you don't remember me, but that's not surprising. You were eight years old and having riding lessons while I was at your father's estate to discuss a job."

She extended her hand, "Mary Carr—"

He kissed her hand. "An honor, to be sure."

She dimpled. "Why, Harry, you sound like a fan of my work."

"As much as William Pinkerton admired my father, yes."

The waiter came to their table and Harry had him bring a fresh pot and second cup. "The lady and I have much to discuss."

Once they were alone again, he continued. "And what of Colette? She seems rather wholesome to be an Elephant. She's obviously not from England, though her accent sounds more French-Canadian than French."

"Colette came to me quite by accident, and you're right. She was brought up in a proper household, but I'll leave her to decide what to share with you. She's of no interest to the Pinkertons, and that's all you need to know."

"And I should take your word on that?"

They paused as the tea service arrived, and Harry poured Mary a cup. "I won't tell you everything, Harry; but I won't lie to you, either. I had too much respect for your father." She leant forward. "It's not too late to fall in with us. An equal share would pay you far more than you'd get in ten years working as an armed clerk for the agency. I think Colette is genuinely interested in you, but it would never work for the two of you as long as you're on opposite sides of the law."

"So you're the serpent in the Garden of Eden, tempting me with a ripe juicy... apple?"

"She's a good woman, Harry. I said I wouldn't lie, and that's God's truth. You could do far worse." Mary gestured to the elegantly dressed passengers in the café. "Do you think any of these fine ladies would want to spend time in your company if they knew your heritage? You don't belong here anymore than I do. Your father was a fine man. Even Pinkerton knew that. You can make a good living off the wealthy, and they'll scarcely feel it. Look around! Most of these folks got the good life by being born into it, or by the sweat of poor bastards who deserved better than they got."

Harry thought of the men stoking the boilers several decks below while he sipped tea. He shook his head. "My father took care to put me on a different path, Mary. He didn't want me to spend my life looking over my shoulder like he did."

He stood and kissed her hand again. "I respect you, and thank you for coming to me, but my course is set. I pray you reconsider and back away from yours. Enjoy being in the lap of luxury for the next few days in a world where, as you say, neither of us truly belong."

He automatically made for the promenade, the usual place he'd go with Colette. The deck seemed barren without her smile and musical laughter. He was looking out to sea when she appeared beside him.

"No," he said, not turning his head.

"No what, Harry? I haven't asked you anything."

"Mary did. I assumed she was speaking for you."

"I speak for myself, Mister Worth. Surely, you've spent enough time with me by now to know that."

"We've both been less than truthful. Why should you stop now?"

"At least I didn't say I was an office manager for an insurance company like it says on the passenger manifest."

"A necessary deception."

"Still a lie, or do you believe the end always justifies the means?"

"I believe in being truthful to my friends."

"Fine sentiments, Harry, but you have the freedom to live them. I… don't have many choices."

He turned. "Why not, Colette? Can I help you with whatever it is? You know I'll stop you if you try to steal the painting. Do you think the jails in America so fine you want to take a holiday in them because, believe me, they aren't any grander than what you've experienced in London."

"I don't know what you think of me, *monsieur,* but I have never been in a jail anywhere!"

"Then you're an even better thief than I thought. I suppose that shouldn't surprise me. The waltz lesson was a stroke of genius, I admit. You're very good at getting men to tell you what you want to know."

Colette saw the doubt in his eyes and yet—deeply buried—she spied a *soupçon* of hope. "It wasn't genius, Harry, it was a moment of happiness. For a brief while, I was just a young woman enjoying a dance with a handsome young man. Since I left my home, I've had few such opportunities."

"You never said, but you're from Canada, I believe?"

She tensed. The mention of her native country reminded her how easily this man could send her back there. "If you would, Harry, let me keep the few secrets I still have." She sighed. "I must go. It seems we shall meet again tomorrow evening during the card game. I wish you good fortune... at cards."

"*Au revoir,* Colette, but you should know... secrets are like catnip to detectives."

"Then I have been warned, and we both know where we stand. *Au revoir.*"

Harry's hope for a final glance before she left the promenade went unrewarded. *Well, that's that.* He sighed. *I'll never forget her, whatever happens next.* He thought of Colette's slender wrists encased in iron and returned his gaze to the ocean—seeing nothing at all.

***

Sam sat in the Smoking Room alone enjoying a late-afternoon drink before dressing for dinner. With the jewels from the book safely stashed in their stateroom, they would be quite comfortable until the painting's ransom was paid. Best not to risk the big score by sniffing around for random opportunities. She'd make acquaintance with a wealthy man whenever possible for a potential future score but do no more than exchange cards for now. All was proceeding smoothly as long as Colette remembered whose side she was on. Her infatuation with the young Pinkerton man was troubling, yet Mary saw no problem with her dalliance. A foolish indulgence when so much money was at stake. Perhaps Sam needed a guarantee of her compliance, something she could hold over her?

Sam considered this. What was Colette's greatest fear? She smiled, drained her gin and tonic in one long swallow, and headed for the Enquiry Office.

She had a Marconigram to send.

***

Sam was in a festive mood that night at dinner. She'd even had a picture taken alongside Mary and the captain. She and Harry locked eyes across the room during the dessert course, and she raised a glass in a silent toast to her adversary. *I'm going to steal the painting right under your nose and make you the biggest fool in the history of the Pinkerton's,* she thought. Ruining the career of the son of Adam Worth added a touch of sweetness to the heist, much as a splash of brandy in a cup of coffee.

The next morning, Mary and Colette strode the promenade together as both had noticed their clothes a bit tighter, and it helped reinforce the charade of mistress and maid. Thus, Sam was alone when the response to her telegram arrived. She tipped the steward half a pound before ripping it open. *Now I have you!* She thought. But her sneer faded as she read the brief message before mashing it into a ball. She was about to fling it into the waste container but reconsidered. *I'm a gambler, and who knows how to bluff better than I when you've got nothing in your hand?*

The ladies returned soon after, and once they sat down, Sam held the crumpled Marconigram aloft.

"What's this?" Mary asked. "Making plans without telling me?"

"Not exactly. You could call it an insurance policy," she said, before turning to Colette. "I have here a response to a telegram I sent yesterday. You'll notice it's from the Prefect of Police in Montreal."

The rosy glow Colette had earned from her walk faded as she stared at the yellow paper. "You have something to tell me?"

"I do. I inquired about the murder of a *Monsieur Duval* one year ago, and if the killer had been caught." She placed her thumb carefully over the center of the message but left the final sentence visible, reading it out loud for Mary to hear. "Killer still at large." She leaned forward. "They're still looking for you, Colette. Every day, every night. Relentless." She folded the message carefully inside her jacket. "Just a reminder of your situation. Play us false with your Pinkerton beau, and I'll show this to him. However long I may go to prison, at least I'll get out alive. Do we have an understanding?"

Colette swallowed. "We do." She rose and turned to Mary. "My apologies. I think I'll take my tea in the pantry with the other servants. I'll be back in time to dress you for lunch." She looked at Sam. "I know my situation. You didn't have to remind me."

Once the echo of the door's slam faded, Mary turned to Sam, "That was unnecessary. By showing you do not trust Colette you were showing you don't trust my judgment. That you don't trust me." Mary folded her arms, "You still deserve your share from our take, whatever it is, but you're on thin ice. There can be no confusion who's in charge here. There can only be one Queen, and it's me."

"Queen for now, Mary, but how much longer? I've got to make plans for the day you step down."

"What? So you can take over?" Mary laughed. "You're good at following orders... most of the time, but the other girls don't trust you, Sam. You never put anyone before yourself. You'll never be Queen. Accept that and it'll go easier for you when I'm gone." She rose. "I'm off for a spot of tea to cool down. I'll see you at lunch."

Sam sat silent as Mary left, but once alone pulled out her boot knife and—taking a stone from her valise—focused on perfecting its edge.

Chapter Twenty-Four

April 14

COLETTE ENJOYED HER TIME in the pantry with the members of the victualing department. It was a safe haven and a club every bit as exclusive as the Smoking Room for the male first-class passengers. Here, the role of dutiful servant could be set aside. For a brief time she could speak with other women as an equal and think of something other than larceny, or the deep brown of Harry's eyes. Violet Jessup became something of a big sister to her, sharing stories of her many adventures at sea and of the people she had served.

"Never forget," she said to Colette, "few see us as real people. I once sat up all night with a rich woman after she'd gotten a telegram her husband had died. She asked me to visit her the next time I was in New York, and—foolish girl I was—I did." She shook her head. "I rang her up at her posh apartment and she let me in, but I could see right away she had no idea who I was. I said we'd met on a crossing and after a drink, took my leave."

"Why didn't you remind her?"

"Why embarrass myself any further? To her I was an amenity to be used. Once I'd served my purpose, she forgot me. But I'll always remember how my passengers see me—or don't."

She laughed. "Oh, I've had my share of marriage proposals, I can tell you, but I suspect they were looking for a live-in servant they wouldn't have to pay. I'm at the beck and call of anyone with the money for a first-class ticket, but I've seen the world, and the money I earn is my own. Ashore, I'm answerable to no man."

"You've no desire to settle down?"

"Oh, someday I'll quit the sea, when my joints and back can't take it anymore, but I'll not 'swallow the anchor' for a good number of years yet. There's much of the world I still want to see. My greatest fear is being old and saying, 'I could have done this' or, 'I wish I'd gone there.' No. Now is my chance, and I'm going to make the most of it. I've had some nice passengers and some not so nice, but no matter how bad or good, they get off the ship and out of my life at the end of the crossing, and I pocket the tips and memories.

"But what of you? It must be a grand adventure, traveling the world with a wealthy widow and her son. I bet you have your own stories to share."

"Oh, she's a lovely lady who treats me well. Her son..." Colette shivered.

"He seems pretty full of himself," Violet said, "but it's what you'd expect from a wealthy man, used to getting his way. Not to worry. I suspect his mother sees that he behaves himself. I like her. She treats me like a person."

"She wasn't always wealthy."

"I thought as much. A woman who's done honest labor appreciates those who do it still."

***

Mary found Maddie Astor in her usual spot in the Reading Room.

"So good to see you, Mrs. Bayer, I was wondering what your plans are, once we arrive in New York. I'd so love for you and your son to visit us in the mansion. I'm sure John wouldn't object."

Mary paused. A man like Astor would have them checked out before associating with them in public. "We will only be in New York a short while, I'm afraid, Maddie. I have some business dealings in Chicago I need to address right away. Perhaps I could contact you when we return to the east coast, before we return to England?"

Maddie's smile faded. "I understand. Not many people are willing to be seen in public with me. That dreadful woman you chased off is of the majority opinion back home, which is why John took us to Europe for an extended honeymoon."

"No, Maddie, you misunderstand me." Mary cleared her throat. Leaning close, she whispered, "It's just that my late husband was the black sheep of his family. If the papers go into his background it could make things uncomfortable for Sam and me. He's gotten into brawls in the past, defending his father's name and I'd rather avoid tarring you with our family issues."

Maddie nodded. "If anyone could understand the sting of public disdain, it would be me, my friend, for friend you shall always be to me—and champion."

They toasted one another with their cups of tea, the scandalous child bride and the fake widow, and each saw only a kindred spirit in the other.

***

The florist was a kindly man and had taken a liking to his temporary assistant, so when Jenny told him she was no longer employed to help around the ship, he asked her to work for him at a shilling a day and offered to teach her how to properly arrange a bouquet. Though now accustomed to higher wages, it gave her something to do during the day, and she agreed. Thus, she was busy with a vase of flowers when Harry passed her in the café.

"What game are you playing at now?" he asked.

She jerked up, deep in contemplation of her masterpiece. "Mister Haskell hired me to help 'im out. He even taught me how to shift a bouquet proper-like!" She sniffed. "You ain't the only man what's got a shilling in his pocket. I reckon I'll need a few more pounds than what you paid me if I'm to go back to London..." She glared. "Where I belong. If he's willing to pay, I'm happy to sort some daisies. Between the flowers during the day and Mister Dickens at night, I'm staying busy... and out of trouble. That's what you wanted, right?"

Harry laughed. "You are a determined young lady; I'll give you that. Good to see you're behaving yourself. How's the book so far?"

"I like the Artful Dodger." She shivered. "I met a man who reminds me of Fagin, though. He weren't near as nice. If you didn't make your daily lot, he'd beat you. He only did that to me once before I left and didn't go back... after I left a dead cat in his bed."

"I don't reckon I'd go back after that either. Seems things are better now, though. Maybe you've been saved from a life of crime."

Jenny shrugged. "It's nice working with Mister Haskell. He explains things to me like I have a head on my shoulders, and no one bothers me while I'm with the flowers." She looked at Harry. "Almost no one."

Harry bowed. "Then I'll leave you to it. Looks like I'll have to pay up when we reach New York. Carry on!"

***

Colette fumbled with the button hook as she dressed Mary for dinner.

"It's not too late to call this off," she said. "You could just play cards, even win back what you lost so we'll be comfortable until we can sell the jewels."

Mary turned around and laid her hand on the young woman's arm. "I know what we're asking you to do seems dangerous, but I promise we won't go through with it if Sam can't pull off her part, and even if young Mister Worth sees through our plan, I can deny you had any part in it. My sentence wouldn't be any longer if it's just me, and I have the funds to hire a good barrister. This job could allow me to retire from the game for good."

She turned around to finish dressing. "I won't let you swing for me. If this goes off like we hope I may buy a bookstore and become an honest, tax-paying, God-fearing citizen." Mary laughed. "Rule Britannia!"

Colette's shoulders relaxed. "I can't imagine you wearing pince-nez glasses on your nose as you wrap a book in brown paper."

"Oh, I might have a private selection in the back for special clients," Mary said. "I wouldn't want to become too respectable."

She admired herself in the mirror. The dress still fit well, but Mary suspected she was a tad too old for the style. Almost a matron now. Soon, other women would notice and whisper at her fashion choices, if they weren't already.

She turned. "But tonight, I'm still Mary Carr, Queen of the Forty Elephants, and if this is to be my last score, let it be one to be remembered for."

Sam entered, already dressed for dinner and Mary gave herself one last look before rustling out the door, dressed to kill. "To quote Lady Macbeth," she said, "'if it were done, when 'tis done, then 'twere well it were done quickly.'"

***

Harold Bride was on duty in the wireless room at 7:20 PM when a message came from the Leyland Line steamer *Californian* under the command of Captain Stanley Lord.

"Three large bergs five miles southward of us, regards, Lord."

Bride, busy with messages from the passengers, didn't inform the captain, but twenty minutes later when he heard the *Californian* send the same warning to another ship, he relented and informed the bridge of the ice ahead.

***

At dinner Harry and his adversaries exchanged a silent salute across the dining room, combatants trying to weaken the confidence of the other as they prepared for the struggle to come. When it was done, Harry forgot the meal almost immediately, and he declined the coffee after. He had no need of stimulant.

Chapter Twenty-Five

April 14, 9 pm

THE WHEELHOUSE WAS KEPT in darkness at night, to protect the night vision of those on watch. Even lights on the boat deck and promenade below were shielded to prevent them from affecting the bridge or lookouts. When a new shift reported for duty, those being relieved remained until the eyes of their replacements fully adjusted.

Captain Smith, having just left a dinner party, was on the bridge with Second Officer Lightoller.

"There's not much wind," Smith said.

"No. It is a flat calm as a matter of fact."

"A flat calm," the captain repeated. "If it becomes at all doubtful, let me know at once—I will be just inside." Then the Captain headed for his quarters behind the bridge.

***

Stateroom C 52 was one of the smaller first-class cabins, so Mary's table in the center left just enough room around it for four seats occupied by Mauritz, Sam, Harry (sitting opposite Sam) and Mauritz's friend and cabinmate during the voyage, Hugh Woolner.

Mary and Colette sat on the sofa behind Woolner, and the star attraction—Blondel's painting—was set up on the lower berth. Its top rested against the stowed upper.

"Go easy on us," Woolner said. "If we were wealthy men, we wouldn't have to share a cabin."

"If you were poor men," Sam said, "you wouldn't be sharing your cabin with such a lovely young woman."

Mauritz chuckled, and looked to the painting. "It's my father's. I'm only bringing it to America for him to ensure delivery to its new owner and see a bit of America."

"Well then, gentlemen," Sam said. "I'd be happy to loan any funds you might require... with the painting as collateral, of course!"

Mauritz smiled with thin lips. "This is merely for recreation, Sam," he said. "I'm usually not one for the gaming tables, but..." He nodded towards the painted lady to his right. "I confess I'll miss the sight of this beauty once I deposit her in New York."

Mauritz brought out a bottle of twelve-year-old Scotch and the other three players readily agreed to a tumbler before starting the game. "What was it Napoleon said?" he asked. "In victory you deserve champagne," he gestured to two bottles in the ice bucket beside the bunk bed. "In defeat, you need it. As for me, however, I'll begin the battle with a quality Single Malt."

The four cut the cards to see who would deal first. Harry drew a Jack, Mauritz a five, Woolner a ten, but Sam—with the Queen of Spades—won the honor.

"Five card draw, Gentlemen. I like simple games with simple odds." Sam drew up her sleeves before dealing. "If only the rules in life were as clear."

After every hand, the dealer changed, moving to the left, and each new dealer chose the game. Mauritz preferred whist; the others stuck to poker. After the deck had gone around twice, Mary had Colette open the champagne, "To celebrate the winner and comfort the losers," she said, before pointing to the Scotch in the men's glasses, "I don't know how you men can drink such strong, peaty liquid, but if you refuse the champagne in favor of that highland potion, that only leaves more champagne for us ladies."

Sam looked at her shrinking stack of chips, "I may be the one in greatest need of comfort." She smiled. "But we're not done yet."

Colette made the rounds, each player emptying their tumbler of Scotch before accepting a flute of sparkling wine. When she got to Harry, she poured his glass with great precision without meeting his eyes. When he raised his glass in silent thanks, Colette gave a slight curtsy, but as she turned to pour the next glass, he smelled something unfamiliar at first, then it hit him. Beemans chewing gum.

When they resumed, Harry watched Sam closely. She was slowly losing, but that meant nothing; a common ploy by card sharps to increase the next wager. After another hour Sam was down about two hundred pounds, the average pot less than thirty. Harry, unsure if he could send a voucher to the Pinkertons for losses at cards as "undercover expenses," usually folded early and often, pressing his luck on one strong hand that allowed him to be about even.

Looking at the growing piles of chips beside Woolner and Mauritz, Sam said the words Harry had been waiting for.

"You chaps seem to have the better of me. Care to raise the stakes before we adjourn, to give me a chance to win some of my money back?"

Woolner laughed. "What was that you said about collateral? Do you have anything of value you'd like to throw on the table?"

"I don't think that'll be necessary," Sam said, in a soft voice. "Let's increase the maximum bet from ten to one hundred pounds, shall we?" She nodded to Mary, who'd been silent until now.

"Notice the pendant my mother is wearing."

Mary placed a protective hand on a gold chain supporting a red ruby the size of an acorn.

"The chain is worth four hundred pounds, the stone another six hundred, so if my luck turns severely against me, I could request a loan of eight hundred pounds against it. Does that strike you as fair?"

Mauritz cleared his throat. "How does she feel about this? I wouldn't hazard her jewelry without her permission."

"If fortune is against him tonight," Mary said, "I'll be sure he recompenses me, later."

"Brava!" Woolner said. He turned to Sam, winking.

"Very well, I accept. You sir, have been warned."

"Five card draw, Gentlemen," Sam said, ignoring the man's jibe.

The pot quickly grew to three hundred pounds, and the chip piles of the younger players were each half of what they had been, while Harry folded after getting a truly nothing hand.

Woolner asked for two cards, Mauritz three, and if Harry had been studying his own hand, he might have missed what happened next. After dealing the other two what they'd requested, Sam said, "Dealer takes one." She slid the rejected card into the pile of discards and, as the other players watched that card slide across the table, the thumb of her left hand slid to the bottom of the deck and flicked a card out.

As she reached for the card, Harry's hand slammed down on top of the dealer's.

"Stop!"

Sam jerked her hand back.

"What are you doing? You folded."

"I'm willing to wager all the money I have that this card is exactly the one you need for a winning hand."

Sam leaned in so that the two were staring eye-to-eye across the table. "I certainly hope so, else why would I keep playing?"

"I saw you deal that card from the bottom of the deck."

Sam spread her hands, turning to the other two players. "Did either of you two see anything wrong with how I dealt the cards?"

Both shook their heads before Mauritz said, "But I think I speak for my friend here when I say I'd very much like to see what you're holding... without any money changing hands."

Sam turned over an ace of hearts. Her other cards: an ace of spades and three queens.

"It proves nothing." Sam said, shrugging. "My luck was bound to change."

"Perhaps not. Then again, perhaps it does," Harry said as he gathered up all the cards on the table and began running through them.

"Ah," he said, holding up a card from the middle of the

deck. "A second ace of hearts."

"Sam!" Mary called out. "How can I hold my head up in public after this?"

Sam sneered at Harry, "You accuse me in front of my own mother? I find your speculation absurd and offensive. If we were in Heidelberg, I would challenge you to a duel."

Harry slapped his Pinkerton badge on the table. "But we're not, and what I have here trumps everything else. My real name, gentlemen," he said, addressing the other two, astonished, players, "is Harry Worth, and I'll ask you to accompany me to the office of the Masters at Arms, where they can find suitable accommodation for this woman cardsharp masquerading as a man, and take your statements before we reach harbor."

"A Pinkerton agent!" Mauritz said, eyes wide, "And a woman..."

"It's true," Sam said, smirking. "You thought only a man could shuffle a deck of cards?"

She turned to Harry, "You have no jurisdiction at sea, Pinkerton man!"

"Actually, I do, as I'm under direct contract from Mister Ismay, the White Star director."

He turned and looked at Mary, shaking his head. "As you, madam, were well aware before this evening."

Harry indicated the two spectators, "I see no need to hinder your freedom, ladies. I have no proof of your cooperation with this person's behavior, but I'll have to ask you to leave, as the room will be empty until after Mister Findlay and Woolner give their statements. Please don't give me a reason to change my mind."

Mary and Colette rose stiffly and made for the door. Colette turned before leaving, looking at Harry, then—without a word—slipped out of sight.

I'll probably never see her again, Harry thought, and he turned to Sam and the task at hand. "I have manacles, but if you promise not to struggle or make a scene, we can go down to E Deck without raising anyone's suspicion. Agreed?"

She shrugged. "As you wish. I'm tired after all this excitement. A nice rest before we reach New York sounds wonderful."

Harry walked closely behind his prisoner as they headed towards the stairs, hearing the door close behind them; the two witnesses followed. "I'd have a steward secure the painting in the hold as soon as we're done here," he advised the young Findlay. "I believe the card game was a ruse to steal the painting."

Mauritz nodded, calmer now. "Of course, Mister Worth, as you wish. I can't wait to tell my friends in America of my adventure onboard. To think, I was playing cards with a Pinkerton agent, just like in the dime novels."

"Please, sir," Harry said. "Not so loud. We're not in New York yet, and I've no guarantee this felon is the only one worthy of my attention."

"Ah, certainly, sir," Woolner said as he touched a finger to his nose. "Mum's the word."

***

On the *Californian*, at ten minutes past ten PM, Third Officer Groves spotted white patches in the water ahead, and pointed them out to Captain Lord.

"Look sir, porpoises!"

Lord grabbed his binoculars, and, after a quick scan said, "That's ice, you idiot!" He grabbed the engine room telegraph and ordered, "Full speed astern," while his junior officer cringed.

After surveying the situation, Lord ordered the ship to halt for the night, determining it to be too dangerous to proceed in the darkness. Justified prudence, for the *Californian* was on the edge of a twenty-eight-mile-wide icefield.

Titanic was one hour behind and moving at full speed.

***

Mary and Colette had gone but a short distance down the corridor into a side passage, and once the noise of the men's departure faded, Colette hazarded a quick glance around the corner.

"They're gone, Mary. Let's go!"

Colette tested the handle, and the door to the stateroom opened noiselessly.

"It worked!" she whispered as she removed the gum she'd stuck in the latch.

The copy of the painting slid smoothly out of its hidden compartment as did the original from its ornate frame, but when the two tried to slide the original into the table its internal frame was too thick, and it didn't fit.

"What do we do?" Colette said. "We only have a few minutes."

"We don't need the frame, not all of it anyway. Hurry back to your cabin and fetch me the tube where you keep the deck plans while I'm busy here."

"What will you be doing?"

"Undressing a nude painting," she said as she removed her cigar knife from her purse.

When Colette returned Mary had placed the fake into the original's external frame. The real painting was cut free of the sides and bottom portions of its internal frame and the painting was rolled tightly around the top fragment.

"Let's hope this fits in the tube," she said. "If not, I can cut it away from the top piece and slide it into the table, but if I fold it, it'll leave creases."

After the deck plans were removed the remaining frame and painting fit snugly within, and both breathed easier.

"What about the rest of the internal frame and the plans?" Colette asked.

"No worries," Mary said, opening the porthole and tossing them out. "The sea can keep our secrets. Now let's clear off!"

***

Harry stirred the Masters at Arms at his knock.

"What's this all about?" Mister King asked through bleary eyes as he studied the four standing before him. "I don't see no blood, so I reckon no one's been murdered."

"No blood," Harry said, "but plenty of larceny. "This 'gentleman'," he nodded towards Sam, "is actually a woman I just caught cheating at cards. The other two, actual gentlemen, were her intended victims. I need you to place the woman into custody and take statements from the men so she can be prosecuted once we reach New York."

"That's a bit harsh for card sharping, don't you think?" King asked.

"I have my reasons. As soon as we're done here, I'll go straight to Mister Ismay. If he says otherwise, you can always let her go later."

King shrugged and barked into his office, "Ron, wake up! You've got some paperwork to do."

Master Donachie remained to take statements while King accompanied Harry and Sam to the far end of Scotland Road. Harry was so focused on his prisoner he momentarily forgot his fear of the long narrow passageway near the bottom of the ship.

"I protest!" Sam said. "I paid for a first-class cabin."

"Third-class accommodations are good enough for the likes of you," King said as he applied the hasp and lock to the outside of the door. "It's still better than what you're likely to get once we're in New York." He gestured at the bunk beds, a pair facing each other across the room. "But at least you get your choice of bunks." He pointed down the corridor. "And being next to the kitchen means your food'll be nice and hot." King turned to Harry. "Mind staying here for a moment? I need to get the lady a bucket for... necessaries."

"A bucket!" Sam fumed. "Despicable!"

"Don't worry, miss," the Master said, grinning. "I'll make sure it has a lid."

Once the man trudged off, Sam turned to Harry. "What happens when we arrive in New York?"

"I'll have you escorted off after the first-class passengers have disembarked. There'll be a police van to transport you from the dock to jail for booking." Harry shrugged. "Cheating at cards is not a capital offense. Mary can get you a lawyer, and you'll probably be out by the next morning."

Master King returned with the bucket and after he'd presented it, Harry turned to go when Sam held his arm.

"Please convey my apologies to Mary and this cabin's number so she can bring me whatever I require. Oh, and tell her what's to happen in harbor."

"Of course. Anything else?"

She smiled. "No, thank you. That will be all," dismissing Harry as though he were a steward.

She's too comfortable, Harry thought. Then it hit him. She'd expected to be caught, and Harry bolted from the cabin as his father's advice returned to him. "No man is easier to fool than one who thinks he's winning."

***

Sam surveyed her new lodgings with mild distaste. She'd been in real jails before, and while this wasn't the fist-class stateroom she'd just left, it would be reasonably comfortable until the ship arrived in New York in three days' time.

She hadn't been searched and still had her boot knife and lock picks. *Amateurs,* she thought. A night in jail in New York City was worth her share of the two-hundred-thousand-dollar ransom they'd demand from the painting's owner. She'd give her contraband to Mary when she came to visit, or *proper* jailors in New York would relieve her of them.

***

After the real Blondel was secured in the container, the fake in the gilded frame, and the frame fragments and ship diagram disposed of, Colette fetched a steward. The young man was easily persuaded with a one pound gratuity to return the table to the storage hold while the two ladies—Colette carrying the metal tube with the painting—repaired to Mary's cabin to drink the remainder of the champagne.

By the time Harry returned to the stateroom, Mauritz and Woolner were already there, and a steward was packing the Blondel away in its travel case.

"Please," Harry said. "I'd like to have a quick look at the painting before it's taken below."

"Really now, detective," Mauritz said. "It's lovely, but you had plenty of time to admire it during the game."

Harry looked around. "Where's the table?"

"I just took it down to storage, sir," the young steward said. "I hope that's alright. The lady had the claim check for it."

"I must examine the painting now!" Harry said. "I suspect the arrest was a distraction, so we'd leave the painting unattended."

"I think I'd recognize my own painting," Mauritz said. "Are you such an art expert you could identify a forgery?"

"Well, I'm no expert, but I know a bit."

"No thank you, Agent Worth. This has been a jolly evening, and I thank you for a story I'll enjoy telling my mates..."

"If I don't tell them first!" Woolner said, chuckling.

Harry turned for the door, defeated, when he caught a familiar aroma. He turned to the latch and saw some moisture... that smelled of Beemans.

"If you'll indulge me a moment longer," Harry said. "I'd like to inspect the frame."

Mauritz frowned. "Just the frame? Very well, but if you find a secret message, you must share it with me!"

Harry nodded absently as he motioned for the steward to reopen the painting's case. The steward gave him a resigned look, then obeyed.

Harry sniffed the portrait but caught no aroma. No fresh paint, no varnish. He examined the back, but the wooden frame was covered in canvas of unknown vintage. He was about to step back to allow the steward to repack it when something caught his eye.

"When was this painted?" he asked Mauritz.

"1814. Why?"

Harry shrugged. "Oh, nothing. Just curious, thank you. I wish you a good night, gentlemen." He nodded a farewell, and smiled once he was in the corridor.

Then it hit him. He now knew enough to have the two women arrested as accessories to an art theft worth tens of thousands of pounds—enough to send them all to prison for years. What to do? Ismay would want to hear of Sam being detained for cheating at cards, but should Harry also tell him of the stolen painting?

He could confront Mary with what he knew and have the real Blondel restored to its case, and no one would be the wiser since it was going down into the hold, probably next to the table the thieves had used to smuggle the real one out. That would save Colette from a prison term, but would that satisfy Ismay?

Harry sighed as he considered his options. He'd learned not to make big decisions when he was tired, and it was getting late. Best tell the director a half-truth now and plot his course tomorrow when he was rested.

***

At 11:10 pm Captain Lord of the *Californian* saw ship lights approaching from the east and went to the radio room.

"Know of any ships nearby?" he asked his operator.

"Only *Titanic,* sir."

"Inform them of the ice. There's a good chap."

His ship stopped for the night, Captain Lord retired to his cabin.

***

On *Titanic,* wireless operator Jack Philips received the message.

"Say, old man, we are surrounded by ice and stopped." Nearly deafened by the strength of the signal from the *Californian* due to its proximity, Philips answered testily, "Shut up, shut up. I am busy working Cape Race on the US mainland."

Philips had just been informed there was an ice field forty-five minutes in front of his ship's path, but as the message lacked the MSG code signifying immediate notification of the captain, he ignored it, thinking the earlier message should suffice.

***

Harry knocked at Ismay's suite and heard a voice call, "Come in." He found the director in a silk dressing gown slouched in a comfortable chair beside a glowing electric heater, a tea service on the table beside him. It was a cold night, and Harry looked forward to returning to the comfort of his own cabin once he'd finished the evening's adventures.

"What news, young man? Stop any bank robberies tonight?"

"No, sir. No banks aboard that I know of. I just wanted to inform you I've placed a passenger into custody."

Ismay sat up, suddenly all business. "Tell me."

"A card sharp at a private game in a stateroom."

The director cleared his throat. "Did the stateroom belong to one of my principals?"

"Yes, sir. It was the cabin of the young man with the Blondel."

"And you think the card game and the painting are related?"

"I do, sir," Harry said.

"Why would you think that?"

Harry was unable to meet Ismay's direct gaze. "I... well, based on an investigation I'd undertaken, I had my suspicions."

"And you felt that cheating at cards was crime enough to confine a man? Please, Agent Worth, give me more credit than that."

Harry sighed. "I was of two minds what to tell you, Director Ismay, but you deserve a full explanation. I believe the card game was a ruse to steal the painting."

"Why the hesitation?"

"The woman I confined is a seasoned criminal and con artist who was masquerading as a man to gain entrance to the First-Class Smoking Lounge, where she could mingle with the wealthy male passengers. The woman pretending to be her mother was once a criminal associate of my father's and is currently the head of a female gang called the Forty Elephants."

Ismay whistled. "Perhaps we should lock them all up. I see that hiring you was a stroke of genius."

"Thank you, sir, but there is a young woman with them, posing as their maid, who is new to a life of crime. I believe she could be steered back to an honest life, if given the chance."

"I see," the director said, nodding. "And is this young woman you're so concerned about pretty?"

"I can't deny it."

"And you're attracted to her? No, don't answer. Your face betrays you, Mister Worth. Have you told her?"

"I scarcely know her. What could I say?"

Ismay sat back in his chair and indicated Harry was to sit on the lounge beside him. "Share your true feelings. I've found that to be the best approach in all matters of the heart." Ismay reached for his teacup. "As for me, I'll be satisfied if the card sharp and her leader are publicly tried for attempted robbery."

He sipped his tea.

The director put his cup down before rising and extending his hand. "I'll be sure to give Mister Pinkerton a glowing report of your performance, and look forward to traveling with you on the return trip." He smiled. "Tell your young lady you've spared her from the gaol this time, but that you cannot guarantee such good fortune if she persists in larceny. Short of giving you a suit of shining armor, it's the best I can do to help you win her heart."

Harry shook Ismay's hand warmly. "Thank you, sir. I'll see to it the painting is restored before morning. It'll be as though the theft never happened."

***

Able Seaman Frederick Fleet and his watchmate shivered in the cold up in the lookout's post beneath a thin crescent moon. Ninety-six feet above the still, dark water, there was nothing to block the wind and their breath was whisked away before it had time to fog. Neither of the men had ever seen an iceberg before.

Fleet saw something first, dead-ahead. It didn't look very large, just a dark shape within the blackness of the night. Fleet looked closer and realized the shape rose above him.

He rang the brass bell above him three times before grabbing the telephone and calling the bridge, reaching Sixth Officer James Moody. It was 11:39 pm.

"Yes. What do you see?"

"Iceberg dead-ahead!"

"Thank you."

Moody relayed the report to the officer of the watch, First Officer William Murdoch who immediately ordered the helmsman, "Hard a starboard!" before grabbing the twin handles of the engine room telegraph and signaling "Stop." The engine's drag and the tiller's extreme deviation together dragged the bow to the left.

Back in the crow's nest, Fleet replaced the telephone while he and his mate watched, breathless, as the ship crept slowly to port as the iceberg approached rapidly.

"I think we're going to make it," he said.

***

At 11:40 pm forty-two thousand tons of metal, wood, and humanity collided with five hundred thousand tons of ice. The lookout mast quivered like a fishing pole in the hands of a titan as the ship slid along the berg on its starboard side. The screeching of tortured metal was like giant fingernails on a chalkboard, the ice ripping through the ship's double hull, causing a narrow rent no more than an inch wide but extending over two hundred and fifty feet. The resulting gash down the side of the great ship resembled a partially gutted fish. The ship could remain afloat with up to four compartments flooded. The collision breached six.

The unsinkable *Titanic* was four hundred miles from land.

***

First Officer Murdoch stared at the iceberg as it passed by, its peak level with the wheelhouse. He shouted, "Hard a port!," unclenching his jaw when the noise of ice grinding metal stopped as the stern fishtailed away from the ice. Murdoch pulled the lever to close the *Titanic*'s watertight bulkheads.

Captain Smith ran out of his quarters to the wheelhouse.

"Mister Murdoch, what was that?"

"An iceberg, sir."

"Close the watertight doors."

"They're closed, sir."

"Good. Have the engineers do a damage assessment immediately." The captain ran his hand over his face, still not fully awake.

"Your orders, sir?" Murdoch asked.

"Remain calm until we see what we're dealing with." Captain Smith looked out the window as the ship idled in the water. "Then remain calm, regardless."

***

Harry had just turned towards the stairs when he felt the ship give a slight lurch to port, accompanied by a low-pitched rumble. He stopped and noticed the engines go silent, the quiet in sharp contrast to the bass rumble he'd ceased noticing over the past few days. Unsure what else to do, he made his way back to Ismay's suite as the engines resumed their labor at a lower frequency. The door to Ismay's suite opened as Harry raised his hand to knock, and the director stepped out in pajamas, a heavy coat over them.

"Mister Worth," he said, his dignity no less for the informality of his attire. "I'm on my way to the bridge to see what's going on. Walk with me."

"Yes, sir," Harry said, and as they made their way toward the bridge together, the engines stopped again, the silence like a heavy cloak descending on Harry's shoulders.

He noticed crewmen whispering amongst themselves as they got closer to the ship's helm and assumed this was due to Ismay's casual dress. When they entered the wheelhouse, he saw a cluster of senior officers—Captain Smith in the middle—adjacent to the white-knuckled helmsman. The crewmen turned as one as Ismay approached, Harry a step behind. Those surrounding the captain stood back to allow the director a clear path.

Smith's bearded face was impassive.

"What's happened, Captain? Why have we stopped?" Ismay asked.

"We have struck ice," Smith answered hoarsely.

"Do you think the ship is seriously damaged?"

Smith locked eyes with the director. "I think she is."

"Where is Chief Engineer Bell? What is his opinion?"

"Bell is inspecting the damage, sir. I expect his report in the next ten minutes." The captain gestured to his side and said, "But I fear it is serious. We are already listing five degrees to starboard."

"Right. I understand you need to stay here. I'll be off to see if I can find Bell." Ismay turned to Harry. "Come along, Worth. You might prove useful."

The chief engineer was easy to find, moving up the main stairway as Ismay and Harry descended. Harry noted the British reputation for a stiff upper lip appeared merited as the engineer gave no notice of the director's motley appearance.

Ismay wasted no words. "Is it serious, sir?"

Bell nodded once. "Aye, Mister Ismay. It is."

"Will she founder?"

Bell paused. "I believe the pumps will keep her afloat a while yet. At least long enough for assistance."

"Good. I'll not keep you then."

Bell nodded and resumed his ascent to report to his captain about the fatally wounded ship.

Harry and Ismay stood in silence, digesting what they'd just been told. A silence abruptly broken by a sound like a locomotive going through a tunnel.

"What's that?" Harry shouted over the din.

"The emergency steam valves. They're venting the boilers through the funnels, so they won't explode."

Harry stared at the director; their situation made clear by the man's calm explanation.

Ismay gazed at the trappings of the stairway; the chandeliers glistening on the deck below and the thick carpet beneath his feet. He shuddered for a moment, then—as though speaking to himself said, "When I discussed our proposed three ships in the *Olympic* class with the head of the shipyard, we spent two hours on the carpets for the first-class cabins." He wiped his forehead. "I think we gave the lifeboats fifteen minutes."

He looked at Harry as though seeing him for the first time.

"Young man, you are relieved from my service. I think it wise to dress warmly and prepare to abandon ship. It's scarce two degrees above freezing tonight! I wish you Godspeed and good luck, both to you and your lady thief!"

With that, Bruce Ismay, director of the White Star Line and the gored *Titanic*, ascended the stairs to rejoin the captain and see how many of her passengers would live, or die.

***

Violet Jessup dressed quickly to see what the commotion meant. Just as she reached the stairs she recognized her friend from other crossings, a young Scottish musician, Jock Hume, violin at hand.

"What going on Jock? Has anyone told you anything?"

"Och!" he said, always one to lay on the brogue for a pretty young woman. "I dinnae ken, but we're off to give the passengers a lively tune or two while the officers get this sorted out. I'm sure it's naught to worry about. They keep telling us this ship is unsinkable, and they couldna lie about a thing like that."

***

Margaret Brown put on seven pairs of woolen stockings. She knew from her time in Colorado that wool would help keep her warm even when wet. She donned a velvet two-piece suit and a sable stole, then took five hundred dollars from her room safe, putting it into a wallet around her neck before putting on her lifebelt and taking a blanket from the bed.

She reached the door to her stateroom and was about to exit before pausing to pick up a small turquoise statuette she'd bought in Egypt.

For luck.

***

Colette and Mary were finishing the champagne in Mary's stateroom when there was a knock on the door.

The two thieves looked at each other before Mary slowly rose and opened it. A young steward held a note addressed to Mary.

"Sorry for the late hour, Mum," he said, "but Master King insisted I bring this to you straight away."

He paused, expectant.

Mary found Sam's cabin number inside with the message that she could visit whenever she liked with a Master of Arms, as they held the key.

"Thank you, young man, that will be all," she said, and the steward left without his expected gratuity.

She closed the door and passed her hand over her face. "I was sure that was Harry with manacles for us both."

She returned to the sofa and raised her glass containing the dregs of the champagne.

"Now we can enjoy the rest of the crossing, just like any other passenger, the hard part's over."

"God, I could get used to this," Colette said as she poured the dregs of her bottle into her glass, her words slightly slurred as the icy wine numbed her tongue.

Mary yawned. "After all this excitement, I'm ready for a nice long sleep. Finish your glass, then off with you. We'd best appear normal tomorrow." She rose to visit the Lady's room when the floor swayed slightly beneath her. *Odd,* she thought, *I can usually handle my liquor better than that,* then a sound like an enormous beast growling told her the fault wasn't in her legs.

"What was that?" Colette asked.

Mary looked out the porthole and froze as a wall of ice slid past, gleaming faintly by moonlight.

"Nothing good," she said. "Follow me."

"Where are we going?"

"We just hit an iceberg, and I doubt your Mister Worth will take the time to get Sam out of her hole if we start to sink. Good thing you kept your picks, in case the gum didn't work. Bring the painting along because we might not be able to return to the cabin later."

She patted her bosom. "The jewels are in a safe place."

They passed a steward on the stairs bearing life belts as they made their way down to E deck. The man seemed unconcerned as he handed one to each of them.

"Just a precaution, ladies," he assured them, "but you should make your way to the boat deck to be ready to board if the captain gives the order to abandon ship."

They said nothing until they reached E deck.

"I doubt they'd mention the lifeboats, if it wasn't serious," Mary said, and paused before putting on her life belt. "Best you do the same."

***

Harold Bride was awakened by the roar of the funnels venting the underworked boilers.

"Might as well be useful," he muttered, dressing before stumbling into the wireless room.

"How are you getting on, Jack?" Bride asked.

"I could use a hand. I just got a slew of messages from the land station at Cape Race for the passengers. Since we came into range, it's been non-stop."

"Anything I should know about?"

"Oh, I forwarded an ice report to the bridge a while back. You know, the usual stuff."

Chapter Twenty-Six

April 15, midnight

HARRY DESCENDED THE STAIRWAY and made for Jenny's cabin on deck E. Then he halted. Mary's confederate was being held in the same corridor. Cheating at cards—or even art theft—did not merit being trapped inside a sinking ship. The office of the Masters at Arms was on the same level, on the other end of Scotland Road. Harry might not have time to get the key, ascend one deck, make his way to the other stairway, and then go back down. He'd have to walk the length of Scotland Road. Alone.

One thing at a time. The key first.

Harry found the Masters gone, but the spare key to the Chubb lock hung from the hook he'd seen Mister King hang it on after Sam was secured. He snatched it, then remembered his revolvers. Sure enough, they were still there inside the glass case. Harry had no time for finesse and, using his elbow, smashed the front of the gun case, retrieved his weapons, sticking his .32 in his jacket pocket and .45 in his belt.

He was sure the deck was swaying beneath him as he headed down Scotland Road, but when he stopped and closed his eyes, the deck was steady as stone. He opened them again and hunched over so that he could only see about ten feet in front. Crewmembers rushed by, hurried but not panicked, some thinking this a drill. None paid the small man creeping down the passageway a second look except as an obstacle to avoid.

Just as he reached the galley, he heard a sudden 'whoosh' and looked back. Ten feet behind him was a torrent of steam pouring out of a ruptured pipe, blocking the way behind him. The strain on the ship's frame from the uneven load of inrushing water was causing parts of the ship's infrastructure to buckle.

I can't go back that way, Harry thought, and continued aft, his hands shaking as he crawled through the dim passageway; the ship's funnels bellowing above him making the walls tremble.

He crept past the far side of the galley and the ship's stores before he was completely through. *Finally.* The stairway at the rear of the ship would take them to A Deck and lifeboats easily enough.

His escape route clear, Harry straightened and wiped sweat from his brow. *Thank God I don't have to go back there!* he thought and went directly to Jenny's stateroom. He hammered on the door and it flew open on the fourth blow.

"Mister Worth?" a tousled Jenny asked, rubbing her eyes. "What's wrong?"

"Get dressed for cold weather. Now!" The other young woman sharing Jenny's cabin sat up and stared at him.

"Sorry to wake you, miss, but the ship's hit an iceberg, and we must get on deck." He returned his gaze to Jenny. "Once you're dressed and ready, join me at the end of the passageway to your left."

As Harry turned the corner to head for the make-shift brig, he saw Mary and Colette, both wearing life belts and Colette with a long tin cylinder on a strap over her shoulder. Colette was bent over the lock while Mary looked on.

"Good evening, ladies," Harry said, holding the key aloft. "Looking for this?"

"Damn right!" Mary said. "A steward was passing out belts on the stairs saying we should prepare to get on a lifeboat, and I reckoned in the confusion you'd let poor Sam drown." She pointed to Colette's lock picks. "God helps those as helps themselves."

"And you're very good at helping yourself, I'm sure. Well, not to worry about me, madam. Mister Ismay has released me from his service. I'm now just a passenger, the same as you. So, you can tell me now. The real painting is in the table, isn't it?"

Colette and Mary exchanged a look.

"Right you are," Mary said. "You're a clever lad."

Harry smiled then sprang the lock and opened the door, leaving the Chubb dangling in the hasp. Inside, he saw a disheveled Sam assembling herself.

"What's going on?" she asked. "Why have the engines stopped?" She looked up after putting on her second boot and saw Mary and Colette in life vests. "Ah. Mister Pinkerton man. Looks like your plans and mine are both undone. We going down?"

"The ship's hit an iceberg." Harry said. "The engineer thinks the pumps can keep us afloat long enough for help to arrive, but we'll have to transfer to another ship by lifeboat. Come along and we'll get you a belt as well."

Jenny popped her head into the room. "Is the ship really sinking? How exciting!"

Sam stood and looked at Mary. "And our valuables? Your pendant? The...?" She looked at Harry.

"No time for that, Sam," Mary said, giving a side eye to Harry. "Our lives are more important."

"We can discuss all this once we're aboard a lifeboat," Harry said. "I don't relish swimming in the North Atlantic!"

"I agree," Sam said. "We haven't much time," She looked at the container Colette carried.

"Why are you carrying that thing? It'll just get in your way."

"It floats," Colette said. "I can't swim, so I'll take all the help I can get."

Sam snorted, then strode to the doorway. Looking back at Mary, she said, "please fetch my hat off the bunk."

As all inside the cabin turned, Sam stepped out into the passageway, shoved Jenny onto the deck, slammed the door, and thrust the lock into the hasp.

The three inside stood motionless for a moment before Mary shouted, "Sam, what are you doing? You'll not face charges for the card sharping." She glanced at Harry. "Nor the painting. He'll have no evidence unless the Pinkertons hire mermaids."

"The jewels in the cabin will see me back to England in style and with you out of the way, who knows? Maybe I'll be the next Elephant Queen. You won't be around to stop me!"

Sam turned to Jenny, still lying dazed on the floor. "Run if you want to live. I've never killed a child, but if you get in my way, I'll start with you."

"You bitch," Jenny hissed, before springing up and running towards the aft stairway, disappearing into the crowd.

"You know I'll find you, wherever you run!" Mary shouted from behind the door.

"I doubt that very much," Sam said. "Not in this life, at least. Goodbye, Mary. I'll need to hurry to get the jewels before the ship goes down."

"See you in hell, Sam!" Mary yelled as she pounded on the door. When she stopped, the roar of the boilers was joined with the ship's groaning as the weight of the water slowly bloated and twisted the *Titanic* in two.

***

Mauritz assured his cabin mate, Woolner, while they waited on the First-Class Promenade that they had nothing to worry about. "This ship is unsinkable, and even if she isn't, it would take hours and hours for her to go down. Plenty of time for others to come to our aide."

Woolner nodded towards a group of men covered in black soot as they made their way up the stairway. "Those fellows may have a different opinion."

Chapter Twenty-Seven

April 15, 00:15

SAM WENT TO THE entrance to Scotland Road, but when she saw the steam curling along the top of the passageway, made for the stairs. She shoved her way through the panicked crowd to D Deck, where she could make for the stairway and her stateroom on Deck C.

Harry, Colette, and Mary looked at one another. The slight vibration beneath their feet told of the water's approach. Soon, it would rise to their level. Harry kicked the door several times, but it held fast.

"Damn Andrews!" Harry said. "The man couldn't build an unsinkable ship, but he certainly makes sturdy doors."

I need to do something, Harry thought. *And fast!*

"Stand back!" he ordered, pulled out his.45 revolver, and aimed for the door handle. He carefully squeezed the trigger and was rewarded with a loud 'click.'

"Bloody hell! I forgot they'd unloaded the guns when they took them," visualizing the bullets still in his stateroom.

Colette placed her hand on his arm. "We haven't much time, Harry. I don't want to die tonight, but if I must, I would have you know why we could never—"

Harry smiled at Colette. "Let's survive the night, then you can tell me anything you'd like."

There was a sudden banging on the door. "Mister Worth!" Jenny shouted. "I'm back. What can I do?"

"Pull on the door as hard as you can, while I shove from this side!" He heard her jerking on the door handle, but it didn't budge. He wiped the sweat from his brow as he imagined the water seeping through the ship towards them.

"I still have the key to the lock, Jenny. Let me pass it to you under the door." He bent down and noticed a raised lip along the floor at the threshold, blocking his effort to slide the key through.

"Just a moment while I pry a board loose!" Harry pulled out his pocketknife, but no matter how hard he thrust, the seam was so tight he couldn't wedge the blade underneath. Then he took his.45 and, grasping it by the barrel, used the butt as a hammer. He tapped the knife carefully and, as soon as the blade was halfway under the board, he tried to pry the ledge up.

It snapped.

"Quick, try the other blade!" Mary said.

"I used the larger blade the first time. This one's even thinner."

"There's nothing we can do on our side. It'll have to be opened from the passageway," Colette said. "Jenny!" she shouted, "Find a fire axe and bring it to us straightaway!"

They heard her footsteps rush off.

***

Jenny rushed desperately about, looking for a fire axe when a steward saw her and cried out.

"See here, miss! All children to the boat deck for the lifeboats!"

"I can't! I've got to help my friends trapped in their cabin!"

"And how is a little girl like you going to do that? Come with me. Now!" He grabbed her by the arm.

"You can't stop me!" Jenny snarled and kicked his shin as hard as her wooden-soled shoes allowed.

"Shite!" the steward cried as he released her to rub his assaulted leg. "To hell with you, then! I'll not be responsible for your death." The man limped off, seeking others more amenable to salvation.

Jenny turned to go in the opposite direction of the

limping steward when she saw an axe attached to the wall. After wrestling it down, she stopped. In the heat of battle, she'd lost all direction.

Where was she?

***

Violet Jessup—after seeing that her passengers were on the boat deck with lifebelts properly fastened—returned to her cabin to find something to wear. She sorted through her clothes, carefully folding her nightgown. Panicked, her friend and fellow steward, Stanley, rushed in and grabbed her.

"My God! Don't you realize the ship is sinking! You need to go to the boat deck now."

Violet said nothing, still looking for a proper coat.

Stanley grabbed the first coat he saw and shoved it into her arms. "This'll do!"

"Now, Stan, this is far too gay for a shipwreck," Violet said, trying to keep the mood light, but Stanley was having none of it. She chose a scarf and headed for the stairs. Stanley stalked back down the corridor to warn others.

"Come along soon, won't you, Stan?" she said, but he stood, silent at the end of the corridor, his arms crossed. As Violet turned away, she thought he looked very tired.

***

Mary collapsed onto a lower bunk. Hot tears slid down her cheeks, noiseless. Colette tried not to stare at this proud woman she'd so admired. Now she felt only pity for her mentor and friend—the Queen of the Elephants brought low by a traitor. Was that the fate of every woman, her destiny decided by others? If Mary could never be truly free, what hope was there for her?

***

Jenny found her way back to her cabin. "Down one corridor and turn left?" she said to herself.

She saw a cook rush by with his arms full of bread, and she remembered it was one passageway closer to the galley.

Got it!

"That's company property!" the cook said, looking at the axe. "What are you doing with it?"

"Our steward asked me to fetch it so he could get into a room with a jammed door. My little brother is trapped inside."

"Ridiculous! Come with me!" the cook ordered. "These..." He lifted his bread-laden arms, "are for the lifeboats, and I can shoo you in beside them."

"My mother will be right along with the steward," Jenny said. "She told me to wait right here if I found an axe. I'm to wait until she or the steward come for me."

The cook shrugged. "Very well then," and handed her a fresh loaf of bread. "Sorry I don't have any butter or orange marmalade." He smiled. "Share some with your brother!" And he was off.

***

Colette was drawn from her reverie by the sound of a tapping at the door.

"I can hardly lift it!" Jenny said. "It's barely scratching the wood."

Harry imagined the young girl in the hallway, heavy axe in hand, the lock and hasp about even with her shoulders. Yes, the hasp. It wasn't the lock that was holding them in; it was the hasp.

"Jenny, take the pointed end of the axe and push it through the hasp from below. Got it?"

"Yes, Mister Worth. I see what you mean. Hang on!"

Jenny grabbed the end of the axe handle and put her full weight on it.

The hasp held.

She jerked as hard as she could.

The hasp held.

She jumped and landed on the axe handle with her stomach and there was a satisfying clatter as the hasp sprang free and Jenny sprawled upon the deck.

Harry felt the door slacken and threw it open, nearly hitting the girl.

"Thank God!" Colette said. Then she saw Jenny face down on the deck. "What are you doing with a loaf of bread?"

"Long story," she said. "I can tell you later."

Mary raised her head, wiped away her tears, and stood. "Well, Sam," she said. "Now it's my turn."

***

First Officer Murdoch was having a hard time convincing passengers to enter the lifeboat that dangled seventy feet above the cold, dark water, so Mauritz and Woolner were given seats to encourage others to follow. The American movie actress Dorothy Gibson sat behind them, repeating over and over, "I'll never ride in my little gray car again." Finally, Woolner snapped: "Please keep a stiff upper lip, Madam" a very polite, very British way of saying, *Shut up.*

***

Jenny left the axe on the floor as they made straight for the aft stairway. Passengers struggled upwards. A pistol shot once, twice, a third time, and the crowd turned into a swirling knot of panicked humanity.

"The officers are shooting men trying to board!" someone shouted, and nearly as many people fought to go back down the stairs as tried to ascend.

Mary shook her head, "This won't do." She asked Harry. "Any ideas?"

He looked back to the narrow entrance of Scotland Road, his mouth suddenly dry. "There's a passageway that runs the length of the ship, but it's blocked by a ruptured steam line."

"Well, we're not getting out this way. Let's have a look."

Harry flinched at the thought of returning to the narrow tunnel deep within the belly of the sinking ship, then looked at the panicked swirl of passengers on the stairway and nodded.

"You can see for yourself, but I tell you we can't go that way."

"We've escaped one trap tonight," Mary said. "Perhaps our luck will hold. I've got a score to settle, and it'll take more than a broken pipe to stop me."

Harry took the lead until they reached the entrance to

the passageway. He could hear and feel the steam escaping before he could see it. He peered into the dim tunnel, imagining a dragon jealously guarding its horde, and froze.

"I can't," he panted, clinging to the wall. "I just can't."

"Look at me," Colette commanded. He did so and noticed the glow in her eyes he'd seen at the end of their dance lesson on the promenade. "We need you, Harry. I need you." She put her hand in his and squeezed. "I play to win, remember? Now come. Let's go together."

The four crept forward into the belly of the sinking beast, unsure if they could reach the far side of the ship before she slid beneath the waves.

Chapter Twenty-Eight

April 15, 00:35 am

HARRY AND COLETTE WENT first, with Mary and Jenny close behind. They reached the pantry and saw the broken steam pipe running vertically along the left side of the passage towards the galley.

Harry's heart sank. "You see? There's no way past. We have to go back!" He hugged Colette fiercely before turning to retrace their steps. "I'm sorry. But there's no other way."

Mary refused to leave. "You might be a fine detective, Mister Worth, but you'd make a poor burglar. How do you bypass an alarm?"

"Alarm?" Harry asked. "What's an alarm got to do with a steam pipe?"

"Both are part of a system. If you want to prevent an alarm from going off, you—"

"Cut the wire between it and the power source," Harry said. "So?"

Mary pointed to the gushing steam. "This pipe here..." She indicated the broken one. "Is fed by the one up there." She pointed to the ceiling. "If we can take the pressure off upstream, so to speak, it will reduce how much steam spews out of the one in front of us."

Colette studied the pipes as Mary described them. "She's right. Making another break in front of this one might let us get by."

"And how do we do that?" Harry asked, looking aft.

Mary turned to Jenny. "Young lady, I need you to retrieve that axe of yours. Now! Run!"

Jenny bobbed her head once before she sped off, pigtails flying.

Harry sighed. "Once more, we're hoping for a girl to save us."

Mary slapped him on the shoulder. "And what of it? She's the Artful Dodger."

***

Jenny came rushing back, face flushed, and Harry grabbed the axe she held in both arms like she was cradling a baby. He swung for the overhead pipe, but the blow sailed underneath, almost a foot short.

"Damn!" He threw it down. "I can't reach it!"

"Let me have a go," Mary said, hoisting the axe. She turned to the others. "Stay clear! No telling how this will play out."

Mary grasped the axe and swung it overhead with all her strength. The first attempt bounced off the pipe, but the second made a crack with the blade. Mary turned it so the pick was in front, and there was a satisfying 'swoosh' and an outpouring of steam with the third try. Vapor shot out across the ceiling before condensing on the right wall, leaving enough clear space beneath for the group to creep past.

Harry leapt forward, his short stature a benefit for once, and saw the way forward partially clear. Steam still spewed from the pipe in front, but with its flow reduced he ran through it without harm. He turned to call the others to follow but they already had. Mary still carried the axe, and Jenny was in the rear.

"I may never leave home again without one of these," Mary said as she slung the axe under her arm.

With that obstacle cleared and Colette's hand in his, Harry led them on, his fear distracted by her firm grip, until they reached a solid iron door blocking their way.

"What's this, Harry?" Colette asked.

"It must be one of the watertight doors Mister Andrews mentioned. I guess the engineers closed it to slow the movement of the water aft."

"I don't see a handle on it," Jenny said. "How do we get past?"

Harry swallowed as his fear returned.

"I don't know."

"Is this door operated from the bridge?" Mary asked. "If so, we're buggered!"

"No," Harry said, thinking hard. Something Andrews had mentioned was rattling around inside his head. He felt around the door and found a large bolt on the wall to the right with no apparent purpose, two feet back from the barrier. Above it, on a chain, was a heavy iron spanner.

"I think I've found the answer," he said. The spanner fit perfectly and, as he cranked, the door began to rise. As soon as the bottom was clear of a small groove in the deck, water flowed underneath past their ankles.

"Stop!" Colette said. "You'll drown us!"

Harry paused and felt along the door. It was cold up to a foot above the deck. He looked back down the long, steam-filled passageway leading to the ship's stern. "We have to chance it, and we have to go now, before the water rises any higher!"

He cranked with a will and after a minute the four were able to creep past and make their way toward the front of the sinking ship. The tilt was increasingly apparent, and when they reached the end of Scotland Road, the water at the foot of the stairway was to Jenny's waist.

"It's so cold!" She said, shivering as they climbed out of the water.

"Up!" Harry said. "Quickly now!"

***

Sam ran to the stateroom, pushing through the crowd like a swimmer in heavy surf. When she reached the passage outside her cabin, she noticed the door to the First-class Purser's Office gaping open, with the safe inside.

Unguarded.

She rushed to her room and threw open Mary's valise, steamer trunk and wardrobe, finally tearing the entire stateroom apart, but nothing.

"Bloody hell!" *To come this far and have nothing to show for it.* Then she remembered the unguarded safe.

I still have one chance, she thought, and raced to the unwatched strongbox full of treasure. Then, like a suppliant before an altar, she knelt in front of the black iron box and laid her ear beside the tumblers.

***

Jenny led the way as they ran up the next two levels to C Deck. When they got there, they paused to catch their breath and Harry was struck by the strains of "Alexander's Ragtime Band" coming from above.

"Who would ask for music at a time like this?" he asked aloud.

Colette squeezed his hand. "Not the best time for a dance lesson, I agree."

Steeling themselves for the climb, Harry and his companions continued on to B Deck and the first-class boarding area but found the Grand Staircase packed with third-class passengers, all male, waiting to be summoned to a lifeboat. More than one had a flask out.

"Wait yer turn!" a man with a thick Scot's brogue, snapped. "You rich sods can't buy yer way through us. A dead man's no use for money, save pennies to cover his eyes."

"What do we do now?" Colette asked.

"I haven't heard any gunshots recently," Harry said. "Perhaps we could go aft and try our luck."

"Good idea," Mary said, "Let's go!"

***

Oblivious to *Titanic's* increasing forward slant, Sam was an island of calm, lost in the mechanical dance of the tumblers rotating inside the safe's steel door. She heard nothing but their silky purring, felt nothing but the ridges on the knob, her face resting against the cool, black metal, at one with the universe—or the safe, at least—which had become her universe.

The ship's slant to port continued until, unnoticed by Sam in her reverie, the door to the office closed silently on its well-oiled hinge.

Finally, she felt as much as heard the give of the final tumbler reaching its release point and turned the handle.

At last! she thought and looked inside at… an empty safe.

She screamed before standing and noticing the closed door to the Purser's Office, and reached for the handle.

Locked!

Water seeped through the door sill, and Sam gave thanks the Pinkerton man had failed to properly search her. The safe was empty, and the jewels weren't in the stateroom.

Mary would not leave the ship without them.

She was owed something after all this, and she knew who held her payment.

The water covered her shoes as she pulled out her picks and her hands began to shake, causing her to drop them.

She looked down as the water lapped at her calves.

So cold. So very, very cold.

***

Harry and his small party wandered through the restaurant reception area, then veered to the left to the Café Parisian, before reaching the aft stairway, thankfully empty. They ascended to A Deck, arriving in the Verandah and Palm Court.

"Where to now?" Mary asked.

"Follow me," Harry said. "You're about to enter forbidden territory. The First-Class Smoking Room."

Four men sat inside, none of them looking their way, nor did they raise a complaint at the sight of two women and a young girl trespassing into their sanctuary. One man sipped a glass of amber liquid in the corner while he read a book as though he hadn't a care in the world. The three others sat at a small table, each with his own glass of brown fluid in a cut glass tumbler, a half-full decanter in front of them.

"Mind if I join you in a drink?" Mary asked, shivering slightly in her wet skirt. "For the chill."

"Anything for a lady with an axe!" the man in the center of the trio said and made for the bar to fetch more tumblers. "But if you want ice to go with it, you'll have to fetch some from the deck."

"Surely you're joking?" Harry asked. "Now?"

"If we make it to a boat, it'll help us to stay warm," Mary said, "and if we don't..."

"Pour me one, too!" Jenny cried. "Time to see what all the fuss is about."

Their glasses full, the man on the end raised his glass in salute. "Good luck!" he said, before the seven of them emptied their glasses in unison.

Jenny coughed loudly, her face reddening as the others laughed.

"Thank you for the drink, gentlemen," Harry said, "but best I get these ladies off."

The committee of three waved them goodbye before returning their attention to their glasses. As Mary left, she noticed the man in the corner turn a page of his book, his glass still half-full.

That must be some book, she thought, leaving the four gentlemen behind, each finding peace in his own way.

***

Once on the promenade, the four found all the lifeboats forward were gone. Water washed over the ship's prow and advanced steadily toward them. While they stared at the disappearing deck, Jenny collected a couple of scattered life belts, and she and Harry put one on. Harry saw a man step out onto the deck, a full bottle of Gordon's Gin in one hand. The man looked about and, seeing no available lifeboats, opened the bottle and slowly downed the entire thing in one long go, while Harry stood, transfixed.

Death will find him ready, he thought. *He may not live long enough to drown.*

"Come, Harry," Colette said. "We must find a lifeboat. They can't all be gone!"

They made their way aft, Colette bringing up the rear as they passed the first-class entrance, and a wet arm reached out of the shadows and grabbed her by the hair.

"Not so fast," a soaking Samantha said. "You haven't paid the toll." She jerked her head backwards. "Let's go inside. We have some matters to discuss... in private."

Chapter Twenty-Nine

1:12 am

SAM LED THEM TO a private stateroom beside the first-class entrance, backing into the room with Colette held in front of her. Once all were inside, she commanded, "Close the door and drop the axe, Mary. We don't want to be disturbed."

"We don't have time for this," Harry said. "Release Colette and if we both make it out of here alive, I promise there'll be no charges against you. You have my word."

"Your word? The word of the son of the mighty Adam Worth? How wonderful! You know, Mary can't say enough good about your father. I find it especially sweet to humiliate you in front of her." Sam gestured to Mary. "I know you wouldn't leave the ship without the jewels. Give them to me, and your little protégé lives, at least long enough to fight for a space aboard a lifeboat." She nodded to Harry. "While Mister Worth will get a chance to take the jewels back." Sam flourished her blade. "Go ahead. I dare you."

"All right, Sam," Mary said. "You win." She reached into her cleavage and pulled out a black velvet bag. She held out the bag. "Take them."

"Excellent. I never expected you to be so reasonable. Walk slowly over here and hand them to Colette, then back away."

Mary did as instructed, and once she'd returned to her previous position, Sam jerked on Colette's hair. "Open the bag and pour a few out. I don't want to walk away with a bag of pennies."

Colette slowly poured a dozen diamonds into her hand.

"My compliments," Harry said. "You've been very busy. If you hadn't tried for the painting, you'd be home-free with an impressive haul."

Sam shrugged. "I'd like to become a woman of independent means, especially if I'm not the next Queen of the Elephants."

"And now?" Mary asked. "You have the jewels. What more do you want?"

"I want to make sure you and the gang don't hunt me down," Sam said. "So... we wait here a while. When there's one boat left, we'll see who gets on it." She lightly rested the blade on Colette's slender neck. "Any objections?"

"I wouldn't recommend that," Harry said, as he slowly pulled his.45 out of his belt. "Drop the knife."

Her grip tightened on Colette's hair. "That was unwise, Pinkerton man. You showed me your ace before I played my trump. I'm betting you care for this woman's life more than these jewels or the pleasure of locking me up."

"Careful, Harry," Mary said. "She'll do it."

"Listen to her, Agent Worth. I've got the winning hand. Now, drop your gun and slide it over to me."

"You'll spare her life?" Harry asked.

"Why not? Why give you a reason to attack me once I've got the gun *and* the jewels?"

"Very well," Harry said. "If surrendering my pistol saves her life, it's a deal."

He bent and carefully slid the revolver over to Sam, who bent and snatched it up, releasing Colette at the same time while placing the knife back into her boot.

"Thank you. This was so easy." She raised the pistol and—pointing it at Harry's chest—pulled the trigger.

The hammer sounded as it struck the empty chamber.

Colette smashed the metal tube into Sam's nose and she dropped the bag full of diamonds as she fell, spilling stones across the floor. Harry snatched the knife from her boot as she lay moaning on her back, gasping for breath.

"My father was a smart man, Sam. It's a shame you never met him, because one thing he taught me was no one is easier to fool than someone who thinks they're winning."

"What do we do with her?" he asked Mary.

"Loan me her knife."

"You're just going to kill her? Without a trial?"

"Yes. Now give me the knife or I swear to God, I'll use the axe."

Wordlessly, Harry handed it over.

"Look away, Jenny," Mary said, "and help Colette pick up the diamonds. This won't take a moment."

She turned to Sam, still dazed on the floor and—in a shaking voice—chanted, "Come, you spirits that tend on mortal thoughts, unsex me here."

Chapter Thirty

1:45 am

SECOND OFFICER LIGHTOLLER BOARDED passengers via a staircase fashioned from stacked deckchairs. Lightoller straddled the lifeboat and the railing, a foot planted on each, and passengers responded to the man's cool competence as he guided women and children smoothly into the boat. John J. Astor came forward with his wife, Maddie, and—after the pregnant woman was safely stowed—the millionaire leaned forward.

"Could I enter the boat to protect my wife, in light of her condition?"

"No, sir. No men are allowed in these boats until all the women are loaded."

"Could you tell me the number of this boat to help me find my wife, should I be rescued?"

"Number 4," Lightoller answered brusquely.

Astor turned to his wife. "Goodbye," he said.

With that, "Colonel" Astor, one of the world's richest men, stood back to join his fellows waiting for a chance.

***

Violet Jessup sat in lifeboat 16 waiting to be lowered while wrapped in an eiderdown she'd taken off a bed when a red-faced steward rushed up to her. "Hold onto this, will you?" he said calmly, and shoved something into her arms before disappearing.

Violet looked down and realized the bundle was a

sleeping baby.

***

After recovering the spilled gems and dragging Sam's body away from the door, the four staggered to A deck to find all the lifeboats gone.

"Look there!" Mary cried, pointing into the water below. "One of the life boats is overturned. We could swim to it and climb on top."

"I don't see any other choices," Harry agreed. "But we need to hurry. I see about a half-dozen on top already."

"But we're so high up from the water!" Colette said. "Can't we wait until the ship is a little lower?"

"The longer we wait, the closer we'll be when the ship goes down, and it could pull us under. It's now or never."

Colette went to the railing and looked down, shivering from her wet clothes, and the distance to the dark water below. "We'll get separated in the dark." She turned to Harry. "Please, go on. I can't do it."

Jenny looked at the empty lifeboat davits. "What if we tied ropes between us? One between you and Mister Worth, and another between Mary and me. That way, we won't get lost."

Harry pulled out Sam's knife. "Colette, can you jump if you're roped to me? Will you trust me?"

She looked forward to the advancing water, then aft at the slowly rising stern. "Get the rope."

Harry cut two lengths from the lines in the lifeboat davits, and soon the four were bound together in pairs. They stood at the railing side by side, looking between the dark water below and the frothing waves creeping towards them.

"Best if we go first, Harry," Colette said, "or I may lose my nerve."

"Right you are. Put your arms by your side until you hit the water, then hold them straight out to stop your descent."

"What should I do with this tube?"

"Throw it away!" Harry said. "It might hit you in the head when you reach the water."

"I'll take it," Mary said. "I'm a good swimmer."

Harry looked from one to the other. "I know you're not telling me something, but you're a grown woman, Mary, and I'm done arguing with you. Let's go, Colette."

"Can't we hold hands?"

"I'm afraid we might crash into each other." He tugged on the rope. "Don't worry, I won't be far away." Then he saw her stricken face. "Very well," he relented. "We can jump holding hands to make sure we leave at the same time, but once we're falling, we need to let go."

Colette turned to Mary and Jenny, to her left. "See you on the other side."

Then before she could react, Harry seized her hand and jumped, pulling her off the railing. He let go once she came free of the ship, but his tug pulled her headfirst, and she found herself diving towards the dark, glass-still waters of the North Atlantic. She forgot what she was supposed to do with her arms and put them across her face to keep the water from hitting her full-on.

Colette landed in the water at an angle, the blow to her chest and stomach forcing the air out. She began choking and panicked, thrashing around without purpose or direction. Then the pull on the rope aided by the life belt yanked her up from one darkness to another.

She surfaced, choking on seawater, and only stopped fighting after Harry pulled her into his embrace. The cold was like a hungry beast, sucking the warmth from her hands and feet.

"You alright?" Harry asked, holding her close.

"Not remotely," she managed to choke out. "I'll n-never understand people's fascination with swimming."

Harry grunted before making for the lifeboat thirty feet away, towing a shivering Colette. As he struggled, an English bulldog came paddling by, making far better time.

Mary and Jenny popped up a little way ahead, both sputtering but alert, and they began moving to the boat straight away, with the metal tube strapped across Mary's back.

Thirty feet. A man might pace that distance in six seconds, a runner in less than three. Fully clothed and wearing a life belt while swimming in water just above freezing, it took the party almost two minutes. Their limbs grew colder, heavier, and clumsier with each passing second. Mary and Jenny reached the boat first, but rather than clamber up out of the cold, Mary held on while Jenny swam back to grab an exhausted Harry so that Mary could tow them all to the craft.

Other survivors clinging to the lifeboat helped them climb out of the water, and one by one they were soon all lying together, shivering. The hull of the overturned boat was sloped, so it was all they could do to hang on to the keel and not slide back into the water. Harry had them lie together to share what little body heat they had with Jenny in the middle, and there was nothing more to be done but await whatever fate the gods had chosen for them.

The deck lights now glowed red and *Titanic* was nine feet down at the head, and sinking faster.

Harry heard a great groaning and noticed the stern starting to sag while the band still played a jaunty tune.

It takes a long time for a giant to die… until it doesn't.

The great ship was like a harpooned leviathan, its bow completely submerged, the stern free, propellers hanging useless in the air. Harry noticed swarms of people still on the ship clinging together wherever there was a handhold, like bees in a hive, while the water below filled with struggling figures who'd either jumped or been washed adrift.

"We should get further away," a man said in the dark to Harry's right, "or she may take us down with her."

"Lend me an oar, and I'll do my best." The two shared a bitter laugh.

They were flotsam and would go where the ocean willed.

Chapter Thirty-One

2:17 am

HARRY WATCHED AS WATER advanced across the foredeck, accompanied by explosions within the ship. When the water reached the dome above the Grand Staircase it collapsed almost immediately, and the ocean rushed in. Now the ship was filling from above and below.

The lights flickered for a moment, then went out forever. Harry wished for total darkness because he still saw too much.

Harry noted a man in a ship officer's uniform and reached down to him.

"Officer Lightoller!" he cried. "Welcome aboard."

As Harry pulled him up, a funnel broke free of its supporting wires, and Harry watched in horror, helpless, as it came straight for their fragile craft.

"Bloody Hell!" Mary shouted. "Hang on tight!"

Lightoller wrenched himself aboard just as the funnel hit the water, missing him and the lifeboat by inches. The wave from the near miss propelled them several yards away from the sinking ship.

"The damnedest thing!" the officer muttered, before turning his head to retch over the side. After his stomach emptied, Lightoller rolled over, his face pale gray in the darkness.

"Are you alright?" Harry asked. "What happened to you?"

"It seems it isn't my day to die; at least not yet. I was

pinned against a ventilation shaft, and my breath was nearly spent when there was an explosion beneath me, and I was tossed clear. I suppose the water reached a boiler, and the reaction broke me free."

He looked up at the stars.

"I'm not a religious man, but if that isn't providence, I don't know what is."

The water was full of swimmers, and the two men watched, impotent, as another funnel broke free and crushed a dozen or so poor souls before sucking several more into it as it sank, reminding Harry of ants washed down a drainpipe. He was grateful the sounds of the ship's death blocked their screams as they disappeared into darkness.

Suddenly, the ship snapped in half, and the bow sank below the water almost immediately. The stern righted itself and, for a moment, looked as though it might miraculously stay afloat before it, too, began its long descent to the ocean floor. As Harry and the other shivering survivors on the collapsible watched, the blue ensign of the White Star Line, which had fluttered so proudly as the great ship sailed from Belfast after passing her sea trials now laid limp upon its pole, the last thing to disappear beneath the waves and into history.

***

"She's gone," Jenny said in awed tones. "The ship. All those people... just gone."

No one spoke as they clung to their fragile refuge, staring at the froth and bubbles marking the grave of the largest moving object ever created by man, lying beneath an ocean made by a force greater still.

"What time is it?" a steward asked.

"What difference does that make?" Colette asked.

"Because my pay stops now."

***

After the stern portion sank from view, those atop the lifeboat were stunned by the sudden quiet... until the cries for help from a thousand throats began to ring out.

"Boat ahoy!"

"Help! My God, help!"

Somewhere in the darkness, a man called out for his mother.

***

Beneath the water, the ship plunged 12,000 feet to the ocean floor, full of the wealth of millionaires and the humble possessions of hopeful emigrants; it carried them all away into the frigid darkness. Into legend.

The final stage of *Titanic*'s maiden voyage took ten minutes.

Chapter Thirty-Two

THE SURVIVORS ABOARD THEIR overturned lifeboat stayed silent as the moaning of the dying slowly faded until there was only the sound of waves lapping against the ice. They understood what the silence meant. Like the lights of the sunken ship, the lives of those in the water had been extinguished, one by one.

Mary rubbed Jenny's back, while they tried their best to stay warm.

"How l-l-long do you think we can l-last like this?" Jenny asked, her teeth chattering as her wet clothes leeched her body's scant remaining warmth into the frigid night air.

"As long as we need to," Mary said. "I'm sure help is on the way."

There's nothing more I can do, she thought as she drew the thin, half-frozen girl close. *If this is where I die, I hope I get a proper burial.*

Colette looked at Harry leaning beside her on the lifeboat's overturned hull, the ropes that bound them still intact and dangling in the water. *I wonder what it would have been like,* she thought, *to wake up beside him, free of fear.* She reached for his hand, and he gave it without a word.

Colette began tingling. *Hot,* she thought. *So hot. Must undress...* She released Harry's hand as she fumbled for her buttons when someone cried, "There's a light!"

Colette saw a... firefly? Fascinated, her hands froze on her still done-up buttons as she watched the faint glow draw nearer. She imagined a wizard with a magic wand showing the way, and slowly she understood the vision was a woman with a lighted cane, standing on a bench in her lifeboat, summoning others to her.

Jenny was barely alert when lifeboat number 14 pulled alongside. Mrs. Elia White, who'd twisted her ankle while boarding in Cherbourg, stood in a pose reminiscent of Lady Liberty atop a bench while steadied by fellow passengers, her light serving as a rallying point for the drifting survivors.

"We need to transfer as many as possible," Lightoller said. "How many can you take?"

"All of you, easily," the crewman at the tiller said. "We could use some men to help row. Just take it slow."

One by one, the wet and shivering survivors crept aboard. The seaman manning the boat helped the passengers unfold the sails, and those who were wet huddled within its folds.

"Come, Harry, join us beneath the sails!" Colette cried out.

"That's likely to be my best offer tonight," he said. Soon, with Jenny between them, the four huddled within the canvas as their boat resumed its wandering into the dying night.

"Colette, you were going to tell me why we couldn't be together." Harry said.

"N-n-now you want to talk, when we're about to die!" Colette stammered, between chattering teeth. "Men have no sense of timing!"

"What better time?" Harry replied, "than when we are about to live." He noticed her trembling lips and sagging head. "Colette, stay with me. Don't you dare drift off."

"Why? Why do you care?" she mumbled. Just before the darkness claimed her, she heard Harry say, "Because I want to..."

***

As dawn broke, the survivors found themselves drifting among great cathedrals of floating ice glowing in the pink light, at once magnificent and terrible as they stood silent vigil over the indifferent ocean. As the sun rose, so did the wind, and those already numb with cold felt themselves drifting in and out of consciousness, the frigid touch of the north breeze lulling them into a sleep from which some would never wake.

The passengers took turns rowing and steering under Lightoller's direction, who had taken command as senior officer. The direction was less important than that they traveled in company with the other boats.

It was now seven hours since the *Titanic*'s sinking. No one spoke, only the creaking of oars broke the silence as they moved slowly through the ice field.

"We're doomed," a woman moaned, shivering as she cried.

Harry was fighting to stay awake. At his request, Jenny had shifted to the right so they could keep Colette's frigid body between them, with only her shallow breathing telling him she yet lived. A man next to Harry nudged him gently before opening his coat, revealing a holstered revolver. "Worse comes to worse," he said, "you can do for you and your lady after my wife and I are done with it."

Harry didn't know which affected him more; the man's offer, or how calmly he made it.

He felt himself drifting away as slowly as the icebergs when he heard a crewman cry out.

"A light! I see a light!"

Harry turned his head and squinted, fearing to believe his eyes when he saw the vague outline of a ship on the horizon. His cheeks were suddenly warm, and realized he was crying.

"Do they see us?" Jenny cried.

"Hard to tell," Mary said, squinting. "We're a small boat in a big ocean."

Lightoller stood and shaded his eyes. Just then the ship fired a rocket and he slumped.

"We're saved," he said. "God be praised."

Jenny had the sharpest eyes among them, so she sounded out the name of their rescuer as it drew nearer. "Carpet, no. Carp something?"

"*Carpathia*," Lightoller said, "of the Cunard Line. She's about half the size of *Titanic*, but a good deal bigger than this lifeboat. I don't reckon anyone'll complain."

Colette stirred slightly, but when the *Carpathia* came alongside, two crewmen lowered a rope sling, and Harry loaded her into it so she could be hauled up. A small child—unable to climb the rope-ladder—was shoved into a canvas bag and hauled aboard, his terrified screams wrenching hearts, while his flailing caused the bag to sway until he reached the deck and was set free into his mother's waiting arms.

A female passenger tried to reach the ladder, but her skirt was too tight for her to step to it. Harry brought out Sam's blade and slit the side of the skirt from mid-thigh to the hem. The woman's mouth made a perfect O as she looked down at the alteration, then nodded.

"Thank you, sir," she said. "I understand it's the latest fashion."

When it was finally Harry's turn, it took all his strength to climb aboard before he collapsed.

Safe.

The deck was crowded with women and children searching for their menfolk as each lifeboat came near. With rare exceptions, they turned away, their arms and hearts empty.

***

Violet Jessup placed the baby she'd been holding into one of the bags but reclaimed it once she boarded. She had scarcely staggered to a bench on deck when a woman rushed up.

"My baby!" she cried and wrenched the infant from Violet's arms, disappearing without a backward glance or word of thanks.

How typical, Violet thought.

***

Many of the *Carpathia's* passengers surrendered their cabins for the survivors but there weren't enough to go around, so Harry, Mary, Colette, and Jenny were taken to a saloon to warm up and sleep. After a change into donated dry clothing and some hot tea and soup, they looked for a quiet corner on the floor or a chair where they could curl up.

Mary found a spot for her and Jenny, arranging some cushions from a sofa. Jenny was outfitted in the striped flannel pajamas from a young man half again her size, and it took several turns of the cuffs to free her hands and feet. Mary noted Margaret Brown tending to a pair of third-class women and their small children, bringing them hot soup in thick porcelain mugs and dry clothing donated by the *Carpathian* passengers.

"I'm still cold," Jenny said, curled into a knot on the cushions.

Mary saw a pile of blankets in the corner about the same time as Mrs Brown. Atop the woolen mound a fat, middle-aged man was blissfully snoring. The two women exchanged a quick glance.

"After you, Mrs. Bayer,"

"No, Mrs. Brown. After you. I insist!"

"Then let's do the deed together."

The two ladies each grabbed a corner of the top blanket and unceremoniously dumped the man onto the floor. He rose, snarling, fists at the ready, but was staggered back by Margaret Brown's left jab. He readied a return swing, but before he could get it off, Mary's haymaker snapped his head to his right, and he went down without a sound.

"Nice form, Mrs. Brown," Mary said.

Brown nudged the supine form with her toe. "Thank you, Mrs. Bayer, but I believe you struck the winning blow." She smiled. "If we were in the ring, I'd raise your glove in triumph."

The wealthy divorcé and the Queen of the Elephants shook hands and put the blankets to good use.

Harry and Colette sprawled together on the floor, beside Mary and Jenny. The ship's doctor assigned to their area handed out sedatives to all who asked, as several were unable to sleep, flinching at every noise. Soon the saloon was filled with the snores of exhausted, drugged, survivors. Mary's snores quickly joined the others, and Jenny's sagging face revealed no signs of life.

"How strange life is," Colette whispered. "This time last night, Mary and I were finishing the champagne from the card game, celebrating our success. Since then I nearly drowned, had a knife against my throat, then almost died from the cold. Yet here we are, like mice in the hay, safe and warm."

She snuggled closer to Harry, savoring his body heat in the dim light of the saloon, the tranquil rise and fall of the ship, the deep rumble of its engines, drawing her closer and closer to oblivion. "My life has been anything but dull since we met, Mister Worth." She yawned. "I hope you don't try to outdo yourself after this. I doubt I could survive it." Just before she drifted off, she said, "I dreamt you proposed to me while we were in the lifeboat, Harry. Isn't that strange?"

He kissed the back of her head as she lay in his arms. "Then you're still dreaming."

Chapter Thirty-Three

April 15-18

THE CROWDED SHIP MADE its cautious way through the ice fields, fog, and worsening weather towards New York and Harry's throat tightened as the fog closed in. He saw Director Ismay briefly when he first boarded the ship, but the man's eyes stared straight ahead, seeing nothing... remembering everything.

The four slept until late afternoon, filled their bellies, then slept through the night. No words passed between them as each came to terms with what had been lost, and what remained.

The next morning as Mary and Colette were washing up in the toilet outside the library, Colette turned to her mentor.

"I'm sorry about Sam, Mary. I can't say I ever cared for her myself, but I never wished her dead, at least not until she tried to kill us. Still, I know that must have been hard for you."

"I don't regret a thing. I can't imagine a worse way to die than being locked in that room while the water rose, unstoppable, to the ceiling. If it wasn't for Jenny, we'd be there yet." She shivered. "Compared to that, a quick blade was a mercy."

She scrubbed her face, savoring the warm water on her skin. "Harry couldn't do enough for you back in the lifeboat. You'd be a fool to let him get away."

"But what about—"

"The Elephants will do just fine, though I'll miss you holding our fence's feet to the fire when we have something sparkly to sell. Harry's asked you once, and he'll ask again before we reach land. Best have your answer ready."

"Like the Lady of Shallot, it's time to leave my tower? She died, remember."

"Well, Colette, being with the Elephants ain't exactly safe, either, but the Lady preferred to die truthfully rather than living a lie." Mary put her hand on the young woman's shoulder. "You can be safe, or you can be brave. You can't be both. You've a place with us for as long as you want it, but I wouldn't want you to stay just because you were afraid to try for something better."

***

Most passengers preferred to spend the day topside staring into the fog as the ship crept its way home, so Harry found Colette, Jenny, and Mary in the saloon by themselves after he returned from his own ablutions. He looked at the tin container lying on Colette's pallet. "I must ask. After all we've been through, is the Blondel rolled up in this tube? That's the only reason I can think of that you'd have carried it off a sinking ship."

"You're not going to arrest us now, are you?" Mary asked. "That would be bad form after all we've been through."

"I'm off the case, Mary." He shrugged. "Call it professional courtesy."

Colette opened the carrier and carefully extracted the rolled canvas. She felt it cautiously. "Still dry!"

Harry spread it out slowly onto a table. He studied the surface and frowned, then examined the two ends of the frame fragment. He turned to the other three and began to snicker, then laugh, then roar as tears streamed from the corners of his eyes.

"What?" Colette demanded. "What's so funny?"

"It's fake!" Harry said, winded from laughter.

Mary glared. "How can you tell?"

"Look at the surface. Blondel painted the original almost one hundred years ago. You just rolled it up like a sausage and look at it. Not a single crack."

"You also studied the frame," Jenny said. "What did that show you?"

"The nails are round. A hundred years ago nails were rectangular."

"That's why our forger, Carol, had the right tints when I asked her to make a copy," Mary said. "She already had!"

"Your former employer was going to sell a copy and keep the original to himself," Colette said.

"And that's why Mauritz was so nervous when I asked to examine the painting in his cabin," Harry said. "He knew the painting he was carrying was fake."

Colette slid the canvas back into the carrying case. "What do we do with this now?" she asked Mary.

"I'll keep it as a souvenir. Why not, after all the trouble we went through to get it?"

"I'd rather have a snow globe of the statue of Liberty," Jenny said, before turning to Harry. "Which reminds me, you still owe me a dollar."

***

Mary approached her new friend, Maddie, huddled under a blanket in a deck chair.

"You should be inside," Mary said.

"I can't relax inside. It's better out here, where I can look for icebergs."

Mary nodded. "Your husband?"

"No. Your son?"

Mary coughed, her throat suddenly tight as she remembered the feel of the knife as its blade slid to the hilt. "No."

"You're still welcome to stay with me in New York until it's time for you to return to England."

"I'd like that."

***

That afternoon, Colette and Harry stood together at the railing beneath a blanket.

"About that dream you had," Harry said.

"Oh, that." Colette blushed. "We were about to die. Think no more about it."

"I've thought of little else," he said, "but you didn't answer my question then." He knelt. "Will you now? Will you marry me?"

"Nothing's changed, Harry."

"What's stopping you from saying yes? Why do you say it's impossible?"

She turned towards him, her hands trembling as she prepared to destroy the love in Harry's eyes forever. "I'm wanted for murder back in Montreal."

"Murder? But you're innocent, surely!"

"It's worse than that, Harry. It's for killing my father."

"Did you do it?"

"I killed him, but it was in self-defense. He came home drunk one night, as he often did, and he began hitting my mother, also as he often did. This time, she'd had enough and told him my younger sister wasn't his."

She turned away, unable to sustain the shock on Harry's face and began to sob, choking out her words.

"He was like a wild beast after that! He knocked my mother unconscious, grabbed a hammer, and was coming down the hallway to my sister's room. I'm sure he was going to kill her." She let out a shuddering breath. "At least that's what I tell myself. I had a pistol my father kept for burglars. I don't remember pulling the trigger, but it went off, and he lay dead at my feet."

Harry pulled her gently around so they faced one another again, then drew a handkerchief from his jacket and handed it to her. "Sounds like you were protecting yourself and your sister. Then what happened?"

Colette's eyes were large and moist, her tears giving them a luster that pulled at Harry's heart.

"My sister came out and saw everything. She told me to run, and I've been running ever since."

"I can—"

"You can do nothing! You understand nothing! You're a man! Do you believe twelve men will find me not guilty? I'll either spend twenty years in prison, or hang. I'm not sure which would be worse. Yes, we are alive, but nothing has changed. I was a wanted murderer before, and I am now. Do you want to go through life fearing your wife may be taken away from you without warning? It would ruin you!"

"You're right, Colette. I wouldn't like to go through life like that. Which is why we need to go to Montreal to clear your name. Together... with you as my fiancé."

She studied his face, his brown eyes open and honest, and recalled his kindness to others who could never repay him. Was he merely being charitable now?

"You adopt strays like Jenny," she said. "Am I another?"

"You are a stray, Colette, but I'm being selfish. I want to save you for myself." He took her hands in his. "You walked me down Scotland Road when everything in me said to run away. You saved my life, but it cost me my heart. Please accept the rest of me so I can be whole."

Colette lacked words to match, so her kiss served as an answer.

After the kiss, she could speak again. "Very well, *Agent* Worth. I place myself into your custody." She gave him a coquettish smile. "I hope I get time added to my sentence for bad behavior."

***

On the seventeenth of April, two days after their rescue, the four were taking the air when Colette shouted out, "Look, seagulls! We must be approaching land,"

"I heard a steward tell another passenger that we should reach New York tomorrow," Harry said. "Not long now."

"That's not all," Mary said, pointing out an approaching naval escort. "We must have someone important aboard," she said, "for this kind of treatment."

"Either that or they want to make sure no one escapes," Harry replied. "The public will demand a scapegoat, and Ismay is the likeliest target. I don't envy his position."

Chapter Thirty-Four

THE SHIP ENTERED NEW York harbor late at night on Thursday, the 18th, passing through a gauntlet of small boats shooting flares, reminding several survivors of the rockets fired by the *Titanic* in its final moments. These lights, however, were not so much in celebration; they were to assist photographers in capturing the moment.

Harry and Colette joined the throng at the rail, and by the light of electric torches and headlights they saw a vast crowd teeming at dock 54, the Cunard line's dock, then looked on in amazement as they steamed past to the White Star Line's dock 59. Only after the remaining lifeboats were offloaded did the ship turnabout and make for the dock where family, friends, and the world awaited. Once the gangway was secured, two officious-looking gentlemen came aboard, asked for Director Ismay's whereabouts, and made straight for his refuge.

"So it begins," Harry said. "They couldn't give Ismay one night's rest ashore before going after him."

The four of them went with the surge of fellow survivors to the gangplank, only to suffer a final indignity. "Debark by ticket-class, please, the purser announced."

Such was the numbed state of the battered passengers that they staggered off as directed with scarcely a murmur.

Once ashore, Jenny saw a woman with a sign bearing her name. The woman stood beside a large man with a Prussian-style mustache.

"Aunt Gladys?" Jenny asked while Mary stood silently behind.

"Yes, girl, that's me," the woman answered curtly.

"Where's the money?" the man asked. "The money we're to use to feed an extra mouth."

"It didn't make it, uncle," Jenny said, chin up.

The man backhanded her before anyone had a chance to react. "You worthless bit of bone! I've already lost a day's work because of you." He reached to take off his belt. "I'll take it out of your hide!"

A fist came out of the dark, knocking him flat. When his sight cleared, he saw a woman standing over him.

"I think not, uncle," Mary Carr snarled. "If you don't want her, then she's coming with me." She looked down at him, hands on her hips. "Any objections?"

She took his silence as agreement and, turning to Jenny, asked, "That's if you're up for it, Jenny. Would you rather come with me?"

The young girl took Mary's hand and nodded. "If you're going back to England, I'm ready. Can I go first-class this time... with you?"

"By all means!" Mary turned to Jenny's relations. "What are you two still doing here? Go to bed. You don't want to miss another day's work, I'm sure."

Without another word, the couple disappeared into the throng, and Jenny hugged her new guardian tightly.

"How will you get back, Mary?" Colette asked.

Mary reached into her skirt and produced the gem-filled bag. "Never fear, Colette, Jenny and I will travel posh for sure." She winked. "I may even buy my own lifeboat." She gestured to Harry. "If it wouldn't offend your new fiancé's honor, I could pay you your share. If you're going to trial, you'll need a good barrister."

Harry shrugged. "Anything you've got would have been lost to the sea, and as Ismay no longer employs me, I've no reason to report a theft."

Mary patted his cheek. "Your father would be proud."

After giving Colette a handful of gems scooped from her bag, Mary handed the metal tube to Jenny and curtsied to the young couple. "Now, madam and sir, we two ladies will spend some time in New York with my new friend, the widowed Lady Astor, until I can book passage home. Cunard, I think. *Au revoir,* Colette! Look me up if you ever make it back to London."

Her business concluded, the Queen of the Elephants—and the gang's newest, youngest member—slipped away into the dark.

Colette and Harry accepted free lodging in the Jane Hotel, temporarily available to unaccompanied survivors.

"What now, Harry?" Colette asked as they sat down to breakfast the following morning.

"For now, a steak on a table that doesn't move, then we'll see to your situation in Montreal."

"I'd hardly call being wanted for murder a 'situation,' my dear," Colette said, laying her hand briefly on Harry's arm. "But at least I won't be facing it alone."

"You won't. I'll be with you as long as necessary to resolve this. After breakfast, I need to book a telephone call to Montreal."

"A telephone?"

"I'd like to know what we're walking into. Wouldn't you?"

The clerk at the hotel's reception desk was happy to arrange the call. "Do you know how long you'll be staying with us?" he asked while waiting for the operator to respond.

"That depends very much on how this call goes," Harry replied, then turned to Colette.

"The agency has a lawyer on retainer in the city. Using a lawyer associated with the Pinkertons will give our case more credibility."

Colette noted how Harry said "our" case without thinking. She'd been a thief long enough to know the things people say without reflection are the most honest. She studied the subtle hue of his eyes. Once she surrendered herself to the authorities, who knew when she would see them again?

The barrister, Jon Fontaine Esq., was happy to discuss the case. "I'll send my clerk to the Palais du Justice this afternoon. Call me back tomorrow afternoon at one o'clock and I should be able to discuss the young lady's situation."

"Could you ask Colette's mother and sister to your office so that she could speak with them when we call back?"

"Certainly." Harry heard the man clear his throat. "At my standard billable time, of course."

"Of course," Harry agreed. Nothing earned a lawyer's loyalty quicker than the promise of payment. Harry put Colette on the phone to give her home address before she handed the phone back to Harry.

"*Bon,*" said the barrister. "Unless there's something else, I'll wish you *au revoir* for now, Mr. Worth."

***

"I'll have a difficult time going to sleep tonight," Colette said, once the connection was ended. "The phone call tomorrow will be the first step towards surrendering my freedom."

"I disagree, Colette, I'd look at it as your first step towards complete freedom. Freedom for us to be together."

She smiled at him, then she looked away, biting her lip.

"What is it?" he asked. "Having second thoughts?"

"it's only... well, I've gotten used to being my own person, coming and going as I pleased. You're a fine man, Harry, but I fear I'll go insane at being just a housewife. I admit I enjoyed the game of wits. I'll miss that if we marry."

Harry said nothing for a moment, then he took her hand. "I may have an answer for that as well. Trust me?"

"I leapt into an ocean with you."

"I suppose that's a yes. Good. First things, first."

"Don't you have to report to your office?"

"Not yet. They probably consider me dead and I'm finding that very liberating." He laughed. "I may take a while before I tell them otherwise."

The papers were full of the *Titanic* and the Senate investigation already underway, but the two lovers turned their back on the tragedy, preferring to dream of their future. The next morning was spent with a leisurely breakfast followed by a stroll in Central Park until finally it was time to place their call to Montreal.

One o'clock found them crammed together in the telephone booth of the Jane Hotel. Neither seemed to mind.

The clerk answered on the first ring. "Mister Worth? Yes. Monsieur Fontaine will be with you shortly."

Soon, the barrister's voice was on the line, and Harry and Colette resumed breathing at the same moment.

"Mister Worth. Before I tell you what I've found out, there is the matter of payment. I've found it better to address that issue before I close a case."

"Close the case? You're refusing to represent Miss Duval?"

"I'll discuss that in a moment."

"Very well. You can bill the Pinkerton's, and I'll have the fee deducted from my pay. Is that acceptable?"

"That's fine. I already have their address."

"Now can you tell us what you've found out?" he asked, sharing the earpiece as best he could with Colette, pressed tightly against him.

"Of course. I'm closing the case as there are no charges against the young lady. Her mother and sister are waiting—impatiently, I might add—in my outer office. I thought it best to relate what my clerk learned yesterday before they can overhear."

"*Mon Dieu!*" Colette said. "Get on with it!"

"The police report of the incident states that Miss Duval's mother was found unconscious, the result of a vicious attack. The father, meanwhile, was dead from a single gunshot wound at close range. Miss Duval's younger sister, Marie, reported a burglar came in through a window, and her father pulled a gun to defend his family, but in the ensuing struggle the gun was turned on him. The robber then beat the mother to find out where the key to the safe in the jewelry shop was held, but he knocked her unconscious, and she has no memory of the assault. Marie states that she went for the police while the man was beating her mother. By the time she returned with a constable, the robber had fled with several valuable jewels missing from the safe and he is presumed still at large."

"How was Colette's absence explained?"

"Marie said her sister was with family in Quebec City and would return the following day. The police posted Marie's vague description of the assailant, and the case is no longer being actively pursued."

The lawyer coughed slightly.

"As an officer of the court, I must advise you not to tell me anything that might conflict with the official version of events." After a long silence on the New York end of the line, the lawyer asked, "Hello? Are you still there?"

"More than ever," Colette said. "May I speak with my family now?"

Suddenly, Madame Duval was on the phone. "COLETTE, *C'EST TOUS*?"

"*Oui, Maman*," Colette said. "You don't have to shout. That's not how a telephone works."

"Ah, pardon. I've never spoken on this device before. The lawyer said you are in New York. Why are you there? Where have you been? Are you alright?"

"*Tranquille, Maman*. In answer to your questions, *oui*, I am in New York. I just returned from abroad, where I was working in London, and... yes, I'm fine." She put an arm around Harry. "Never better."

"Why did you leave? I was devastated by your father's death, but when Marie told me how he died defending his family, I realized that—despite his temper—he loved us all very much."

"I left... because of my guilt."

"Guilt? What did you have to feel guilty about, *mon cher*."

"I should have been there with you. I blame myself for his death."

"Ah, *mon petite chou*. You cannot hold yourself responsible for the evil of others. It is well you were away, so you did not see your father's death, or you might have been attacked by that monster yourself."

"*Merci, Maman*. It bothered me greatly."

"Nonsense. Now, when are you coming home?"

"Excuse me, Madame Duval," Harry said.

"Who is this?"

"My name is Harry Worth, Madame. If you'll allow me a moment to ask Colette a question, then we can answer yours."

Harry covered the mouthpiece just as Mrs. Duval, shouting once more, began a litany of questions. "Colette, you're free. Free to come and go as you please and stop looking over your shoulder." He blushed. "There isn't room enough in this booth for me to go to my knee, and I don't have a ring in my pocket, but would you marry me? We could travel to Montreal for the ceremony before I return here to New York to settle affairs."

Colette looked up into Harry's eyes, and fell into their gentle depth. It was as though he was holding her with those eyes.

"*Mais oui!*" She smiled. "My mother will be overjoyed and furious at the same time."

"Furious? Why?"

"Because she won't have time to panic about the wedding ceremony." Colette kissed Harry until the squawking from the earpiece reminded them both of their situation. She gently shoved her new fiancé out of the booth, but before closing it, she said, "Best you leave this to me, but don't go shopping for a ring." She winked. "I think we can get a good price in Montreal!"

Chapter Thirty-Five

London

May 30, 1912, 8 pm

RANDOLPH FINDLAY WAS IN his study going over his accounts. The large payment he'd deposited in his account that morning from the *Titanic* settlement would soon convert several of the red numbers in his ledger to black zeroes. He was calculating how much he'd have left when there was a knock at the door.

"Bugger!" he grumbled as he reached for the bell pull, then remembered he'd let everyone go save the cook, and she lived elsewhere. Mauritz, as usual, was at the theater, his actress lover all the more ardent after his exaggerated tales of heroism.

When he flung the door open to give a piece of his mind, his words stuck in his throat when he saw a short man in a brown tweed suit and two constables on his doorstep. Pulled in front of his home was a police van with another constable at the wheel.

"Wh-what's all this then?"

The young man in tweed pulled out a badge. "Harry Worth, Pinkerton Detective Agency, here with Constables Cross and Beaverton. We have reason to believe you've just defrauded the White Star Line to the sum of sixty-thousand pounds and my agency has been contracted to recover it."

"While we," Constable Cross said, "are here to take

you into custody."

"That's preposterous!" the man spluttered. "You've no proof of any of this."

Cross produced an official-looking document with a seal, "We have a warrant to search your home, Mister Findlay, if you'll kindly step aside, or would you like me to add 'obstructing an officer of the law' to your other charges?"

"Other charges?" he said, his face growing pale, and he staggered aside as the three men brushed past him and made straight for the stairs. He tried to protest, but felt a sudden heaviness in his chest, and sat down.

The cry of discovery from his bedroom told him everything, and soon he heard the stomp of heavy boots as the Pinkerton man came down the stairs, followed by the two constables carrying the painting.

They set it down beside the man, frozen in his chair. "This looks like the painting you just claimed went down with the ship," the Pinkerton man said. "Do you deny it? I can easily get an art expert to verify it if you'd like."

"This is it," Findlay gasped. "The Blondel."

"How long you reckon he'll go to prison for this?" The Pinkerton asked Constable Cross.

"Oh, ten years, I'd think," he grinned. "It's a lot of money."

"If you wouldn't mind, Constable," Agent Worth said, "I'd like to discuss our situation with Mister Findlay while you secure the painting in the van, as evidence."

"Right you are, Sir. Please don't take long, my shift's nearly over and it will take a ton of paperwork to get this lot locked away until his barrister can get him bail." With that the two bobbies lugged the painting off, leaving the sweating Findlay alone with Harry, and his fate.

Agent Worth coughed. "The complaint was lodged by my client, the White Star Line. If they were reimbursed for their loss, they might see their way to let this go."

"All of it?"

"All of it."

"Who should I make the cheque out to?"

"Forgive me, sir, but a man who would defraud us is not a man we'd trust with a cheque. I'll need to accompany you to your bank tomorrow for you to pay me in cash."

"And the charges will go away?"

"They will."

Findlay swallowed. "What about the painting?"

"I think after all Mister Ismay's suffered, he'd like it for the board room of the Line, but if the payment goes through smoothly tomorrow, I can probably convince him to drop the charges and return the painting to you. He's spent enough time in tribunals of one sort or another to last him the rest of his life."

He patted the wilted man on the shoulder. "I expect you at your bank tomorrow morning at ten. Do we understand each other?"

"We do." Findlay ran his hand over his gray, moist face. "If there's nothing else, I'll ask you to leave now. I have some accounts to examine, and a good deal of Scotch to drink."

***

The next morning a subdued Mister Findlay slowly handed Agent Harry Worth a locked canvas bag holding sixty-thousand pounds.

"My painting?"

"Is waiting for you at your home, with Mister Ismay's blessing. You'll just need to sign for it. It'll be waiting for you inside the police van outside your door. I can give you a lift home if you like."

"Thank you, Agent Worth, as I currently can not afford a taxi."

The back of the van was closed but opened at Harry's knock. Findlay started when he saw no painted lady, but two flesh and blood ones. One he recognized immediately as Henrietta. The other, middle-aged woman holding a long tin canister looked familiar...

"Hello, Rudy," Mary said. "For once, it's nice to see you."

His mouth gaped. "Mary? Mary Carr? You've aged well," he said, glancing at her bosom.

"And you've just aged."

"The painting?" he asked at last.

Mary laughed. "Oh, the painting you claimed was lost was in fact, saved." She opened the canister and showed him the canvas rolled up on part of the frame. "It's right here." She hoisted the tube, "the carrying case is no extra charge."

"But, the bobbies," he turned to Harry. "The Pinkerton man."

"Oh, the badge is real enough," Harry said, "but I'm not a Pinkerton, or not any longer. Now if you'll forgive me, our business is concluded. I'd remind you if you went to the actual police, you'd have to explain how you were robbed of a valuable painting you'd been reimbursed for. Good day!"

Mary and Henrietta savored the view of Rudolf Findlay staggering back to his house, a metal tube under his arm, before Mary opened the canvas bag full of pound notes and carefully paid Henrietta her share.

"Pleasure doing business with you," Henrietta said. "Seeing his face turn from red to gray was glorious."

"Stay in touch," Mary said. "Our art forger has contacted a private collector who's willing to pay us another sixty thousand for the real painting. We should have the money within the week." She smiled, "You know, I may not open a bookstore after all. An art gallery has a lot of potential."

***

Harry admired the glint on Colette's left hand as she shifted gears on the fake police van, the wedding ring the result of a *very* good deal in Montreal.

"You're wrong, you know," she said as she sped to the warehouse where they'd repaint the truck.

"Wrong? How so?"

"I think you were never more real."

Harry agreed.

Today he'd seen justice done and he'd helped make it happen. He was no longer just a guard dog with an impressive pedigree.

He was Harry Worth, proud son of a good man and master thief, and husband to Colette Worth, recently of the Forty Elephants.

"What now, Harry?" Colette asked as she steered the truck around a pothole. "After my time with the Elephants, I could never settle for a life of ironing your shirts and burning dinner."

Harry laughed. "Is that why your mother never let you in the kitchen?" He squeezed her arm. "As for me, I could never stay with the Pinkertons. Mister Andrews was right, sooner or later I'd be sent to bash the head of a good man trying to feed his family."

He cleared his throat. "How does the sound of Worth & Worth Detective Agency strike you? With our share of the painting's payoff we could open a small office in New York. That way," he coughed, "we could avoid dealing with old friends on the other side of the law."

Colette drove in silence until they reached the warehouse. Once she parked the truck, she turned and kissed her new husband. "Why not? They say it takes a thief to catch a thief, and it seems to me *Agent* Worth, we've caught each other."

Author's Notes

This manuscript was my thesis project as I completed a Master's in Creative Writing at Napier University in Edinburgh, using the last of my GI Bill benefits to good effect, and my ability to portray British dialogue was much improved by my "study sessions" at the Canny Man's pub in Morningside. I hope, by mentioning him here, I'll get a free Scotch from Alex, the barman, who taught me the proper way to drink, and spell, "whisky."

My time in the UK also afforded me the chance to visit the Titanic Museum in Belfast, and the SeaCity Museum in Southampton. I recommend both highly.

One of the frustrating things about writing historical fiction is finding interesting things and people, not all of which can fit inside your story. As a means of easing my conscience, I like to include snippets about them in the back of my books.

Objects

Alfred Hitchcock coined the term "MacGuffin" to describe the item that drives the story. In the *Maltese Falcon*, for example, it is the small bird-shaped statue. In *Raiders of the Lost Ark*, it's the Ark of the Covenant. You get the idea. In my story, I was extravagantly fortunate, as I had two MacGuffins: the jewel-encrusted copy of Omar Khayyám's *Rubaiyat* and the painting by Blondel. These were not the only valuable items lost, but they are the most famous, and their stories are both worthy of a book in themselves.

The Illustrated *Rubaiyat* of Omar Khayyám

(Image: British Library. Used with permission)

In 1907, Francis Sangorski met John Stonehouse, manager of Sotheran's bookshop, founded in 1761 and still in business today. Sangorski told him of his dreams for a book whose origins went back to the 12th Century. While Sangorski had previously bound some versions of the renowned Rubaiyat of Omar Khayyám, the master craftsman said this time he wanted to create a work "such as had never been seen before."

Stonehouse agreed to commission the book with the following guidelines:

"Do it and do it well; there is no limit. Put what you like into the binding, charge what you like for it—the greater the price, the more I shall be pleased—providing only that it is understood that what you do, and what you charge for it will be justified by the result, and the book—when finished—is to be the greatest modern binding in the world."

Measuring 16in by 13in (40cm by 35cm), the book was encrusted with 1,050 jewels, including specially cut rubies, topazes and emeralds. About 100 ft.^{2} (9 m^2) of gold leaf and some 5,000 pieces of leather were used in its creation, and it took the firm two years of continuous work to finish.

Sangorski agonized over every detail, at one point borrowing a human skull so he could accurately depict it. He even bribed a keeper at London Zoo to feed a live rat to a snake so he could capture the image first-hand. The Daily Mirror considered the finished work to be "the most remarkable specimen of binding ever produced."

On March 29, 1912, just twelve days before the *Titanic* set sail, the book's British owner consigned the bejeweled Rubaiyat to Sotheby's rare book auction in London, where it sold for just £405 (around $2,000 in 1912) to Gabriel Weis, an American. The New York Times reported the final auction price was barely a third of the book's worth. Many found the book too excessively ornate, including Sir John, the Royal Librarian to King Edward VII, who was offered an early chance to procure it, and he would later declare the bottom of the Atlantic: "The best place for it."

Since the discovery of the wreckage of the great liner in 1985, numerous dives to the scattered wreckage have brought up a vast number of precious artifacts from the ship, but thus far, there's been no trace of the *Rubaiyat*. Many paper products, including money, playing cards, sheet music, and letters have miraculously survived after being submerged underwater for 75-plus years. Paper has survived, however, only when it was discovered stored within heartier containers, such as leather suitcases and handbags. In fact, most leather objects have survived the wreck incredibly well, as oceanic microorganisms can't digest the tannins used in preserving animal hide.

The precious stones embedded on the book's cover are likely still present if the book was not destroyed upon impact. Since the book's binding was fine leather, even after 100-plus years at the bottom of the sea it's possible that if the book is ever discovered, the binding may be identifiable, if not the pages within. The book, with its remarkable history and tie to the *Titanic,* would command a huge amount at auction, with rare book collectors and *Ti-*

tanic enthusiasts in a bidding frenzy.

But the story doesn't stop there.

The book's illustrator, Francis Sangorski, drowned off a beach in England ten weeks after the ship sank. A replacement was finished at great expense by the late 1930s, but it was incinerated by German bombers during the Blitz.

Stanley Bray, nephew of one of the two founders, made the second copy, and later—in his retirement years and after four thousand hours of meticulous labor—completed the third using the original illustrations and designs used by Sangorski. The only difference from the first is the lack of jewels, Bray not having the resources to duplicate the extravagance of the original.

Bray lent the third Omar to the British Library, and it was later permanently left to the institution after the death of Bray's widow, Irene, in 2004. The book remains among the library's collection, although access is rarely permitted.

La Circassienne au Bain, The Circassian Woman of the Bath, or Une Baigneuse.

(Copy by John Parker, in the public domain.)

The painting was a large work in oil rendered in the Neoclassical style, produced by the French artist Merry-Joseph Blondel. It depicted a life-sized young Circassian woman in a Roman-style bath. The painting was first exhibited at the Paris Salon in the Louvre Museum in November of 1814. The initial critical reaction to the painting was muted, but by 1823 critics began talking more enthusiastically about the painting, due both to the popular reception to printed reproductions, and to Blondel's improving reputation.

The painting was lost aboard the *Titanic*, and in January 1913, a claim was filed in New York against the White Star Line, by Titanic survivor Mauritz Håkan Björnström-Steffansson for compensation. Steffansson's claim form described a substantial painting "8 x 4 feet," which explains the difficulty my thieves would have had in getting it off the ship unnoticed. I changed the name of the painting's owner to make it easier to write, and to give the owner a personal relationship with Mary Carr.

The claim was for $100,000 (equivalent to $3.3 million in 2025) making it the most valuable item lost, which would also explain why my felons would choose it for their big heist. Mauritz did not receive the compensation he asked for, however, as all the cases against White Star were settled for a combined amount of $644,000.

The Titanic

Much has been made of the lack of binoculars for the lookouts. They were there in their perch, secured in a locker, but the ship's officer with the key was transferred to another ship at the last minute, and he didn't hand them off. I know from my brief time in the infantry in the US Army that binoculars improve your night vision, as they gather more light, but in the inquests held on both sides of the Atlantic, seasoned mariners testified that field glasses wouldn't have made a difference (which makes me wonder why they were a standard-issue, but I'm not a sailor). Those who testified had no reason to lie, so I'll leave it to you to ponder if a misplaced key might have been the final straw that doomed the great ship.

The 'smolder' in the coal bunker by Boiler Room #5 is another source of controversy. At a recent conference I attended in Las Vegas, a naval architect who'd done extensive forensic analysis of the wreck stated the death blow was when the internal bulkhead between the bunker and the boilers failed. The bulkhead hadn't been made to withstand the pressure of the ocean twenty feet below the surface, but it does at least raise the question as to how much the fire contributed to a fatal structural weakness.

A lifeboat drill for the crew was scheduled for the fourteenth, the day of the disaster, but for some reason the captain cancelled it. Therefore, the only crew who had any experience with the procedure on that particular ship—which featured new, improved davits—were those who lowered two nearly empty boats in the harbor under the supervision of the Board of Trade. One reason the lifeboats were lowered with less than full capacity was because the officers lacked confidence the new davits could support the weight of a fully loaded boat. Captain Smith's instructions to the crew manning the lifeboats to go around to the gangways to take on more passengers were ignored, and the boatswain and crew sent below to open the entrance on D Deck were never seen again. A dive to the wreck in 1998 found the door was open, telling us the men accomplished their final orders before dying.

At the time of its sailing, the Titanic had more lifeboats than legally required. The British Board of Trade specified that ships over ten thousand tons should carry sixteen lifeboats plus enough capacity in rafts and floats to accommodate fifty percent of the total on board in the case of watertight bulkheads, which the ship had. The Titanic had twenty lifeboats, plus additional floats and collapsibles to exceed that number with a total capacity (if loaded properly) of 1178 souls. The ship carried 2224 on its maiden voyage.

The general manager of the Harland and Wolff shipyard had proposed forty-eight lifeboats, which would have provided enough seats for everyone, but the White Star Line opted for fewer, so as not to disturb the views from their more expensive first-class staterooms. Given how chaotic the loading process was, it probably wouldn't have made much difference as many passengers initially refused to board, thinking the situation wasn't as dire as the crew said. By the time the sinking was obvious to all, there was little time left.

Still, the White Star Line seems very prudent when compared to its competitors. Cunard's *Carmania* had only 29% lifeboat capacity of its maximum passenger load, and if the Hamburg Line's *Amerika* sank, it would have left 2,000 without a space.

The Inquiries

Commissions were established on both sides of the Atlantic. The one in the US was headed by Senator William Smith of Michigan, a member of the Commerce Committee, who had previously made inquiries into railroad accidents that led to significant safety improvements. He initially had difficulty convincing President Taft of the need for a commission until the president learned that Major Archibald Butt, Taft's military advisor and a passenger aboard the ship, was not listed as a survivor. Taft arranged for a naval escort of the rescue ship, Carpathia, and Senator Smith personally boarded the rescue ship as it entered the New York harbor, informing Ismay and the ship's officers they would be forced to remain until they provided testimony at the hearing, which began the following day, April 19, at the Waldorf Astoria Hotel in New York.

Upon return to England, the process was repeated, this time by the British Wreck Commissioner on behalf of the British Board of Trade, the commission chaired by Lord Mersey. The two inquiries had roughly similar findings:

- Ships should slow when entering areas with drifting ice.
- There should be enough lifeboats for all aboard.
- All ships with wireless radios should monitor distress frequencies constantly.
- Boat drills should be conducted with passengers aboard.

- Rockets should only be fired aboard a ship in times of distress.

The recommendations were incorporated into the International Convention for Safety of the Life at Sea, or the SOLAS Convention. Initially ratified in 1914, it has undergone successive updates since, the most recent in 2015. It affects only merchant vessels, not military craft, but ninety-nine percent of all merchant vessels sail from signatory states.

The US Navy began ice patrols along the Grand Banks for the rest of 1912, then the duty was assigned to the Revenue Cutter Service, the forerunner to the US Coast Guard. They continue to perform this service as the International Ice Patrol, which is jointly funded with thirteen other nations interested in maintaining safe passage across the Atlantic.

People

Samantha (Sam) is a fictional character, but professional gamblers (boat men), and con men were very much part of the milieu aboard luxury liners of the day and I think my fictional thieves would have fit right in with their real-life inspirations.

Colette is also a fictional character, based upon no one in real life, as far as I know.

Margaret Brown

Margaret Brown, known as "Maggie" to her friends—not "Molly"—was the divorced wife of a man who'd made his fortune in mining in Colorado. She'd married for love when they were both young and poor, and their divorce was amicable. She had worked in a dry goods store in the rough and tumble of Leadville when it was a mining town, and the elite of society in Denver never fully accepted her due to her humble start, which she found amusing.

Known throughout later life for her many charities, when the *Carpathia* arrived in New York harbor, she refused to leave the dock until she'd made sure every third-class passenger had a place to spend the night.

Mary Carr and the Forty Elephants

The Forty Elephants began as the women's auxiliary of a gang of highwaymen operating out of the Elephant and Castle pub in South London during the late eighteenth century, but they soon established their independence from the other, and by 1912 were infamous for their brazen shoplifting, blackmail, and lavish parties thrown in some of the poshest establishments in London. These women grew up in poverty, and crime offered them an attractive way out. Life for them was hard and often short, so when they scored, they celebrated in grand fashion.

As a young woman, Mary Carr worked as an artist's model during the day and as a criminal at night. She would often dress as a well-to-do young lady and ask a prosperous gentleman to walk her home to keep her safe. Once at the door of a home, she would threaten to scream if the man didn't pay her the contents of his wallet. She is even said to have ensnared a member of Parliament in this manner.

Once she became Queen of the Elephants, she ran her organization by the "Hoister's Code," paying legal fees of gang members from levies she imposed on all thefts and ensured rents were paid while an Elephant was incarcerated. Those in the gang were punished for drinking on the job or partying excessively the night before an operation, either through fines, beatings, or banishment. The worst offense was to marry someone outside the criminal world, as they were seen as a potential snitch, thus Colette would never be allowed to consort with a law-abiding man, if she wanted to remain in the gang.

I do have them violate a part of the "Hoister's Code" in my story however, which stated one was not allowed to wear clothing they had lifted, but I made an exception for an exceptional journey.

Fences were critical to their income. A fence who paid less but never revealed a source was highly valued. When you couldn't find a reliable fence, the Caledonian Market in London was always an option. It had an infamous reputation as a place where stolen goods might legally change hands, owing to an obscure medieval law known as market overt (or marché ouvert). This law guaranteed a buyer title of ownership if an item was bought in good faith between sunrise and sunset, whatever its provenance. The law was finally abolished in 1994, after which the market was said to have suffered a damaging drop in trade. I suspect eBay has done much to fill the void.

J. Bruce Ismay

The director of the White Star Line has alternately been portrayed as a hero and a villain. Miss Jessup commented that during the disaster he treated the female crew and third-class passengers with the same care as for those in first-class. He boarded the last lifeboat that would otherwise have departed with empty seats, and only after making sure there were no women yet to board.

Despite his portrayal in James Cameron's epic movie, Ismay did not pressure the captain to increase speed. The *Olympic* class ships—of which the *Titanic* was the second to be built—were designed in response to the German "Greyhound" liners, such as the *Kronprinz Wilhelm*, that set speed records for transatlantic crossings. Ismay decided not to compete with the Germans by making his ships faster, but more luxurious. The captain's decision to speed through a known ice field was unwise but a standard practice at the time (since discontinued). The unusually calm sea meant no waves crashed against the ice, making them harder to detect in poor light.

Ismay retired from public life shortly after his return to England, and his mixed legacy continues to frustrate those who like life and people in neat boxes.

Violet Jessup

Miss Jessup was a stewardess on various ships of the White Star Line, as well as others. She was aboard the *Olympic* during its 1911 collision with the HMS *Hawke* as well as on the *Titanic's* maiden and only voyage. In 1916, while serving as a nurse, she survived the sinking of the *Britannic*, which had been converted into a hospital ship, after it struck a mine in the Aegean Sea off the Greek island of Kea. She was nearly killed when her boat was drawn towards the exposed propellers as the ship sank, suffering several blows to the head. Years later, a skull x-ray revealed an old fracture, probably incurred during the sinking.

The incident of the baby thrust into her arms only to be reclaimed by an ungrateful mother is true.

Miss Jessup's memoirs offered me a rare look at life below decks among the victualing crew who provided services to the passengers. I'll leave it to you to decide if she had very good—or very bad—luck.

She seems to have been a kindly soul, and I hope I'm forgiven for portraying her placing flower petals in Mrs. Cardeza's pillowcase (who was a real person). As for the subterfuge of the pantryman adding fresh melted butter to make a passenger think their meal was freshly prepared, I worked as a waiter during my university years and used my own experience to add such details. I'll claim the right against self-incrimination if pressed for particulars.

Second Officer Charles Lightoller

Charles Lightoller went to sea as a young man, and even if he hadn't been aboard *Titanic,* he would have been credited with having an eventful life. As a young man, he was shipwrecked on a deserted island off the coast of Brazil and was rescued eight days later when a passing ship saw smoke from his campfire.

He later tried his luck as a gold prospector in Alaska and as a cattle wrangler before returning to sea. He was demoted to Second Officer aboard the *Titanic* as I relate in my book, and therefore his wife received conciliatory telegrams after news of the sinking was released, as the First Officer was listed among the casualties. It was only after he arrived in New York that he was able to send her a wire

informing her otherwise. He was never made a captain by the White Star Line but was placed into command by the Royal Navy during WW I and awarded twice for bravery. In June of 1940, he was part of the Little Boats flotilla that assisted in the evacuation of British and Allied forces trapped on the beaches of Dunkirk, rescuing 130 men with the help of his eldest son, Roger, and an eighteen-year-old Sea Scout. A character in the recent movie, *Dunkirk,* is based upon Lightoller.

Steward Littlejohn

An experienced steward of the line, Mister Littlejohn came to my attention on a Facebook site dedicated to all things *Titanic*. The site showed two pictures of the man,

one taken about six-months before the sinking, a second some two years after. In the second, he appeared to have aged over twenty years, his once thick dark hair turned thin and white, his face lined and thinner. I know a smattering of Latin, but one phrase I often use seems apt here: *res ipsa loquitur*—the thing speaks for itself.

Adam Worth, father of Harry

Adam Worth was an American of German extraction who was probably the inspiration for Sherlock Holmes' arch nemesis, Professor Moriarty, though he began his life of crime by accident. He enlisted in the Union Army and was wounded in the Second Battle of Bull Run. After recovering from his wounds, he discovered he'd been declared dead and decided on a serial military career by enlisting in various Union regiments and collecting his one-thousand-dollar bounty, then deserting and joining another.

Once the war ended, he turned to pickpocketing but soon branched out to bank robbery and became so successful he began planning and bankrolling the robberies himself. His career took a turn when he broke into a Boston bank from an adjoining shop (which calls to mind the plot of The Red-Headed League), and stole cash and securities valued at $200,000. With the Pinkertons in hot pursuit, he fled to England.

Worth adopted the name Henry J. Raymond, settled in London, and lived a lavish lifestyle, which included running a string of racehorses and sailing in his steam yacht.

His home became the meeting place of the leading thieves of America and Europe and a clearing house or "receiver" for most of the big robberies in Europe. In the latter-1870s, and all during the 1880s, one major theft followed another that implicated Adam Worth, but his involvement could never be proven.

Perhaps Worth's best-known crime was the theft of Thomas Gainsborough's painting of Georgiana Cavendish, Duchess of Devonshire, painted in the mid-1780s. It was stolen by Worth and his henchmen from an art gallery on the night of May 25, 1876, with the aim of using it to ransom a gang member in jail. The charges against Worth's associate were dropped soon after the theft, however, and Worth was left with a painting too famous to sell, so he decided to keep it for himself.

Georgiana Cavendish, Duchess of Devonshire

At the time, nobody knew who'd taken the picture though rumors pointed the finger at Worth. In 1892, he was arrested in Belgium for a botched robbery and sentenced to seven years hard labor. While in prison, he was approached by the Pinkertons with offers of freedom if he would return the Gainsborough, but he always denied any knowledge of the painting.

In 1899, after being released from prison broken in health and penniless, Worth contacted William Pinkerton, agreeing to meet with him in America to discuss the disposition of the portrait. It was ultimately returned for $25,000, exemption from prosecution, and the promise that Adam's son, Harry, would become a Pinkerton agent when he came of age so he would escape his father's life of crime.

Worth was completely opposed to violence. William Pinkerton described Worth in a posthumous pamphlet (Adam Worth, alias "Little Adam" 1904).

"In all his criminal career, and all the various crimes he committed, he was always proud of the fact that he never committed a robbery where the use of firearms had to be resorted to, nor had he ever escaped, or attempted to escape from custody by force or jeopardizing the life of an official, claiming that a man with brains had no right to carry firearms, that there was always a way, and a better way, by the quick exercise of the brain."

During a transatlantic crossing, Arthur Conan Doyle fell into conversation with William Pinkerton and first heard of the real "Napoleon of Crime," as Pinkerton called the master criminal, both due to his brilliance and short stature. Whether Worth was the model for Moriarty, he was clearly—like Doyle's creation—a master criminal sitting at the center of a web of crime in London. Unlike Moriarty, he spent time in prison and was loyal to friends. As Pinkerton comments in his pamphlet, "This man was the most remarkable criminal of them all."

Harry Worth

As for Harry Worth, I can find no record. Whether he became a Pinkerton man or chose a different path is—like the bejeweled edition of the Rubaiyat—lost in the murky past.

The story of *Titanic* is one of tragedy and loss, so I'll end our time together with the words of an ancient sailors' blessing: *May you have fair winds, and following seas*.

Bradley Harper M.D.
COL (Ret.) US Army Medical Corps
Fellow, Royal Scottish Society of Arts

About the Author

Bradley Harper MD is a retired US Army pathologist who began writing at sixty-three. His debut novel, *A Knife in the Fog* published in 2018 placed a young Arthur Conan Doyle on the hunt for Jack the Ripper. The book was a 2019 Edgars Finalist, and is a recommended read by the Doyle estate. The audiobook won Audiofile Magazine's Earphone Award. Dr. Harper completed an MA in Creative Writing at Napier University in Edinburgh in 2021, and this novel was his Masters thesis. You can follow him and learn of his other works at http://BHarperAuthor.com